THE WILD HUNT

A PROCESSION OF FAERIES ~ 5

THEA HUTCHESON   ANTHEA SHARP

BRENDA CARRE   DEB LOGAN   LINDA JORDAN

REBECCA M. SENESE   SHANNON LAWRENCE

DEANNA KNIPPLING   LOUISA SWANN   KIM MAY

BRIGID COLLINS   JAMIE FERGUSON   ANNIE REED

Edited by
JAMIE FERGUSON

COPYRIGHT

"My Last Hunt" © 2020 by Thea Hutcheson

"The Faerie Invasion" © 2016 by Anthea Sharp
First published in Fiction River: *Visions of the Apocalypse*, July 2016

"Gigglebark Tea" © 2020 by Brenda Carre

"Emma: A Feyland Dryad" © 2018 by Deb Logan
First published in *Feyland Tales: Volume 1*, November 2018

"The Turning" © 2020 by Linda Jordan

"Take a Walk on the Wild Side" © 2020 by Rebecca M. Senese

"Of Earth and Fae" © 2020 by Shannon Lawrence

"The Last Private in the Gray Hoodie and Blue Jeans Brigade" © 2020 by DeAnna Knippling

"Scraggle Goes Hunting" © 2020 by Louisa Swann

"Of Blood and Bone, Earth and Air" © 2020 by Kim May

A fierce host rides across the winter sky at night
In wild pursuit of whoever crosses their path

Peals of thunder follow the horses as they gallop through the clouds
Fire flashing from their hooves

The baying of the hounds echoes across the sky
Their sharp teeth glinting in the light of the moon

The Huntsman blows his horn, and the Fae ride behind him
Their faces both beautiful and terrible to behold

When the nights are long and the winter winds howl, stay inside
Lest you cross the path of the Hunt...and become their prey

CONTENTS

INTRODUCTION

The Wild Hunt contains thirteen stories based on the wide and varied folklore of the Wild Hunt. In some tales, the leader of the hunt is Odin; in others it's King Arthur, Herodias, or Herne the Hunter. Sometimes the riders are Fae; sometimes they are specters, or skeletons, or strange beasts never before seen by mortal eyes.

But no matter who the hunters are, you definitely don't want to be the one they're after...

Let the Wild Hunt begin!

—Jamie Ferguson
Editor

MY LAST HUNT

THEA HUTCHESON

I lie on the floor of the kennel, in a pile of fresh hay. The kennel master is coming down the aisle, trundling the water barrel. He has no food, so I know that we will hunt. The hunt master says the hounds must be hungry in order to find their prey the quickest.

I think this will be my last hunt. Not because I am old, or infirm, or pregnant, but because the spell is fading, and I am starting to remember before. When the spell was strong, the magic smelled of spiderwebs and anger, shame and green grass. I knew only my pack-mates, the kennel, the gentle touch of the kennel master, and the joy of the hunt.

I have no memory of spells before. I was just a mortal human then. After the magic, I became a dog in the Fae's pack.

The master stops at my kennel. He is large for a Fae—muscular, with strong legs, and kind hands. His silver braid falls over his shoulder as he works, and I always like to sniff it when I get the chance. It smells of wondrous things, like cold biting air, freshly turned earth, and a thoughtfulness that I don't ever remember from before and have only smelled on him.

He opens the gate, takes out the old bowl, sets down a fresh one, and ladles cold, clear water into it.

"Annsalas, girl, this will be your last hunt." So I am right. A worry from before pricks at me. What will happen to me after this hunt? Fear rises and I leap up to confront whatever it is that frightens me, my claws, all red except for the silver middle claw on each paw, digging in to the hard-packed dirt.

But I can see or smell nothing imminent, and he smooths the dark silver hair on my head as I glance about for danger. He scratches behind my velvet silver ears, flapping them. I have no worries now as I lean into his hand.

I decided long ago that all those wondrous things I smell on him add up to the scent of love. I nuzzle against him, and lean against his knee, giving him that love back in the only way I know now.

With a last scratch and a pat along my darker silver flank, he backs out, shutting the gate firmly behind him.

I am both happy and sad. I whine a little as I settle back down in the hay.

Just then the kennel master's apprentice brings Dimoso, the top stud of the hunting pack, back to his kennel.

He trots down the aisle, his white coat gleaming, his red ears pricked, and his crimson tail held in a high arc. His gait makes it seem like his red paws are attached to coiled springs instead of legs.

This was not just because he is the alpha, but because he has just been bred to Canoie, the top bitch of the pack.

I am a part of the pack, but always on the outside. I don't look like any of them with my silver fur. The kennel master has never bred me, and while the other dogs allow me a place in the pack, they hold me more in awe, or perhaps look at me with a faint condescension.

This makes me sad, because everyone wants to fit in, even dogs. Dogs know right from wrong, but they're opportunistic. This doesn't mean they don't love each other and others. I have only memories of loving my parents from before and I am certain I don't want to lose the love of the kennel master now. He is my master, and he is kind, and deserving of my loyalty.

Let me tell you a story I have just remembered. The memory makes me growl low in my throat, and my tail goes between my legs in shame as I think of it. The memory has lots of smells, but none of them smell like love.

The night was dark, the low hum of traffic whirring along the avenue two blocks over. I walked down the street, my new high heels clickin' on the sidewalk. I could smell the junk, the scent so thick it laid over the block like a blanket.

That told me right there T-Jack's boys had made a new batch. It smelled like acme shit. My eyes itched thinkin' about the high just one drop would give.

It smelled like vanilla mixed with vinegar, and it would be strong enough to make your eyes burn and water when you dropped it, and sour enough to make the back of your throat hot and scratchy. But, oh, the buzz! The buzz would make it worth all the tears and coughin'.

I walked faster. A stiff breeze stirred-up the leaves and scraps of paper into little dirt devils. I swore as little rocks and twigs pelted my naked legs. The skirt was short and did nothin' to protect my legs, but T-Jack would like it. And that was what counted. Luckily, it didn't seem like any of the rocks cut my skin.

He had dumped Lila right off his lap when I showed up at his digs two nights ago, wearin' that blue dress that fit me like a second skin. She had shot me the look, but it didn't matter; she was on the floor and I was standin', arms akimbo, my legs strong and trim, my hips wide, my narrow waist widening up to my full bosom that offered up mounds of joy like ripe fruit.

Now I was gonna go sit on his lap and make some scratch. I was his best delivery girl. He had told me so weeks before. But I wanted to be more than a delivery girl, and the only way I could see to do that was to be T-Jack's woman.

Not only did bein' his woman mean you'd rate the cream junk, but he showered you with presents like rain. I didn't like rain, but I did like presents. God knew I didn't get any from anywhere else, with my parents both dead, and no relatives or anyone else that gave a shit about me. So what other choice did I have? And I could sell whatever I didn't want for enough to keep that tiny roof over my head and food in the tinier fridge.

No, my best path lay in T-Jack's lap. I think he knew it. He had always told his guys that he liked it when they showed initiative. So how was that different for me? I knew what I wanted; I also knew what I would do to get it. And what I wouldn't. I might trade my body, but I wouldn't lie or steal.

T-Jack's house was old, not quite fallin' apart, which had made it a cheap buy. He said it gave him an air of legitimacy. Personally, I thought it tied him down and gave the cops a way to tag him when the payoffs weren't big enough. It was big, brick, lots of windows, three stories, and had a dirt basement where the boys made the junk.

As I got close, I nodded at Pelo, tonight's gate guard. He leaned against the fence, vapin' somethin' that smelled like a cherry Jolly Rancher. He nodded back with a little smirk. Pelo had hit on me once, but I'd shut him down. He opened the gate, still smirkin'. "T-Jack's waitin' for you. He said to come right on in when you get here."

I sashayed through, my hips swingin', my heels clickin'. Pert manned the door. He was a short little skinny guy, as gay is the day was long, and totally wicked with a knife. T-Jack had put him high up in the gang. He smirked at me too, as he opened the door. "T-Jack's waitin' for you. He's in the den."

I stepped inside. The junk smell was so thick here it was like wadin' through fog. My eyes burned and the back of my throat started to scratch. I coughed, and got a buzz just bein' in the house. I stood for a moment and breathed, in and out, as I carefully dabbed my eyes to keep my makeup from smearin'.

My head got light, my heart got full, and everythin' was dee-light-ful. I was climbin' up to the top of the world. I felt so good, I could feel the future. Things were gonna turn around for me.

I saw clumps of people sittin' around in the living room to my left doin' junk, three or four lollin' on the couch, a few playin' some game on a screen that took up most of one wall.

I walked on. To my right, in what would've been the dining room, a bunch people sat at a table and passed a tiny bottle around, takin' turns droppin' the junk in their eyes. I would never share a bottle; you never knew what kind of a disease you could get. And longtime droppers, they got infections, weird ones, that turned their eyes green. Gross.

Past the dining room there was a dark, tiny hallway with a set of really narrow, steep stairs goin' up the back of the house. T-Jack said it had been the servants' stairway, but it was a quicker way to get to his den, so I didn't mind usin' it.

My shoes clicked hollowly on the worn wooden steps. I held onto the handrail because my head was light and climbin' the stairs felt like I was walkin' up a mountain. I could feel the burn in the back of my calves as I went up. I was glad no one was comin' up behind me because they would've seen up my skirt. Not that I was commando, but the G-string was barely there and it was brilliant white.

I'd been savin' it for a special occasion. And I expected that T-Jack was gonna want some sweet stuff. That was good, because I knew that I could wrap him around my little finger. I was good at the sex stuff. I'd watched a lot of YouTubes, and I'd shared a ton of sweet stuff with a lot of guys to learn what they liked and how to do it the best.

Not that T-Jack would ever be owned, but if I could cement a position on his lap long enough to get a decent stash of my own, maybe I could turn my life around. Maybe I could get more out of life than just bein' a delivery girl.

That was a lot of maybes, but I had no plans for bein' a delivery girl all my life. That was a dead-end for sure, if not by gettin' tapped by the cops then endin' up on the wrong of end a deal.

At the top of the stairs there was a bathroom on my left, and a long hallway to my right. On either side of it were rooms. On the left side T-Jack's den had been created out of three rooms with the walls knocked out between them. From the right side of the hallway I could hear someone havin' sex; they were tryin' to be quiet but you could tell somebody was really gettin' it. On the left, from the closed door of his den, I could hear laughter and the murmur of conversation.

I stood in front of the door, adjusted my skirt, fluffed the girls, and ran my fingers through my long hair, which I'd had dyed a burnished silver yesterday. I lifted one hand, admired my four red lacquered nails and the one silver one on the middle finger, shook my six silver alloy bangles, and tapped with my knuckles three times.

The conversation shut off quick, and M-low opened the door. He looked at me from top to bottom and then back again, with a long stop starin' straight at the girls. He smiled, a kind of half-leer, half-smirk. I made a face, and he stood back and gestured me in like he was some kind of fancy butler instead of a fixit man.

"She's here."

"I can see that," said T-Jack. He sat in this old leather La-Z-Boy recliner against the wall. He straightened up, looked at me from top to bottom, and waggled his eyebrows in appreciation. I smiled and

7

licked my lips coy-like. I wanted to wink, but the other guys would see. No, I was all for T-Jack. Nobody else was gettin' get anything close to a taste.

"Clear out, guys. The lady and I have some private business to attend to."

I suppressed a shudder of excitement, and smiled at the sudden warmth I felt. I was right. He wanted some sweet stuff, and I would be as sweet as he wanted.

A couple of the guys made noises, like teenagers. They were just jealous. Maybe Lila was upstairs. Maybe one of them would get lucky with her.

But, to a guy, they all smirked at me as they went out, one or two winkin'. The last one out closed the door and we were alone.

I stood, not quite breathless, but certainly a little buzzed from all the junk in the air. T-Jack looked at me from out of one eye, and smiled. "Well, don't you look nice."

I added little smile and an eyebrow waggle of my own. "All for you, T-Jack."

He didn't waste any time and he took it all, and then some. Later, when all the hard breathin' was done and we had settled down, he gave me a bottle while I sat in his lap. It was brand-new, never been cracked. I held it up to the light and shook it. The junk was all pearly with little flecks of gold in it. This was good stuff. Like champagne compared to the beer they were droppin' downstairs. I opened the bottle and put two drops in each eye and closed them. It burned like I had gotten embers in my eyes.

That had happened to me once, back when my folks were still alive. Dad took me and Mom camping up in the mountains. We were sittin' around a campfire, and Dad was tellin' us ghost stories. One of the logs popped and shot a spark right into my eye. Oh God, it hurt so bad.

My mom rinsed my eye out and put drops in. She gave me a cloth with ice cube in it. I kept gettin' new ice cubes and held them against my eye for the rest of the night. I hardly remember any of the stories Dad told, because my eye hurt so bad, throbbin' in time to my heart.

But this burn was different. The junk was totally good. I sucked in a deep breath and kissed my careful makeup job goodbye as my eyes ran like faucets. If I got a buzz just breathin' the air downstairs, that was nothin' compared to this.

My whole body felt weightless, and it felt like only T-Jack's hands on me kept me from floatin' away. I squirmed a little on his lap. Exultation. That's what I felt. A big smile plastered over my face. The dim room seemed shot with a glow that made my heart thump fast and hard.

"It's called Nirvana."

"I don't think I've ever done anything that good in my whole entire life." I relaxed back against T-Jack, my head nestled in the crook of his shoulder and his neck. I breathed in; he smelled good, some kind of fancy cologne that smelled like the sea on a bright summer day, a breeze blowin' the scent of a spicy flower in my face. I just kept breathin' him in.

"You like that shit, huh?"

It took me a minute to process his words. My brain was thrummin', no, it was purrin' and I was ridin' it along with the afterglow of all the sweet stuff.

"Oh, yeah, I like this a lot," I said, the words fallin' out of my mouth like syrup. "Thank you, T-Jack." That was somethin' my mom taught me: givin' lots of gratitude. "You catch more flies with honey than you do vinegar," she always said. It made sense if you thought about it, but who wanted to catch a fly anyway?

Except, this was one fly I was not only gonna catch, but I was gonna milk for all it was worth.

He chuckled. "Well, there's more where that came from. But first, I want you to do a little delivery for me."

I sat up slowly, feelin' a bit irked that he got me high then talked business. I didn't like to be high when I did business. Too many chances to screw your own pooch.

But this was T-Jack and so I would talk business. I struggled to get up because, even high, I knew you didn't discuss business sittin' in anybody's lap.

He had his hands on my hips, and he gave me a little lift so I could get out of the recliner easily. I struggled to get control of my legs, and managed to sit reasonably gracefully on the hassock next to him so I didn't appear taller than he was.

He reached down onto the floor beside him, and lifted up a square package about as big as my hand wrapped in packing paper. "I want you to take this down to Fourth and Jackson. A guy'll be waitin' for you just past the Pizza Bomb. Skinny, silver hair, like yours. You tell him 'Crackerjack'. He'll ask you if there's a toy inside. You tell him, 'Yeah,' and give him the package."

I nodded. Fourth and Jackson wasn't all that far, although with my heels, it made me wish I'd brought flats.

I hadn't forgotten this was business though, so I said, "And what's the rate?"

He smiled and reached for his wallet. He lifted out five bennies. I watched him count them. I'm sure my eyes got really wide. That would pay the balance of the rent on my tiny house, the phone, and utilities for this month.

This must be some delivery. I wondered if Lila had been gettin' this kind of rate all along, and that I'd moved up to it by sittin' on his lap.

I took the bennies when he handed them over, makin' sure that my nails grazed his hand and that I made eye contact with him, lettin' him know what he got with me.

He smiled with one side of his mouth, and winked. We read each other right.

"Now get along, this guy won't wait long."

"Shall I come back here when I'm done?" I raised one eyebrow, smiled a little bit, and licked my lips. Maybe I'd overdone it, but I wanted him to be sure he knew what he got.

His smile got bigger. He laughed. "Sure," he said. "Come on back if you want."

I wished he would have said he wanted me to come back instead of makin' it seem like I was somebody's little sister gettin' to hang out with the big kids. I nodded anyway and gave him a bigger smile. "Okay, then."

I walked toward the door, gave him a wink and a smile over my shoulder, then closed the door behind myself. I swear I heard him laugh as I went down the stairs. All the guys were downstairs. They all looked at me; they knew what we'd been doin'. I hope they were jealous. I was finally gonna get something out of life.

If it took sittin' on some guy's lap and givin' out sweet stuff, that was a small price to pay for movin' on up.

The Uber guy was friendly, almost too friendly, but I showed him my mace and he cooled off.

I got out of the car at Third and Jackson. The Pizza Bomb was on the right side of Jackson, a little more than halfway down. I crossed Third and made my way up Jackson. There were tons of people out and I got a lot of eyes from both gogas and jeffries, but I was doin' business, so I ignored them. Plus, T-Jack would be waitin' for me when I got back.

I passed the Pizza Bomb, and looked in the boutique window, like I was admirin' the dress on the mannequin. It was kinda cute, but a little too Japanese schoolgirly for me.

I smelled him before I heard him. He smelled like green things, kinda like my Gramma's garden, but spicier.

"You have a package for me?"

I turned around and looked at him. He fit T-Jack's description— tall, thin, really lean, with a long pale silver braid down his back. Nice dye job, but his hair was a little too long for me. He wore black skinny jeans and some kind of slinky tunic top that shimmered in the light. I wanted to touch the fabric, but this was business.

He had lavender eyes set in a face that was all angles, with cheekbones like they had been cut with knives. This guy was super danzig, but I remembered T-Jack and my goals.

"Yeah, it's crackerjack." I smiled, because it's good business. Plus, it never hurts to show a nice face when business is so good-lookin'.

"Has it got a toy inside for me?" He said it with a half-smile, his lavender eyes diggin' right into me. When he lifted his eyebrows, I noticed they didn't arch; they were like slashes. I wondered if he'd had them threaded that way, or if he plucked.

"Yeah." I handed him the package. We touched fingers as he took it. His were cold, not like ice, but too cold for such a nice night. I wondered if he was sick or somethin'.

It didn't matter; I had done the job and could go back to T-Jack's with five bennies in my pocket. I turned away and started walkin' up the street. I heard somebody shout as I turned the corner, but shit like that happened all the time. I had my phone out to call for a car when I heard someone say, "Hey," right behind me.

I stopped and turned. It was the danzig. He wasn't smilin' now.

"There's no toy in here," he said. "And if T-Jack thought he could trash me with a crap spell like that, he's made a big mistake."

I shook my head, his words not makin' any sense. I scrambled for somethin' to say. This was crazy. It should have been done biff, bam, boom, super easy, real slick. I'd done everythin' T-Jack said to do.

"He said to deliver the package. He put it in my hand, told me what to say. I came here, I did the deal just like he said," I said to danzig man.

His face turned ugly. I looked around. There were a few people across the street; they looked and kept on walkin'. I flicked the latch on my purse. I could get the mace out and squirt him if things got bad. I sure wished I'd worn flats; I knew I'd never be able to run far in those heels.

He shook his head. "That's still no toy, and it wasn't funny. I'm Rasmon," he said like I should recognize him. "You don't fuck with me. He made a deal with me, and if he didn't like it, he should have looked at the details better."

I made calm motions with my hands. "I'm not fuckin' with you. I'm tellin' you, I did the deal, just like I was told. You have no beef with me." I wondered now exactly what kind of a deal T-Jack had sent me on.

And suddenly all those smirks, the grins, and those winks, they all made more sense. I was a stupe, a queen stupe. I couldn't believe it; was T-Jack fuckin' with me? I didn't know, but I felt my face heat up, even considerin' that it was a possibility.

Rasmon flipped the remains of the package at me. It smelled like somethin' curdled and black ash fluttered out of the paper. "Whether you just did the deal or not, he tried to shiv me. And as his bitch, you're gonna pay." He pointed one graceful finger at me that was tipped with a long, sharp silver nail.

I stared at it. I wanted to turn, to run, but I couldn't move. My heart started thumpin' really hard. I lifted the can of mace out of my purse, but he started snarlin' words in some language that I didn't understand.

I felt sharp stings, like his words were shootin' into me. Everything went all wavery. My muscles started crampin', the can fell from my hand, and my back jerked. I bent over, fallin' to my hands and knees. It hurt like a sum bitch, and I tried to shout at him, but what came out of my mouth was a horrible howl.

I fell onto the ground, the night closin' in with a great boomin' fist on the back of my head.

What had he done to me?

~

The moon is coming up, big and silver. The rest of the pack is getting antsy, barking and dancing in their kennels.

I can smell the Fae outside the kennel. There are only a dozen or so of them, so it's not a big hunt. I hear the horses' harness and tack jingling, and their hooves clopping in the stable yard. The kennel master comes down the aisle and opens the gates. We flood out, barking and prancing down the aisle in our excitement. I bring up the back, a little silver clot at the end of the snow and crimson wave of fur.

All the dogs are milling around outside the kennel grounds in the swatch of grass that surrounds it. The kennel master has his horn. I'm busy sniffing who's there. I smell a couple of princes and their cohorts, but none of the high royalty. So this is personal, not like a solstice hunt, not like a hunt in the deep of winter, when you breathe the air and it's like knives in your lungs, and you howl with joy for the crisp wind that brings the scent of your prey.

Rasmon mounts his milk white stallion first; he's the highest prince in the group. Then Cailen, acting as Rasmon's hunt master, mounts and calls out to the rest of the gathered Fae.

Once they're all sitting their horses, they drink goblets of wine that smell rich like honey, but with a bite that's sharp in my nose. They start bantering, working themselves up. The magic is thick, a mixture of flowers, grass, apples, and snow, and burning leaves in the air. This is definitely personal.

Personal hunts are different. They target a specific prey, not like on the other hunts, where we chase whomever we come upon. Sometimes when we catch someone, the Queen makes them do her a favor, like steal another Fae's cows, or find some impossible treasure. Sometimes we tear them to shreds for her pleasure.

The kennel master shouts, "Aiyup, gather round, ye hounds."

We obey, coming to cluster around him. He leans down and offers each of us a cloth to sniff to get the scent of the prey in our noses.

When it's my turn, the kennel master stares at me, touches my chin, and offers me the cloth. I take a big breath in, and smell the sea on a bright summer day with the breeze of some spicy flower over the top of it. I know this smell. It dredges up that story I just remembered. The rage and humiliation that had been long buried flare up, like a hot flame in my heart. My belly feels tight and my legs shivery, while my tail arches high with tension.

The kennel master is still holding my chin, so I have to look up to him. I try to look away, because it's poor manners to meet your better's eyes, but he forces me to meet his gaze.

"Tis your last hunt, Annsalas," he says softly. "Tis your hunt, too, and your time to take the lead; no one will deny you that." He stares at me, his pale blue eyes lit from within with a glimmer than makes my heart leap.

He looks sad; he smells sad, too. I don't know what he means. I lick his fingers even though I'm confused. I've always run at the back of the pack.

But this smell, I know it from a long time ago. I want to run this prey to ground, and catch it in my mouth and shake. I want to feel the bones crush in my jaws, the blood wash over my tongue.

I want T-Jack to know what he did to me.

And then Cailen shouts to the kennel master, who stands and blows his horn. He shouts, "Away with ye, to hunt, to hunt," and we're off, racing across the cool green grass. Dimoso is the first to leap into the night sky. The rest of us trail behind, howling and barking as we cast ourselves into the night, searching for the scent. I'm the first to catch it, and I turn and race away, my paws scattering clouds as I follow that scent, and the memories it brings me.

Soon we pass over the forest, crossing a stream that is silver in the moonlight. The shimmering curtain of Other When is in front of me. I gather my haunches under me and feel the power coursing through my body as I leap forward and rush through it.

Every time I cross over to the mortal land, I feel like a weight has been lifted from my senses. Everything is less bright, less charged, but clearer and sharper.

The lights of a city are bright below me. The air is thick with scent: people, food, smoke. But through it all I smell that scent of sunlight on the sea, and that spicy flower filling my nose. I lift my nose and breathe in with my mouth open to hone in on the track and, with a belling bark, I call the rest of my pack after me.

They surge through the curtain into the mortal land and follow me. The scent of the prey grows stronger, filling my nose, making my heart pound, filling it with anger fueled by humiliation.

The princes and their cohorts lash the air behind us on their horses, their joyful shouts filling the night sky as they urge us on.

I can smell their hunger for revenge like a knife newly sharpened. That hunger goads me on like a lash. The scent of my prey is like a line drawn on the air. I follow it, down into the city's lights. It's stronger here. I'm close, so close.

My bark is one constant staccato note that my pack mates echo, calling the Fae to follow us. I touched down to the ground, my claws gleaming as they click on the cement. The silver ones glow like the moon. I lope, my nose down, my mouth open, filling myself with the scent of my prey.

I turn left down a dark street. I hear the pounding of the horses' hooves as they touch down behind me. My heart feels like it will burst, it's beating so hard.

The street opens up onto a green space. I smell the grass, the trees, the moist earth, squirrels and birds bedded down for the night, a fox hunting mice in the scrub. I smell the fox's fear as he catches my scent. But he is not our prey tonight.

More memories crowd back into my mind, confusing me as I run toward that scent, so hot and fresh it suffuses my nose and makes me giddy. He is lawful prey; the kennel master set us on him. I will bring him to bay so the Prince will have his prize.

He hears us. I can smell the sudden fear laid over that sunlight on the sea scent, the spice overwhelmed by the acrid smell of flight or fight.

I tear forward with a growl. I can see him now, outlined against the lights behind him. He smells older, much older, and I pause as I wonder how that can be.

He starts to move, to run, knowing for certain that the pack is after him, but it's too late. I have four legs against his two, and I use them. Running up, I leap upon his back so that he trips and falls with a grunt.

He turns under me, flailing, and I remember he always carried a gun. I grab his hand in my mouth and taste vanilla and vinegar, and a woman's sex.

This makes me crazy with rage and I shake his hand, biting down hard. He shrieks and starts to kick me as the bones of his hand crack. And then the other dogs are on him, biting and snapping. His shrieks turn to moans and wails, and there's the sharp scent of piss followed by the thick odor of shit.

The horses pull up to a stop, encircling us. The kennel master wades in, shouting, "Getaway, getaway, you dogs, back off, back off."

The pack obeys, even I, although I'm last. I let go of T-Jack's hand and back away, growling softly. This is the source of my anger and humiliation. This is the reason I'm in the pack. This is the reason I'm no longer human.

I remember again that it was Rasmon whom I met near the Pizza Bomb that night. I remember how everyone at T-Jack's that night had known, how T-Jack had used me to try to get something over on one of the princes of the Fae.

I had paid the price, and all of T-Jack's guys had known, when I walked out the door, that I was being set up to take a fall. To deliver a spell that they didn't realize had no strength against a powerful member of the Fae.

I had been sacrificed for nothing.

Rasmon jumps down lightly from his horse, handing the reins to Cailen. He saunters up to T-Jack, a big smile on his face as he looks down at the old man lying on the ground in a puddle of his own piss, with his shit stinking up the night air.

"So, T-Jack. You agreed to our bargain in the beginning. We shook on it. I reminded you a second time, after you sent your girl." He gestures at me. I sit, tongue lolling, mouth open, the better to smell what was going to happen.

"I don't know what you're talking about, Raz man."

I can smell that T-Jack has lied. Dogs know lies; they have a smell all their own, even when you can't see someone's body. And a human body tells the truth, every time, even when they try to disguise it.

Rasmon smiles even bigger, his lavender eyes catching the silver moonlight. He tosses a packet down in T-Jack's chest. "You don't know anything about this cheap enchantment?"

"I didn't do nothing to you or yours."

I growl, long and low, my hackles up, my body stiff. Rasmon looks over at me. "Even your girl knows you're lying."

T-Jack glances around and then back to Rasmon. "What girl? I got no girl."

That is a lie too, I can taste her on his hand, smell her on his shirt,

17

on his neck where she'd licked him. He has a new girl sittin' on his lap, givin' him all the sweet stuff.

I should be jealous. I should hate her. Dogs can be jealous. I have been jealous of my pack members, their camaraderie.

But instead I snort with disgust. Because dogs know disgust, too.

Rasmon smiles the smile he uses when it's clear he's won. "It might've worked against an ordinary Fae, if they hadn't been paying attention. But not against me."

T-Jack sets his mouth, ready to double down on his lie.

Remember how I told you dogs have morals? They know right from wrong, they know lying? They know loyalty too. I wonder why I ever thought I should choose T-Jack for my master. He has no loyalty to anyone but himself.

I never loved T-Jack. I had been using him, using him like a ladder to try to make a better life for myself. But the truth is, in his own twisted way, his actions gave me a better life. I have a pack, food, a warm kennel, and fresh water. And I have a kennel master who loves me, who looks after me, who will never let anything happen to me. *He* deserves my loyalty, and I give it every day.

I glance at the kennel master and see him looking at me. Does he know what I was thinking? He reads his pack better than I could read any trail. He knows each of us intimately, better than any lover.

But if the spell is fading—and I can barely smell it now—what will happen to me? What will I do without my pack? Will the kennel master keep me, and care for me, if I am no longer a dog? My heart breaks at that thought, of losing him, of losing that love. A whine escapes before I can stop it.

Rasmon looks at me. "You served your penance, Ann Salas. I release you." He flicks his hand and murmurs *words*.

The words strike me, one after the other, like arrows. I howl in pain and anguish. Everything seems to stretch and shrink at once, cramping, tearing my flesh. What is happening to me?

As I writhe on the ground, I lock eyes with T-Jack. The horror and disgust in his eyes make me wish I was safe in my kennel.

The pain is gone, suddenly, like a switch has flicked. I am lying on the ground, human again, mortal again, and I'm naked.

As I sit up, the kennel master steps toward me, offering me his cape. His fingers stroke my cheek lightly as he wraps it around me. I look up into his eyes, my heart in my throat. His eyes are dark, but his touch is gentle.

"This is the girl," Rasmon says. "The one that you sent to me all those years ago, with the package that had no toy in it."

T-Jack stares at me and makes as if to get up, and flinches from the pain in his hand. Dimoso growls and steps forward, stiff-legged. T-Jack settles for leaning on one elbow.

"We pay you very well to manufacture the little cozies that we ask for. Twice now you have tried to go back on your word and sought to destroy us with paltry magic. Twice now you have been caught. I told you after the first time what would happen if you attacked me again." The prince glances down at me as I huddle beneath the kennel master's cape.

I look from the prince to T-Jack, whose eyes are wide as he stares at me. "You're so young," he says. "How are you still so young?"

I don't know. But T-Jack, he is old, long past his prime. Had it really been so long? Dogs don't live very long. I tried to think back, remember my pack members. They hadn't changed. It had always been Dimoso and his mate and the rest. If it had been that long, then the Fae dogs didn't age, either.

I know that the Fae land is thick with magic, you can't help but smell it. I also know that their queen is old; she looks young, but she smells ancient.

I say nothing and look away from T-Jack. Dogs can ignore the ones that don't deserve notice. I may have been turned back to my human form, but the lessons I learned as a dog are still true even now.

Rasmon kicks T-Jack in the thigh and laughs when the man moans. "Feeling sorry for yourself now? You should, you stupid fuck. You have tried to attack a prince of the Fae. You will pay."

He turned to me. "Ann Salas. He betrayed you. You have spent more than thirty mortal years as a hound in the Fae's pack. You have every right to want revenge on this pitiful mortal. What say you? Do you want to name his punishment? Do you want to punish him yourself? That would provide no small entertainment, I think."

Dogs do not understand revenge. They fight for a position in the pack, they defend the pack and their masters against enemies. They accept their defeats, and try again when the chance permits.

But I am not a dog anymore. And I don't feel human, either. What am I?

I search my heart for what I want. I remember wanting to be in T-Jack's lap, wanting it so badly I can still feel the yearning.

But sitting in his lap had nothing to do with love, and everything to do with opportunity, with survival. And, unbeknownst to me, betrayal lay at the bottom of everything.

I wince as I remember the shame and anger I felt when I realized that T-Jack had sent me on the delivery knowing full well he was using me.

But that shame and anger feels so far away, so small, so insignificant compared to the memory of the hunts I had run in, the cold air tipping my ears, my paws, my tail. I have known joy in running with the pack, leaping into the air and shredding the clouds with my claws. I have known fierce pleasure in bringing the prey to bay.

There is no shame, no anger in my canine days. There is anguish that I was never fully accepted as a member of the pack, but I was never shunned or cast out. I know now they must have always realized that I was a mortal bound to the hound shape. That would explain their good-natured condescension, like adults watching a puppy imitate them.

I shake my head. Rasmon is growing weary of waiting. He expected me to leap and cry, "Yes, punishment, yes, revenge."

I look to the kennel master. His eyes are dark and he gives no sign, no movement, to advise me what to do. But his cape is warm, and he was kind to offer it.

I stand, keeping the cape wrapped around me. My feet are cold, and I step from foot to foot in a vain attempt to warm them.

I bow to the prince as I have seen other Fae do.

"Your highness, it has pleased me to serve in your pack. It was more a gift than a punishment." That is true. I had been going nowhere, and the slightest misstep would have sent me tumbling down a terrible path. "You gave my life purpose and honor that I had lacked before."

I have been a member of something grand and, even on the outside, it was better than being on the inside of my life before, sitting on the lap of a man who would throw me down for no other reason than I was handy. I have been a good hound, a loyal beast, and have been rewarded for that with a warm bed, good food, and a gentle touch from a master who cares about me and my condition. Did the kennel master care still?

His cape around my shoulders says he does.

"Your highness, T-Jack is a terrible person—cold to those who care for him, disloyal to those who serve him, and dishonest with those he would deal with. I do not care one way or the other what happens to him, except that I am sorry for whatever brought him to such a state."

Dogs feel remorse. They have sympathy and caring in their hearts.

"Hey, Ann," T-Jack says, trying to rise up from the ground. "It was never supposed to be like that. You were my best delivery girl."

I stare at him lying on the ground, beaten, bloodied, and stinking.

"And yet," I say, "You sent me on that delivery that night. You knew. All of your gang knew what you were sending me to do."

I turn from him. Dogs do not acknowledge those that do not deserve it.

"Very well, Ann Salas," Rasmon says. "I have offered. His fate is now none of your concern." He gestures, and some of the Fae come and pick T-Jack up.

T-Jack struggles, but they laugh as one ties a cord around his wrists. The Fae are strong for all they are lean, and T-Jack's efforts boot him nothing but a cuff on his head that sends him reeling.

One hands Rasmon the end of the leash, for that is what it is. I hope he will not turn T-Jack into a hound. He would make a poor dog, and cause no end of strife in the pack.

Rasmon gives his heels to his stallion, and the horse takes off at a trot.

"Hey, hey, no, wait, don't," T-Jack screams as he stumbles after Rasmon, the cord pulling him willy-nilly. I watch him running to keep up with the horse. Rasmon's laugh carries on the breeze behind him.

The rest of the Fae follow, laughing and bantering between themselves as they look forward to the sport T-Jack will provide.

I hear the moment the horses leave the ground, their hooves no longer booming on the mortal land. T-Jack's cries grow shriller, and then fainter, as the prince leads the way to the curtain between worlds.

I turn around. The kennel master stands amongst his hounds. Habit tells me to go to them, but I have no place there any long. I am no longer a dog. I am a mortal again, with less prospects than I had before the prince cursed me so many years ago.

The kennel master smiles a bit. "That was well done, Ann Salas. I am proud of you."

Warmth fills my heart as the breath leaves my lungs. He is proud of me? I bask in that glow, replaying his words over and over. I want to lean against his leg and give him all the love I feel in this moment.

"You could have taken revenge on your betrayer," he says. "Not a Fae among them would have denied you that right. But it would have diminished you, and the years you spent as part of the pack."

I nod, feeling his words fan the flames of pride that warm my chest. "Dogs do not know revenge," I say. "They know right from wrong, and how to be good."

"Yes, they do - when they are taught so. You came to me a blank slate. You knew nothing, except your nature. And your nature was good. It *is* good. You have been an obedient and loyal hound. I am proud to have had you as a part of my pack."

The tears come then. "But what am I now?" I say, my voice breaking. "I am no dog now, but I was a poor human then. I have been gone for years, decades. Time has rolled on. Now I am naked in the land of mortals, with only your cape on my shoulders, and no idea of where to go or how to be."

He shakes his head and lifts a pouch from his belt. "This contains all of your belongings. I saved them."

I take the pouch. Inside are my purse and the remains of my clothing, the bangles, the heels. I throw the rotting cloth and the heels to the ground and open my purse. Inside I see the mace, the bottle of Nirvana, my phone—long dead, and my wallet containing nothing but a now expired license and the five bennies T-Jack had given me for betraying myself.

"I was so stupid," I say. "I thought I would find a way up in the world through him."

The kennel master's smile is sad, but kind. "Not stupid, only ignorant. You were young and desperate to better your life. I think you are right. Prince Rasmon did you a favor when he cursed you."

I want to throw the purse on the ground. Then I think of the bottle of junk, and the high it would give me. Dogs do not find highs like cats with their nip, or horses with their speed. No, dogs are made for joy—the joy of the hunt, the joy of the pack, the joy of puppies playing, the joy of the love of the kennel master.

I will not use the bottle. It offers nothing that will help me, and will merely thrust me back to where I'd been with even less than I had then because the world has turned, and gone past anything I know of it.

"But now the curse has lifted and I am human again," I say. "I am human in the mortal land after thirty years. I have no life here."

There is no explanation for my reappearance thirty years later, with a face that has not aged.

He nods. "You have a life, if you wish to take it up."

"What life is that?" I ask, with no irritation, no whining, just the simple question.

"With the pack. With me." His eyes are open, full of something I have never seen. Is it hope?

I stare at him, swallowing hard.

23

"With you? What of your apprentice?"

"He will move on to some other posting." He nodded at me. "Ann Salas, I have known you since the moment you came to my kennels. I saw you for the kind heart you had, for your willing nature, for your desire to excel. You were a good hound, obedient, loyal, and caring, even when the rest of the pack treated you like a pup. You proved yourself willing to learn on the first hunt, and you never failed at any lesson I set for you. How can you be less than that as a human now?"

He smiled at me the way he would when he praised me for a lesson well-learned.

He wants me? He found me to be all those things? He thinks I will be a good human now. I flush. I have never thought of my mortal self as any of those things, except willing to learn so I could rise above my station and reach for something better.

His words make me feel pride, something I had rarely felt as a mortal. Perhaps I had been a good person, but it took being a hound to bring it out. I had found that a dog's nature agreed with me. I felt comfortable within those bounds and, yes, I had thrived.

But he wants me. *Me*. As I am. That means all the times he had praised me, petted me, stroked my flanks and murmured those nothings to me, it meant that he had seen me for who I truly am.

"If you do not care to return with me," he says, "I understand. I can offer you nothing but a life in the kennel, as my assistant."

His eyes are full of hope and I see now that beyond his kind hands, he is handsome in a rough way the other Fae are not.

I realize I have taken nearly too long to answer him, and he thinks I will refuse him. But how can I? He offers me a life I have loved. And more, I heard something beneath his words that I want to understand.

"I know nothing of the kennels beyond my place in them," I say.

He looks down at the ground, certain of my refusal.

"But I am willing to learn, as I was before."

His head comes up and I see happiness glitter in his eyes. His smile splits his face and I see the joy he feels at my answer. I want to fall on him and lick him, and I laugh ruefully, knowing that it will be some time before I remember what it means to be a mortal human.

We stand there for a moment and he reaches out his hand. "Then let us go home."

"Yes, Kennel Master. I would like that."

"You should call me Asteron now, I think."

"I shall be happy to, Asteron," I say, my own smile feeling as if it's making my face glow bright enough to light the night.

I take his hand; it's warm and, when he looks upon me, his love and kindness streams from him. I lift his hand and press it to my cheek.

Together we walk, the hounds bounding around us. Then we run, rising into the air, surrounded by the pack, heading for the curtain to Other When. For home.

ABOUT THE AUTHOR

Thea Hutcheson's story in *Realms of Fantasy's* 100th issue prompted Lois Tilton of Locus to say her work "is sensual, fertile, with seed quickening on every page. Well done..." She has appeared in such publications as *Hot Blood XI, Fatal Attractions, Baen's Universe Issue 4, Vol. 1, Amazing Monster Stories Issue 3, Nuns with Guns, Water Fairies,* and several of the critically acclaimed *Fiction River* anthologies.

She lives in an unscenic, nearly historic small city in Colorado with a 1000 books, four rescued cats and one understanding partner. When she's not working diligently as a Planning Commissioner to change that, she writes, and fills the time between bouts at the computer as a factotum and an event planner.

Find out more about Thea at:
theahutcheson.com

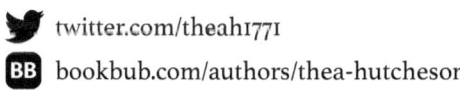

🐦 twitter.com/theah1771
BB bookbub.com/authors/thea-hutcheson

THE FAERIE INVASION

ANTHEA SHARP

R ic Garcia ran, breath scraping his throat as his over-full backpack slammed his spine. Behind him, the heavy tread of his pursuer shook the rubbled streets.

Two months ago, he would have laughed at the thought of being chased by an ogre down Vista's main street. That kind of stuff belonged in sim games or fantasy books, not real life.

But that was before the invasion.

He dodged around a squat, stucco building and forced his legs to pump out more speed. Just a little farther. His iron crowbar might hurt the twenty feet of enraged ogre chasing him, but ultimately he was going to be lunch.

Good thing the crowbar had other uses than defending against the fey folk.

Ric skidded to a stop halfway down the block, in front of a round sewer grate. He forced the tip of the crowbar under the grate and heaved. Dammit! The heavy metal didn't budge.

The ogre rounded the corner. A hideous smile stretched its mouth wide, showing blackened teeth as it reached for its cudgel.

"I see you, youngling. Tender eating, yes."

Desperately, Ric threw all his weight against the bar. With a rusty squeal, the grating lifted. He pivoted, scraping the grate over the pavement until the opening was big enough for him to slip through. He hoped.

The ogre was close enough to smell now, the stench of rancid meat and old sweat wafting down the street. Ric flung himself down and got his legs into the hole, then his hips. Crap, the backpack. No way was it going to fit.

He tore it off and shoved it to the side, hoping the ogre wouldn't crush it under those huge, flat feet. Ric's scavenging had yielded treasure, but his life was even more important.

"Come back, morsel!" the ogre cried, lumbering into a run once more.

Ric's feet found the ladder on the side of the pipe. He forced his shoulders past the grate, feeling his T-shirt tear and his skin burn.

Hopefully there wouldn't be much blood. Goblins could smell it, and track him that way.

He ducked low and began scrambling down the ladder. Overhead, his pursuer flung the sewer grate away as if were a penny. The light faded as the ogre reached into the hole. Thankfully, it couldn't jam its thick hand into the opening, but had to resort to sticking a couple fingers in. One brushed the top of Ric's head and his foot slipped as he pushed himself faster.

He scrabbled at the rungs, caught his balance, then went down a few more feet before he let himself stop. Hooking one elbow through the rung, he hung there, panting. The ogre raged and stomped around above him, but the creature was too dumb to wait for him to emerge. Some unlucky soul would divert its attention and it would leave, forgetting about Ric.

A trickle of liquid sounded from somewhere below the soles of his battered Converse. Just a trickle, not a rushing stream. There weren't that many people left to run the water in their kitchen sinks, or flush their toilets.

Everything was breaking down. Because of the Faerie Invasion.

It sounded so ridiculous. And at first the invasion had only been a little freaky, and a little comical. Water sprites in the drinking fountain at school. Pixies flying around at night, causing traffic accidents.

News reporters said the world governments were "handling" the sudden influx of magical creatures. Stay calm. Nothing to worry about.

Then the mer-folk had swamped New York, the sea-witches had drowned Los Angeles, and most of the broadcasts had stopped.

After that, things had gotten severe pretty quickly. Mortals had learned to stay inside after dark, when the Wild Hunt rode, harvesting souls and sowing madness in their wake. Old lore was rediscovered, and people started carrying iron with them. Before the 'net went down, the main sites were flooded with information about how to repel the fey folk.

Cold iron was one of the best ways, and apparently people broke into museums to steal the armor and swords. Unfortunately, Vista was just a podunk town with only the Museum of Hispanic Art. Ric couldn't see himself fighting off ogres and goblins by brandishing a painting or clay pot.

Salt sprinkled across thresholds and windowsills was supposed to help. Unless the fey folk could dislodge it with wind or water, and then come right into your house.

Supposedly the creatures could be held at bay with various herbs and charms. Too bad they were made of things that didn't grow around Vista, or stuff Ric wouldn't recognize if he saw it.

Going to the supermarket for supplies was too dangerous now. The faeries had figured out pretty quick that humans needed food, and stores were their favorite hunting grounds.

Sure, there were a few crazies that had walked out with open arms, begging the fey folk to take them. Some had been messily eaten. Some had just disappeared.

It was mostly horrible, and Ric was worried the human race was going down. Although, a few times he'd experienced breathtaking things: a beautiful maiden with gossamer wings floating in the moonlight, a strand of melody so sweet he thought his heart would break, a glowing ring of mushrooms in the park, where creatures danced and glimmered.

By the time the ogre stomped off, Ric's heartbeat had calmed to normal. Still, he waited a good fifteen minutes, just to be sure. No way was he leading that thing back to his little sister.

Angelina was probably worried by now. But she was a smart kid, and knew how to lay low in the hiding place they'd found. They'd be okay.

Nothing's ever going to be okay again, his conscience whispered.

Shut up, he said back.

The Garcia family would make it, the way they always had. From wars in Mexico to illegal immigration to full status as U.S. citizens. Some storybook creatures weren't going to take them out. He knew that wherever the rest of his family had ended up—Mama, Papa, Aunt Dolores and his annoying cousins—they were fighters.

Even Angelina was going to get better. His pack was full of medicines from the pharmacy he'd looted. Something in there would help her, would stop her from coughing all the time, and restore her appetite.

Carefully, he emerged from the sewer, the late sunlight elongating his shadow as he crept to the curb. Ric fished in his pocket and pulled out the red knit hat his aunt had made him last year. He jammed it on his head, then grabbed his backpack—thankfully untrampled—and slung it over his shoulders. Then he bent over, cocked one shoulder up, and let his other arm hang down to his knees.

Up close, he was clearly a human, but at a distance he could be mistaken for a redcap goblin. Unless he ran into another ogre, who could smell a human from twenty yards away.

He shambled down the street, taking his time. Down one side street he glimpsed the twiggy forms of spriggans, but they were going the other direction. He skirted the shops where the pixies had taken up residence. They were easy to avoid, the windows glowing with pale silver light.

He stayed away from the residential areas all together. Too depressing, and in some cases, gruesome. Instead, he headed down to Vista's industrial sector.

At the end of the main street, he stopped and glanced over his shoulder. Nothing seemed to be following him. Still lurching, he turned down Coronado Way. The warehouses rising around him were untouched—nothing of interest there for the fey folk.

He picked up his pace, scuttling forward until he came to the boarded-up window covered by bent metal bars. It had taken a lot of prying for him to fit, although Angelina had slipped through, no problem. She'd laughed at him, her dark eyes flashing, calling him *gordo.*

Any extra weight he might've carried was long gone, though. Both of them were getting too thin—especially Angelina. Even though he generally found enough things for them to eat, she was growing more and more listless. Some days he had to spoon-feed her.

But the medicines in his pack would help. They had to.

He rapped out their secret code on the plywood. After a few

moments the board scraped aside, just enough for his sister to peep out.

"*¿Quien es?*" she asked.

"*Soy yo,*" he answered.

They figured the fey folk wouldn't know Spanish. For whatever reason, all the creatures came from British Isles fairy tales and lore. *La Llorona* and the other ghosts and demons from their own tradition seemed to be missing from the invasion. So far.

Angelina gave him a weak smile and pushed the board wider.

"Took you long enough," she said, for a minute sounding like a nine-year-old version of Mama.

"I ran into complications."

He climbed through the bars and into the boxy room they'd claimed as their hiding place. Until a few weeks ago, it had been an office for some warehouse manager. On the opposite wall was a metal door with a wire-webbed window, and another, larger window that looked out into the shadowy cavern of the abandoned warehouse.

They'd covered that window with dark blankets, and put a blackout curtain over the one on the door. The room was plenty big enough for their sleeping pallet, their clothes and few possessions, and their makeshift kitchen: hotplate, microwave, small fridge, and electric kettle, plus assorted dishes and pots.

So far the electricity had stayed on, though a couple times it had flickered wildly. Every time, Ric's heart squeezed tight. Already parts of the town were dead. He didn't like to think about what would happen when the lights finally gave out.

He pulled the board back over the window and set the two-by-four across that held it in place. The room dimmed, and he clicked on the desk lamp they'd found in the office. The illumination made Angelina's cheekbones stand out from the hollows of her cheeks, and he tried to tell himself it was just a trick of the light.

"So?" She set her hands on her hips. "What did you get?"

He shrugged the heavy pack off.

"I got some medicine to make you feel better, *hermanita*." He pulled the plastic bottles out and lined them up on the cement floor.

She made a face. "I don't like pills."

"I know. But I also found these." He held up the three chocolate bars, and her eyes brightened. "And one more thing."

He unzipped the side pocket of the backpack and drew out the best treasure yet.

"Oranges!" Angelina stuck out her thin hand, and he placed one in her palm, trying not to notice how her fingers trembled.

So far, the fey folk hadn't learned to stake out the gas-station convenience stores. They probably had at first, but nobody drove now. Talk about making yourself an obvious target. The store Ric had plundered that afternoon still had a decent stock of snack food. And fruit by the abandoned registers. The bananas had turned to blackened slime, and the apples were all mushy, but the oranges were still good.

The sharp smell of citrus filled the room as Angelina ripped hers open. Mouth watering, he did the same. They sat without talking for a few minutes, a neat pile of orange rind on the floor between them while they savored the treat.

"Don't lick your fingers," he said, when they were finished.

"But it tastes so good."

"And you'll be sticky all night. Come on, wash up."

He dampened one of the dishtowels they'd scavenged. So far, water wasn't an issue, although he'd give almost anything for a hot shower. Sponge baths were getting old.

Angelina let him clean her face off, too, then yawned.

"Bedtime, sleepyhead," he said. "And take a couple pills."

He tapped an antibiotic and a few vitamins out into his palm and handed them to his sister. She obediently swallowed them with a few sips of water, made a dreadful face, then crawled to her side of the pallet without argument.

They both were sleeping a lot. He didn't know if was because they were getting malnourished, or the stress of having to hide all the time.

Sure, they were alive, but it wasn't the greatest life. Angelina hardly got to play at all now, and his days were long swaths of boredom punctuated by moments of extreme panic. The adventure of surviving had gotten old pretty quick.

But he didn't know what else they could possibly do. There was nowhere to go. This wasn't one of those happy stories where a brave enclave of humans holed up in the hills battled off the invaders, and emerged to restore the world.

Ric tucked Angelina's fuzzy pink blanket over her. Good thing they lived in a warm climate. Winter was going to be chilly, but they wouldn't freeze to death.

If they made it to winter.

As his sister's quiet breathing deepened into sleep, Ric rolled over and grabbed one of the books he'd borrowed from the library. It wasn't stealing if there was nobody left to check books out, right?

The shelf of folktales and fairy lore had been partially ransacked by the time he thought of it, but there were still enough books left to take an armful and leave some for the next person. So far, though, he hadn't found any answers about how to stop a faerie invasion.

From what he'd been able to gather before he and Angelina had gone into hiding, somehow a gateway had opened between the human world and the Realm of Faerie. The president and world leaders were planning to negotiate with the king and queen of the Realm, but clearly they hadn't gotten very far before things broke down entirely.

Outside, a long howl shivered through the night. Ric cocked his head, listening. The thunder of spectral horses galloping through the sky, the winding cry of a hunting horn, the shrill yapping of red-eyed hounds drifting through the air. . .

The Wild Hunt was riding.

He snapped off the light. Early on in the invasion, he'd glimpsed the hunt out his bedroom window. The memory still made him shudder—especially the sight of the leader of the hunt, a dark figure with huge antlers silhouetted against the eerily-lit sky.

In the darkness, Ric set the book aside, then kicked off his shoes and pulled another blanket over himself. Not that he'd be able to get to sleep while the night echoed with creepy sounds, but there was nothing else to do.

Still, he must have dozed, because the sound of something scratching at the board covering the window brought him wide-awake. After a moment, the light pawing turned to wood ripping under claws, accompanied by a snuffling and grunts of anticipation.

Ice swept over him.

They'd been discovered.

Beside him, he felt Angelina go rigid. She must be awake and hearing the noise, too. He reached his hand over and felt for hers, then gave it a tight squeeze. The sound of shredding plywood intensified.

Ric slipped his hand free and groped for the crowbar. If this was it, he'd go down fighting.

A hound bayed right outside, the sound jarring through him like a physical blow. Angelina whimpered as he stood up, and he wished he could reassure her—but they both knew the situation was dire.

The cement floor was cold under his bare feet. But not as cold as his heart as he faced the boarded-up window.

With a crack, the plywood fell into three pieces. A sinuous, ghostly hound slithered through the opening in the bars, skinny enough to pass through without touching the iron. It landed on the cement, eyes shining with red light, and growled.

"Stay back." Ric brandished his crowbar.

A hollow laugh boomed through the room, and outside, the antlered leader of the hunt held up his hand. He was surrounded by a dozen elfin knights on shadowy steeds. Their faces were beautiful and terrible to gaze upon, their long, silver hair shining like moonlight.

"So brave, you mortals, always," the huntsman said. "And so foolish. Come out."

"I don't think so." Ric swiped at the hound, but the creature dodged back.

Another one slipped through the window, then another. An eerie glow illuminated the room, and Ric shot a look at his sister. There was no way they were going to make it through this alive. Her dark hair was tangled with sleep, her eyes wide with fear in her gaunt face.

"I love you, Angel," he said, his throat tight. "Always and forever."

Ahh. A sigh swept over the riders outside, and their radiance increased, as though someone had turned up a dimmer knob.

"Come out," the antlered figure said. "Or would you prefer to be rent by the teeth of my hounds?"

The nearest one growled, its red eyes glowing.

"Why, so you can chase us down again?" Ric poked the crowbar at the hound, and it skittered away.

"No. We are charged with taking you to our queen."

Ric hesitated. He'd be an idiot not to take the chance. But everything he'd read about faerie bargains only showed the fey folk were not to be trusted.

"Let's go outside," Angelina whispered. "I don't want to be bitten to death."

"Okay." Ric raised his voice so the huntsman could hear him. "Call off your dogs. We'll come."

"Leave your cold iron behind," the huntsman replied.

Fair enough, though Ric waited until the last hound slunk through the barred window before setting his crowbar down. It clanked against the floor, a forlorn sound. The sound of safety, being abandoned. Not like they had a choice, though. Not really.

Angelina stood up, clutching the thin blanket around her shoulders. She looked more wraithlike than ever in the eerie light.

"Keep your blanket," Ric told her, eyeing the horses and riders.

Wherever the Wild Hunt was taking them, a little protection from the elements couldn't hurt. He snagged his black hoodie and shrugged it on, then climbed out the window.

Turning, he helped Angelina out, then held her hand as they faced the awful beauty of the Wild Hunt. One of the riders urged his mount forward, heatless flames flickering around its hooves. Ric's heart gave a thump of terror, but he stood his ground.

"I will carry the little one," the faerie said, his voice like ice crystals chiming together.

Angelina stared up at the elfin knight, awe filling her thin face.

"You better take us to the same place," Ric said, like he was in a position to make demands.

"Have no fear," the knight said. "All roads lead to the Dark Court."

He gestured with one long-fingered hand, and Angelina rose gently into the air. She gave a small gasp, then smiled at Ric as she floated up to the rider's saddle.

"I'm flying," she said.

Ric blinked fast, clearing the hot tears from his eyes. He had to be strong for his little sister. And himself. He had to stop counting her smiles as if each one were the last he'd ever see.

"Be gentle with her," he said, giving the knight a hard stare.

The faerie only regarded him, centuries fathom-deep in his eyes, until Ric had to look away.

"Have you courage enough to ride with me?" the antlered leader of the hunt asked.

"Why not?" Ric tried to sound casual, despite the fear clogging his throat.

One second he was standing on the rutted pavement, the next, invisible bonds snaked about his chest, pinning his arms tight as he was tugged into the air. He did his best not to yelp, especially as Angelina was watching him.

Instead of drifting gently to land in the front of the saddle, the way his sister had, Ric was roughly deposited on the back of the horse, behind the huntsman. He started slipping off, and the rider reached back with a hand as hard as stone and hauled him back.

"You must hold fast to me," the huntsman said, an echo of deep laughter shading his voice.

Great. Ric supposed it was too late to change his mind. Besides, he was brave enough for this. Really he was.

Clenching his jaw, he grabbed hold of the rider's waist. It was like holding on to an unyielding statue, nothing alive there at all, but Ric made himself hang on.

The huntsman raised one gloved hand, then snapped it down. Instantly, the horn sounded and the horses leaped into the sky. Cold wind whipped Ric's hair and made his eyes water. The hounds yapped fiercely, swirling about the fiery hooves. A sickle moon shone high above the riders, and from somewhere Ric heard the cry and wail of bagpipes.

Below them, the orange streetlights of Vista shrank, ranked in their orderly rows. More than half the city was black, though, and as Ric watched, several blocks of the city went dark.

Then they were speeding over rocky, shrub-dotted hills, gaining altitude until he could see the very edge of the ocean shining to the west.

Something swirled in the air in front of them, half-glimpsed around the huntsman's broad shoulders. Blue fire outlined what could only be a gateway back into the Realm of Faerie. The first hounds reached it, and winked out, and Ric braced himself.

Maybe he screamed—he wasn't sure. All he knew was that every cell of his body felt like it had been dipped in liquid flame. Breathing harshly though his nose, he forced back the taste of orange-flavored bile at the back of his throat.

It took a few minutes to feel like he was all there. He was surprised he hadn't let go and fallen off the fey horse, but somehow his arms still clung to the huntsman's waist. Despite the wind tearing at his breath, he turned his head to make sure Angelina was okay.

The rider bearing her was close behind. She sat upright in the saddle, seemingly unhurt, though her face was pale.

"You all right?" he yelled, the words snatched from his lips by the cold air.

She stuck one hand out of the fuzzy pink blanket and gave him a thumbs up.

Ric closed his eyes for a moment. He couldn't believe this was really happening—but then, life had been a nightmare for the past several weeks. Why not make it worse?

When he opened his eyes again, his breath caught at the view. Stars sparkled overhead, a thousand times brighter than in the human world, each one a laser beam of pure white light. The crescent moon was still there, but it spilled moonlight like water over the fantastical land below.

Groves of tall, pale-barked trees danced, their silver leaves flashing. At the top of a hill stood a circle of standing stones, shining with inscribed runes. Beyond the circle lay an orchard filled with gemlike fruit, a golden apple glowing in the highest tree.

The smell of sweet flowers drifted up as they rode over a field of pale blossoms. The sound of pipes were now joined by a flute and drum, weaving a melody both happy and sad. Giants shambled over the distant meadows, and mysterious lights beckoned from the marshlands.

This was the Realm of Faerie.

Despite himself, the enchantment of it filled Ric's senses. No matter how horrible the fey folk were, and how overrun his own world, this was magic, and part of his soul yearned for it. Had yearned for it his whole life.

The riders began to drift lower in the sky, heading for the dark woods ahead. Gnarled branches of ancient oak trees rose into the night, surrounding a clearing in the center of the forest. As they rode closer, Ric could see a bonfire flickering there, eerie purple flames illuminating long feasting tables and a throng of fey folk.

The far side of the clearing glowed with pale blue light. A throne made of tangled vines rose over the gathering, and upon that throne sat the most beautiful woman Ric had ever seen.

Of course, she wasn't really a woman, but a faerie. He knew that, but still couldn't take his gaze from her as the Wild Hunt landed in the clearing.

That must be the Dark Queen.

The huntsman dismounted, then grabbed Ric's arm and pulled him from the back of the fey mount. He managed to keep his feet, and pulled out of the rider's hard grasp. One thing could distract him from the queen: his little sister. He hurried to Angelina's side.

As before, the knight had gently floated her to the ground. Despite that care, she doubled over in a racking cough. Ric slipped his arm around her shoulders, holding her while her body shuddered.

Finally she straightened. The pink blanket was spattered with blood, but her eyes shone with wonder.

"Hang in there," he said.

His heart wrenched at how pale her face was. Riding through the shivering wind and going through the gateway surely had overtaxed her already weak system. She looked worse than ever, her skin practically translucent, almost revealing the bones underneath her flesh.

"Look at this." Her voice came out barely louder than a whisper as she glanced around the clearing. "It's incredible!"

And freaky. Oddly-jointed creatures danced and shambled around the bonfire. Red cap goblins tore at a haunch of meat with their sharp claws. A pale woman with tears of blood falling down her face crooned a lullaby while playing a harp made of bone.

In the shadows, other musicians played, including a man holding a guitar who looked almost human. Near the throne, a small figure sat upon a red and white-speckled toadstool. His hair was full of leaves, his clothing tatters and feathers. Meeting Ric's gaze, he cocked his head and gave a bright-eyed wink.

Three faerie handmaidens hovered behind the queen's throne, their gossamer wings slowly moving back and forth. White moths wove among the dark branches of the trees, like fluttering stars. The air smelled of frost and roses.

"Welcome to my court, mortals," the queen said. "Come pay me your regards."

She beckoned with one long-nailed hand, and the look in her midnight eyes sent a shiver coursing through Ric. Keeping his arm around Angelina's frail shoulders, they walked the few paces to where the queen sat.

"Kneel," the huntsman said.

Ric didn't particularly want to, but the word carried the weight of command. His knees bent, and he and Angelina ended up kneeling on the velvety-soft moss before the throne. At least his sister didn't have to keep standing. Ric slipped his arm down to take her fingers, her hand cold and delicate in his. He held it lightly, afraid of breaking her.

The queen leaned forward, regarding them. Her black hair framed her face, and her gown swirled about her as though made of smoke and stitched together with spiderwebs and starlight.

"What do you want from us?" Ric asked. His mouth was dry with fear, with awe.

"Your dreams," the queen said.

"Really?" He didn't bother keeping the sarcasm from his voice. "You sure you don't want to, like, sacrifice us at the full moon or something?"

She frowned, and clouds rolled over the sky, obscuring the bright stars.

"There has been bloodshed enough," she said, her voice crackling with disapproval. "Indeed, there are almost too few humans left for our purposes. The denizens of the Realm indulged too freely of their own appetites, once given access to your world."

"Maybe you should have stopped them."

Her eyes narrowed, and frost settled on the nearby branches. "Do not tell me how to rule my court, youngling."

Clearly Ric had hit a nerve. He almost pursued it, but despite her talk of too much death, he suspected the queen wouldn't hesitate to turn him into a pile of ashes if he pissed her off any more. Already he could tell he was riding the line.

He gently squeezed Angelina's hand. No way was he letting anything happen to her. *Hah*—like he had a choice.

"What do you mean, your purposes?" he asked.

"The Realm of Faerie requires the essence of mortality to remain in existence," she said.

"Seems like you've taken a lot of that, already." He had no idea how many hundreds of thousands of people had died, but it was a ton.

"It is not the *deaths* of humans we need—not unless we capture your life essence in the process which, alas, only too few of my subjects have done. No, it is your dreams and hopes, your music and art, which feed the Realm and sustains us. Without that, we shall fade into the shadows and wither in the wind."

Sounded like the queen had made a tactical error in letting the fey creatures run amok in the human world. He didn't say so, though. Clearly she already knew that, and if he got fried, who would look out for Angelina?

Beside him, his sister shivered, then slowly crumpled to the mossy ground.

"Angelina!" He scooped her up in his arms.

Her eyelids fluttered, then opened and she smiled up weakly at him. He could feel her pulse racing.

"*Te amo . . .*" she whispered.

"No. No, you're not dying on me." He didn't care that tears spilled down his cheeks, or that the fey creatures pressed close, their expressions avid. "Stay with me, Angel. Please."

She drew in a long, shuddering breath.

"Save her!" Ric lifted his gaze to the Dark Queen. "I know you can. Please—save her, and I'll give you anything you want."

The air trembled, as though an invisible current coursed through the clearing. The dark clouds rolled back and the stars shone down, showing the last spark of life in Angelina's eyes.

Beware of faerie bargains, his conscience whispered. But it was too late, and anyway he didn't care. He'd give up everything to save his sister.

"You know not what you ask," the small creature perched on the toadstool said.

"Silence, Puck," the queen said. "Mortal, I accept your offer. In exchange for saving your sister, you will dwell here in the Realm forever, giving us the sustenance of your humanity."

"Okay," Ric said. "Just hurry." Angelina felt so light in his arms, as though her soul was already halfway gone.

"Set her on the ground before you," the queen said.

He didn't want to let go of her, but did as the queen bid.

"I love you, *hermanita*," he said, gently brushing Angelina's hair back from her forehead. He wasn't sure if she could even hear him any more.

The queen drew a long black thorn from her sleeve. Chanting strange, liquid syllables, she inscribed symbols in the air above Angelina. They glowed with violet light, then shimmered down like trailing fireworks to settle on her body.

The bright sparks began seeping *into* her. Ric forced himself not to brush them away. He hoped they weren't hurting her. Soon, his sister's whole form glowed purple.

Then she began to change.

"Hey!" he cried. "What are you doing to her?"

"Saving her," the queen said, her gaze cold and implacable. "Her human form was failing, so I must give her another."

"That's not what we agreed to." He glanced at his sister's now-elongated hands, the shape of her face sharp-edged and almost alien.

"You only asked that I save her," the queen said. "Not that she remain human."

The sprite, Puck, gave him a sorrowful shake of the head.

Ric swallowed his useless protests. There was nothing he could do, except watch as his sister was transformed into a faerie creature. Would she even know him when it was done?

Finally, the glow faded. The queen spoke a single syllable more, and Angelina slowly sat up. Her gaze met Ric's, and he braced himself.

For a moment, her dark eyes stared blankly into his. Then something flashed in their depths, and she grinned at him. He tried to ignore the fact that her teeth were now pointed.

"Angelina?" he asked.

"Ric! I feel so *good*." She jumped to her feet and gave him a hug.

He didn't quite know how to hold this new, elongated body of hers. Especially when his hands encountered something strange on her back—a soft, feathery touch against his skin.

"What are those?" he asked, though he suspected he knew.

She pivoted, looking over her shoulder. "Oh my God, I have wings!"

Sure enough. Coming out of her back were two gossamer wings, a rainbow sheen of iridescence on them, like an oil slick on water.

"Now you really are an angel," he said, his voice tight with relief. With regret.

She wasn't the same little girl any more, and he had a feeling that slowly her humanity would fade from her, until she was just another faerie maiden serving the Dark Queen. But it was the bargain he had made.

What would be worse, having her die in his arms, or watching her become something other, each day moving further and further from him? He didn't know. It was an impossible choice.

Angelina waved her wings back and forth, and tilted into struggling flight. Some of the watching fey folk tittered, and Puck bounded into the air. He took Angelina's hand and steadied her, then looked at Ric.

"I will bring her to visit you every day," he said in a high, piping voice.

That didn't sound good.

Ric cleared his throat. "Where is she going?"

The queen laughed, the sound like chiming bells, and Ric turned to face her once more.

"She remains in my court," the queen said. "*You* are one about to depart."

He didn't want to leave Angelina—but he didn't really want to stay in the Dark Court, either.

"Depart to where?" he asked.

The queen tilted her sharp chin and beckoned to a figure standing in the shadows. A human walked forward, a young man who looked a few years older than Ric.

"Royal will show you to your new home in the mortal compound," she said. "Every month, at the new moon, expect a summons to court."

"But I'll see my sister every day, right?" he asked, giving her a hard look.

"As Puck has said. Now be gone. I weary of this conversation."

47

She turned away and one of her handmaidens placed a gem-studded silver goblet in her hand. The music rose, harp and drum and guitar weaving a jaunty melody through the clearing, and most of the watching fey folk returned to their former pastimes. Angelina still hovered lopsidedly in the air, her hand in Puck's.

"Say 'bye to your sister, and let's go," the human called Royal said.

"Is that really your name?" Ric asked.

"Yeah."

Royal didn't explain, just waited as Angelina made an awkward landing and Ric hugged her again. No matter what she looked like, part of sister was still there, inside. At least for now.

"Enjoy your wings, Angel," he said. "I'll see you tomorrow."

Whatever tomorrow meant in the Realm of Faerie. He hoped it would be soon.

Royal led him out of the clearing and through the moon-gilded oaks, toward the dubious protection of the mortal compound.

Behind him, the glimmer of the Dark Court faded.

Before him, the future stretched into forever, an eternity spent dreaming of the lost and empty human world.

ABOUT THE AUTHOR

Growing up on fairy tales and computer games, Anthea Sharp has melded the two in her award-winning, bestselling Feyland series, which has sold over 150k copies worldwide. In addition to the fae fantasy/cyberpunk mashup of Feyland, she also writes Victorian Spacepunk, and fantasy romance. Her books have won awards and topped bestseller lists, and garnered over a million reads at Wattpad. Her short fiction has appeared in Fiction River, DAW anthologies, *The Future Chronicles*, and *Beyond The Stars: At Galaxy's Edge*, as well as many other publications.

Anthea lives in sunny Southern California, where she writes, hangs out in virtual worlds, plays Celtic fiddle, and spends time with her small-but-good family.

Find out more about Anthea at:
antheasharp.com

 facebook.com/AntheaSharp
twitter.com/antheasharp
bookbub.com/authors/anthea-sharp

GIGGLEBARK TEA

BRENDA CARRE

P easewater and me have been arguing "side by each" since the 1960s.

That's when she came over from the old country as a "new-wed, new-widdowed and 'nivver' gone back, more's the pity."

I never knew when she'd be putting out "milk for the Fey," or some kind of gazing "gew-gaw" for the "blessed merfolk." Or, kill me now, trotting out around her property "sky-clad," which was a whole lot more information than I needed in one lifetime. Bad enough in her salad days when Lucy was alive and godmother to Peasewater's one poor scrawny little sprog.

But *now*? *Still*?

Our back doors look out across a mile-and-a-half of Inlet water. Our front rails look out on Ragged Ass Lane. We're part of a huge co-operative called the Islands' Agricultural Reserve. Little farms and a lot of country roads where weekend hoards of bicycle clubs buzz by with their butts in the air and a whole lot of attitude.

Today started with her carping at me through my box hedge for letting "my lame buck" steal into her yard to eat her "potatees."

"That's impossible." I grinned, laying aside my spade as given this was gonna take some time. "You keep your garden locked up tighter than a virgin's hoo-hoo."

"Don't you hoo-hoo me, you old coot!"

Peasewater's disembodied pigeony voice snarked back at me from someplace near the lower middle of my hedge.

"Hoo, hoo!" I shot back, enjoying myself.

I took off my dirty garden gloves and slapped them against my knee. I wasn't above a dig at the supernatural. "How do you know it wasn't kobolds ate your precious *potatees*?"

"Of course it wasn't kobolds," she snapped back, taking my bait. "It's barely September! kobold season happens closer to Hallowe'en. Oh, and another thing, I don't want you feeding catnip to my Spoon-grin! I don't want my mouser *catting* it up over there, getting his dear fuzzy head into 'tinkin your back forty belongs to him."

"I don't have a back forty, Old Woman! What I got's three acres of hops and market garden and a lame buck who needs my help..."

"Three acres of pesticial nightmare!" she shot back without letting me finish. "No wonder you have a lame buck, you agricultural luddite. I bet your catnip is filled with poison."

A tickle at my leg and an *Awrrrowp*, made me jump.

Here was *His Nibs* Spoongrin, the devil cat in question, as if some unholy termagant of an incantation had conjured him up from the pits of fomentation. Some ancient battle had taken the tip off one ear. The other came to a sharper point than usual. The end of his long tail was crooked. One of his fangs was longer than the other. On a regular basis, he seemed to think I needed the gift of his half-eaten mice.

"Hsst!" I glared at him and made a shooing motion with my foot.

"Is that you cussing at me, old man? Have you forgotten the three-fold law?" snapped Peasewater.

"Old woman, why don't you come through the gate and talk to me like a normal human being?"

"The three-fold law...."

"I know about the flippin' three-fold law! We're trying to sort out what to do about that buck! He's sick, and all I was hoping was for one of your remedies. You do still do, those don't you...?"

Spoongrin came back for another pass, stiff whiskers tickling my skin where the shorter leg of my oldest bib overalls hung waving down at my muddy crocs. "*Awrrrupph!*"

I ground my teeth and threw a garden glove at him.

It bounced off his big skinny body and took the head pods off a patch of nasturtiums. Spoongrin went after his "kill," grabbed it up in teeth that had bitten me more than once, and made off under my porch.

"Gawwwdammit!" I cussed.

I threw the other glove onto the ground and stamped on it.

"You have my darling over there, don't you?" warned Peasewater.

"If you mean Spoongrin, that furry son of demon spawn is under my porch and he's not coming out," I said, giving up on the buck. "I can only imagine the horde *your* damned cat's got laid up under there. I could rip up the whole damn porch and open a stolen glove shop!"

A frustrated *tsk* erupted from her side of the hedge like she really believed me.

"You will *not* rip up that porch, Lewis Fumarole. Lucy *loved* that old porch!"

Of course she had, and so did I. Testimonial to Peasewater for knowing zilch about me.

Our porch had seen the birth of Black Cooter's puppies. I'd a chain swing on that porch looked like it might have emerged from the dawn of Canadiana—kinda like me right now.

Lucy and me had canoodled on that swing when we were new-married and making plans for a bunch of kiddles that never came. What came to our house instead were foster kittens, swarms of hummingbirds, and a big vine of concord grapes that won "best wine" awards for Lucy at our local church market. That porch had also brought us Peasewater's little boy, who'd lost his dad before he was old enough to know one.

That porch had brought us a love we thought might conquer time. It hadn't. Lucy had died. Her beautiful herb patch in the back corner that Peasewater was denigrating was now filled with weeds even Roundup couldn't get rid of.

The latch on my cedarwood gate clicked up in a way I can only call pugilant. It squawked open to squish against my yard-thick hedge, and Peasewater stomped through it like a teeny wrinkled gorgon in her oilcloth garden onesie.

After spending what must be a couple of years spitting through that hedge at her, I'd forgotten what a bottle rocket she was up close —frilly flowered bib or no.

"Lewis?" she said, gum-booted to her knobby knees. She eyed me up and down with that green gimlet stare of hers. "What in bejeezzus happened to *you*?"

'You mean this?" I said, pulling at my tangled beard. "It makes up for the scraggles I got left on top."

I tried to remember if I'd been shaved last time her and me had locked horns face-to-face.

That was voting day for Municipal Council. Her hippy-dippy

friend got in as Mayor. Peasewater threw a hippy dippy party right next door in celebration. I'd called the police for noise violation.

"You look like a starved billy goat made out of chalk and piss, Lewis. Are—are—you took sick or just gone to seed...?"

"I dropped maybe a pound," I interrupted her. "Nothing serious. Cat's under there. Go fetch him."

"He'll keep," she said. "How long have you been like this?"

"Day or so," I lied.

I'd "took sick" last week, the same day I'd spotted the sick buck in my apple orchard. Since then I'd dropped twenty-five pounds. Food just wouldn't stay down. For a skinny guy like me that was worrisome, but I'd lay in the dirt before I'd go see a doctor.

"Have you tried Lucy's Gigglebark Tea?" she said.

I opened my mouth to say "no."

What came out was, "Have you tried minding your own damn woo-woo business, old Woman?"

Peasewater glared at me like I'd sprouted a tail. "That's nasty even from you, Lewis. You should know there's an epidemic of something deadly going around, and I'll bet you have it!"

"There's always something deadly going around. We oldsters now live in a gall-danged messed up world, Peasewater."

"Idiot!" She took a couple of steps toward me, and I backed up.

"Mother of Joseph, Lewis, stop!" she cried. "Now I know what's wrong!"

All of a sudden, I felt something big right behind me. Real BIG, with real big HOT breath. My neck hackles about curled up and squeaked. Here was an issue gone waaay out of my field of understanding.

"So. It's you. Why am I not surprised?" Peasewater said to whatever was behind me. She talked with the kind of threat comes out of a warrior's mouth before doing battle with one last halleleujah.

A quick fetch of wind came up from the water, and a flash of lightning pretty much did for what was left of my belief in the sane-dangles of life.

Next thing I knew I was laying on my snout, like I was one of them cardboard stand-ups you can see in the comics shops. A thick wormy smell like compost rot hit me right in the throat—

"You will leave this mortal alone, Herne," said Peasewater, stepping over my prone carcass.

No way, Jose.

Seconds earlier, there'd been nothing behind me but my own familiar garden. Now here was me pushed onto my face and something called "Herne" growling back at us like a junk-yard dog crossed with a T-Rex.

Staggering up, I turned around and about pee'd myself.

The sky had gone thunderous all of a sudden. Our fine fall sun had hid behind a bank of cloud that looked thicker than time. The mangy buck looming over little Peasewater was bigger than moose-sized.

Here's when a memory surfaced that now made weird sense to me. Some myth Lucy had read me once about a horned god called "Herne the Hunter" who gallops at the head an army of avenging Fey known as the Wild Hunt.

"Goofy," I'd said, and laughed in Lucy's face.

No laugh now.

Here was a supernatural critter, with a rack the stretch of my arms and a snout like the nose cone of a Lear jet. He was way more than the wounded buck I'd worried about a week ago. His pelt was coming loose in chunks. He was a mess—flanks oozing with open sores, a terrible, fiery mess.

For a second, I felt the quick bite of kinship for the big festering beastie, until he lowered his great rack in my direction and a buzz of lightning began to flit between his sharp tines.

"Get out of my way, woman. He needs to die," said Herne.

Peasewater stayed between Herne and me like some bite-sized morsel. "This is trice-warded land, Hunter, and this mortal is under my watch! I'd have killed him before this, if I "tought" him a threat," she said.

A threat? Me? Lewis Fumarole, aphid hunter?

What's more, short of fighting the nut-shrinking waters of our inlet in her nothing-at-alls, what was *Peasewater* doing calling me a mortal?

I jumped as something twined around my ankle. Not some tentacle from the dark unknown, but Spoongrin, come out from under my porch.

"*Awrrrrowph*," he said, showing me his fangs.

"You will surrender this aged mortal to our Hunt, Woman of Lir," Herne demanded.

Mortal or not, I felt slapped in the snoot. "Hey Doofus, who are *you* calling aged? You're the one with the weeping sores," I snapped. "According to Lucy *you've* been around since *gawd* was a pup!"

Herne ignored me and glared down at Peasewater, pawing his cloven forefoot into the mud.

"This mortal is the source of the dying. Look at him. Look at the cankers that waste me! I defy your wards. The Wild Hunt is loose."

"Are ya' out of your antlers?" cried Peasewater. "There has to be a better way to deal with this sickness than loosing the Hounds of Annoon. Do you remember what happened when you loosed them last time? They preyed on decent minds and gorged themselves on the blood of innocents. You set off a revolution that started wars that led to more revolution."

"And we are there again now! The Hounds are the devourers of pestilence!" Herne roared over the downpour that now come down in darts, soaking me through from my bald spot to my muddy crocs. "Look at these wounds. Look at the water and feel the wind! This stupid feeble mortal is the source!"

"It's a flu," I shouted.

Peasewater shot me a glare of surprise. "It is *not* the flu, Lewis! Our Mayor's took sick same as you. Get a brain. Now will you shut up?"

Spoongrin hissed and let loose a long, bloodcurdling howl that grew in size. Claws of ice frosted my spine as deeper yowls answered from the dark beneath my porch.

Shadows, big shadows, moved under there—yellow eyes glowed out at me. *The Hounds.*

Peasewater turned to me as the sky split open. Unsinkable, unquenchable Peasewater was afraid for me.

"Run, Lewis," she said.

Right then, I knew two things: I was not the source of this gawd awful sickness and I could *never* outrun *that* look from Peasewater.

She was afraid for me, like I didn't have the chops to stand up for myself.

"Ok then, Janet. This might not be a flu, but I'm not going to run," I told her, using her first name for the first time in dog's age.

"What are you going to do?" she said, surprised.

I picked up my spade and handed it to her. "Stand *with* you like I should have done a long time ago."

Peasewater grinned at me. "You old coot. Now I know why Lucy used to call you "Laying it Heavy" Fumarole."

"Yeah, well...."

I crossed my arms on my chest and scowled way up at Herne like the old beezer I am. "You kill me, Big Guy and immortal or not, your day is done. I'm not the source of your pain, but I have the answers to stop it. The world's going to hell in a handbasket, and Lewis Fumarole and Janet Peasewater are here at the checkout counter waiting to cancel your order."

"Kill him," said Herne. At his command, the eight black Hounds of Annoon slunk through the rain to ring Peasewater and me, tails lashing, whiskers dripping, and wedge-shaped heads low to the mud. These "hounds" were panthers the size of great danes.

Even Spoongrin looked doubtful around them, hissing like a snake and weaving the ground between Peasewater's ankles and mine.

"Hunter, I told you before, this is warded land," said the ever-unflustered Peasewater, lifting my spade to the sky like it was her wand.

"Lir," she murmured, "We need ya."

The air crackled and lit with a flash like the blast of a cannon. Peasewater stood firm as a statue in her baggy-bottomed oilskins. The scoop of my spade glowed white. My ears thudded in pain as the rain turned to fingerling salmon.

They hit in a flurry of flapping and flopping, whacking Peasewater and me and the Hounds of Annoon.

"Payment, Lir, yes, I understand," she said as the fingerlings continued to whack the mud, Herne's bloody chest, and the muzzles of his hell cats.

Peasewater glared at Herne as the Hounds of Annoon leaped and danced at the fish in matted black ecstasy. She pointed the still-glowing spade straight at Herne.

"Better I pay Lir than you, Hunter. You want the Hounds' next course to be venison?"

Herne made a crooning squeal and flinched away.

"So I thought," she said. "Now let's talk like two semi-civilized Fey, and reckon just what we're to do about your wounds."

"They hurt," growled Herne.

"Poor wee fella, lets find you a teensy violin," Peasewater said. "Lewis, since you're in on this now, what's next? I already owe Lir for the fish. I'd like to sort out the rest on our own, if you don't mind?"

"The rest?" I said, scratching the back of my neck in confusion. Seems I'd tricked the wrong Fey into thinking I knew what I was doing.

"Yes," she said picking up an agitated Spoongrin. "You're the one wanted something done about the "sick buck," after all. Then there's dealing with the real source of this plague, and fast if you don't want Annoon's little dearlings over there sniffing you out for their pudding."

'Annoons dearlings' were rolling in the mud, licking chops still coated with salmon guts.

Think of something fast, Fumarole.

"We could, err, um, try some Gigglebark tea on Herne," I said, taking a wild stab at an idea. Lucy used to say Gigglebark could cure the worst case of distemper ever. She was being metaphoric—humans don't get distemper—but there were times she could swear I broke the mold. She used Gigglebark on me more than once, warmed up with a double shot of McCallan's.

"Hmm," said Peasewater playing along, "I doubt the tea's strong enough, but how about Gigglebark salve? If I remember, Lucy used to make something strong out of seaweed and arsenic."

"Yowp," I agreed. "That was her tincture. She used to say it was strong enough to kill rats, and stem the tide of Armageddon. I got some of all three left in the house."

I knew what we were doing was coming up with a placebo—but placebos can work just fine if you believe in them hard enough. Lucy used to give Gigglebark tea to Peasewater's Connor, when he was feeling blue. We'd all drink some, and laugh and laugh until the tears rolled out of our eyes.

It never failed to cure Connor's sullens. I was now beginning to think that like Peasewater, little Connor wasn't actually human....

"I have never heard of an herb called Gigglebark," burbled Herne, salving the hurts on his chest with a long black tongue.

"Oh, and I suppose you've never heard of Lucy either?" I said, laying it on thick. "Finest herbalist this side of the Rocky Mountains? Her tea stopped World War Three. Twice. Impossible to declare war if you're killing yourself laughing." I did my best to keep a straight face.

"I do not laugh," said Herne.

"Then don't, I dare you not to. Just you wait, Big Guy. I'm off to make your day."

While he was still thinking about that, I hopped over the biggest Hound of Annoon and made for my porch, crocs sucking through the puddles like a couple of plumbers' helpers.

I swear, it seemed Lucy was there all of a sudden, giggling with mischief like a leprechaun or something. I felt a bubble of mirth rising up from my toes and took the porch boards at a full-out tilt, careening through the living room and into the kitchen we hadn't renovated since the nineteen-eighties.

I knew which pantry shelf Lucy kept her jar of Gigglebark

mixture on. Untouched for ten years, it still smelled as semi-sweet as I remembered.

"Bwaaahaaahaah!" I guffawed, knowing what was coming. Such a joke. There was nothing in there but comfrey and mint, something fruity, I didn't know what, and a bit of rancid, like somebody had farted in the room and tried to cover it up by looking innocent.

A bunch of little jars of Gigglebark salve were next to it. White plastic with screw-top lids. I grabbed half a dozen of the salves and stuffed them all down the front of my bib overalls.

It was going to take a lot of salve to cover Herne's wounds.

As an afterthought, I grabbed the black bottle on the lower shelf. The stuff I'd lied about stopping Armageddon. If the salve didn't heal Herne I'd dose him with every drop of the tincture in the bottle. It smelled like stinky tofu, and monster or no, he'd have the runs for a year.

Before you could say "squirt the cat," I was back outside.

"Here you go Big Guy. This is my promise you're going to get better if you trust us," I said, stepping over the paws of one of the Hounds of Annoon.

The Hound twitched but he stayed prone, blessed be. The other seven were asleep in a heap, gorged on fish for the now.

Herne bent to sniff the pot of salve I unscrewed. His gums rolled back over his teeth in disgust.

"I'll put some on you myself, to prove it's just fine for the Fey," said Peasewater, taking a dollop onto her fingers and rubbing it onto her face. Then she chuckled. "My sweet mither, I'd forgot how good this is."

She rubbed a dab on Spoongrin's flat snout and he sneezed. I swear he broke into a smile.

"Mmnnerrr nerr nerr," he said, and coiled up between Peasewater and Herne to lick the salve off.

"Here," she said, reaching up to Herne with more salve on her fingers.

"No, it doesn't smell good," he said, shaking his antlers so sparks flew. "Will it hurt?"

"Oh, Muffinn," mocked Peasewater. "Suck it up, Princess, or I swear I'll tell the piskies what a woosie you are."

"Not the piskies," snarled Herne.

"Yes, the piskies, and every leprechaun in the realm of the Seelie. I promise."

"Hoooweee," he replied. He dipped his huge rack, and Peasewater rubbed Lucy's concoction on the sores between them. "Huh-huh!" He started to chuckle as she got him covered from hocks to head. "Howeee haaa haa!"

His laughter was infectious.

Now I was laughing again, the mirth rolling out of me. The sleeping Hounds of Annoon woke out of their fish-spawned stupor and soft-pawed up to investigate their master. The taste acted on them like catnip. All eight pounced off to dab at each other and roll in my chrysanthemums.

Hell, *I* felt like rolling in my chrysanthemums! I hadn't felt this light in years. Where was my flu?

Then it hit me like a ten-ton block of surprise. Gigglebark was no placebo. It was the real thing.

"What is this sweet bliss?" said Herne, sniffing his matted chest, now caked with salve. My whole herbaceous border smelled like Gigglebark.

"It's you," Peasewater told him. "You're the bliss, you crazy animal. The world is as you are. Didn't you know that? You're healing now and so is the world. It isn't war and pestilence making you sick, but the other way round: It's *you* creating the pestilence. Look at Fumarole here. He's grinning like some leprechan flipped him a fortune. Look at your Hounds. Do they look like they want to devour the weak?"

The panthers were chasing each other over my gambrel roof and around my cottage like a kindle of frolicking kittens. Spoongrin had climbed Peasewater's leg and lay twined around her neck like a cat-shaped shrug.

"Go home to *Mrs.* Herne, why doncha?" said Peasewater. "Or, was summoning the Wild Hunt Danu's way of getting *you* outta the house?"

Herne winced at her sarcasm, and so did I. I remembered suggestions like that. There were times even Lucy got sick of what she called my "cantiferous grouching."

"Danu made the suggestion I go do something useful…" he began.

I snorted and shoved a fist in my mouth. Spoongrin blinked. Peasewater wrinkled her snub nose. "And *did* Danu tell you to summon the Hunt, you big stupid?"

"Welll…no," Herne admitted, pawing his hoof on the ground in a hangdog way. "It's too late now. The Hounds must hunt. Those are the rules."

"You know Danu's gonna have your antlers when you get home don't you?" said Peasewater.

He hung his big head. "I know, I know."

Peasewater kept at it. "Now you're for it. Even lice will forsake you…"

It was time to butt in. Right now the Hounds were happy, but clearly a bunch of fish and a bunch of Gigglebark would not a paradise make. "If the Fey fight like this all the time, no wonder we're in trouble," I said.

They both stared at me and I shut up.

"Do you have something useful to add to our discussion, being the mortal among us, Lewis?" warned Peasewater.

"I hope so," I answered her, and meant it. "Doesn't it make sense that if the big Source here is feeling better, then the rest of everybody who got sick this past week might be feeling better too" I mean, won't everyone get better on their own?"

"No," they both said together.

"The sick will die. Kill them now. The Hounds must feed," said Herne.

"Will you chill out, you Unseelie Galloot? The Hounds *did* feed," said Peasewater. "They "hunted" and they dined out at Lir's expense."

"I don't think he has a "chill" setting, Janet."

"*Awrrrowpp*," added Spoongrin.

Herne glared at me. "You are out of salve, Puny Mortal."

I had a bottle of tincture. That might be enough to help our community, but what would I do when that was gone?

"Why can't people just believe they'll get better? Isn't that a part of hope?" I persisted.

The biggest panther—the one I'd stepped over a couple of times now—padded up to crouch, purring on his haunches no more than an arm's reach from me.

"It doesn't quite work that way," mused Peasewater. "The Seelie Fey need a potion to implant the power of hope in folks. That's where things like Gigglebark come in. You have the plantings, but having the recipe to make the tincture, that's another thing."

"Well, the problem is, Janet, I don't have the plants anymore. My whole back corner's gone to weeds—the same back corner you've been razzing me about for years. The more killer I spray them with, the harder those damned weeds grow, overpowering Lucy's poor Gigglebark flowers. I'm sorry, but Lucy's corner now stinks like dirty feet. I've done everything to get rid of the weeds..."

I hesitated at the look of shock on Peasewater's face.

"Those 'stinky weeds' as you put it Lewis, are the essence of Gigglebark. They thrive on mischief and malice. I thought you knew that, but now it appears you've kept Lucy's patch alive by active stupidity."

"You're kidding?" I asked. "Well, then, we are in on making more. I have Lucy's recipe for Gigglebark, tea, salve and the almighty tincture."

"You have Lucy's *recipe*?" asked Peasewater, astounded.

"Yeah, it's in her recipe file. Also, we might be out of salve, but I have her black bottle of tincture right here. What if we hop in my truck and go check on the Mayor? If she's not getting better, we dose her with a drop of tincture. After which she goes all environmental on the news and everybody who needs a dose hears about it. We can make a bundle—a whole bunch of batches. We'll call it 'liquid hope.'"

The purring Hound fixed me with a bright golden stare.

"Bring *him—Whatsisname*, with us."

"His name is Gilnath," said Peasewater. "I don't think that's a good idea."

"Why not? He's big and he's natural. What says 'healthy environment' more than a big, mellow cat? What better proof that Lucy's stuff works? People see the news, they'll all want Gigglebark. Everybody will be happy. Then Herne can go home to his little missus with no harm done."

"Awwrrouph," purred Spoongrin, hopping off of Peasewater's shoulders to go butt heads with the panther.

"You really don't know who Herne's 'little missus' is, do you, Lewis?" said Peasewater.

"No," I said, "Does this make a difference?"

"If you think *Herne* is a threat, you do not want to mess with Danu, because messing with her is to mess with the Fey en masse. Danu is the mother of giants. The Tuatha can poke the San Andreas to send us 'The Big One'. Which they will, if you piss off the goddess by feeding Lucy's mix *holus bolus* to a bunch of mortals."

"Oh."

I tried to process this, and couldn't. Way too much right now for an old codger like me. "Can we use the Gigglebark tincture on the Mayor, or no?"

"Carefully," said Herne and Peasewater.

"First we need a messenger to supplicate Danu." Peasewater looked pointedly at Herne.

"Not me," he argued. "I'm in it right now, remember? I go home and we're all for the Wild Hunt for sure."

"Arrowwph," said Spoongrin.

"Very well," said Peasewater, frowning at the big skinny tom. "You do it, but take care my hinny. You don't want your other ear ripped to smithereens, do ya?"

"Nnnarrrowph," he said, and disappeared. I was starting to think that Spoongrin was not just the devil cat he appeared to be.

"He's gone to the other realm," Peasewater explained to me. "To, um, er, appease the Goddess."

"Yeah, and how long is that going to take?" I grouched.

"Arrrowrr," said Spoongrin, returning.

"Pretty quick," said Peasewater. "Time runs different in Faerie."

"No kidding," I said. "So, what's the verdict, hey?"

Peasewater consulted her pleased-looking tom. His ears twitched like crazy. "Danu gives us leave to develop Lucy's Gigglebark, but the Fey get a fifty percent cut if it succeeds. If it doesn't, Herne here will return. For now, she wants him back home. Him and the hounds."

"Nooo!" said Herne, pawing the ground like mad. The rain had quit a while ago, but the afternoon was cloudy and drear. Perfect climate for moping.

"Go!" she said. He slunk away, with his big tines pointing down. His bulk dwindled into the air until there was nothing left of him but the pong of moldy fur.

"You too," said Peasewater, pointing at the Hounds. "Don't make me ask twice."

Gilnath sent me a dark look and disappeared into the other realm. The other seven hounds, whose names I'd never learned, followed him like dark smoke from a house fire, rising into the air and becoming one with it.

So, yeah, Peasewater and I got into my truck after this.

Spoongrin spent his time snoozing in my crew seat. We visited our hippy-dippy Mayor to begin with. We uncorked a bottle of red wine. With my tongue stuck firmly into my cheek, I helped the ladies discuss the value of gluten-free over paleo, and if carb-rich food done organically could still be a thing.

I slipped a drop of Lucy's tincture into Madam Mayor's wine.

After that and a whole lot of giggling, she agreed that a press release would go out. Organic herbs, heck yeah. We didn't need a big black panther to stress the issue after all.

"Whatever made you believe in me enough to fetch Lucy's salve?" Janet asked me later, her in her flowered oil-cloth onesie and me in my oldest striped bibs. I'd put on a pot of tea and dragged out a plate of stale Weetabix.

It felt good to be "having a coze" as she put it, pouring Gigglebark tea into the cup Lucy always kept for me.

"Well, to be honest, Janet, I decided I'd better not disappoint you, not after you trusted me to help. Besides, I still have to live next to you."

She laughed. "Yes, you do, you old kermudgeon."

I sipped my tea, honey added, just the way I used to drink it. I'd never drunk Gigglebark when I was well and happy, only when I was raspy and feeling the grouch. The difference was noticeable. Life sat on me now like a big cat, reclined belly-up in full satisfaction.

"So where do we go from here? Giving fifty percent of our take to the Fey is cheap if it keeps Mr. Fat Antlers from coming back."

Peasewater frowned, and took a sip from a mug shaped like Betty Boop that said *friends are the boo-boo best.* "There will be a cost that goes even beyond the half shares the Goddess expects. We did stop the Wild Hunt, after all."

A quiver of unease rolled through me. It felt like that indigestion I get after eating ice cream, pigs feet, and pickles, but I knew it wasn't.

"What cost?" I said.

"I might need to do away with my bodily form," said Peasewater. "Until now I've been able to keep low and mind my business. But now that the worlds' become too so dark I might have to send meself to a higher plane. My energy will go into the land to be drawn back up at need, into herbs, into new life, into the ingredients for teas like this. Now you know what I am, now you know the Fey aren't just some tale to be told to little ones, you're in on this. Are ya willing to accept you might be called, Lewis?"

"I'm not afraid to die, if that's what you mean. We all have to go sometime," I said.

"True enough." She grinned. "Do you have family, Lewis? There's going to be quite a pot of gold left behind."

"I'll think of someplace to put it."

Peasewater nodded. "I think Lucy knew this was going to happen. It's why she left her recipe behind..."

I set down my cup. "What you're saying is *Lucy* was like you," I said.

"Well not exactly like me, but yes, Lucy was of the 'Seelie Fey.' Have you heard of the wee folk? The green folk? The leprechauns, if you will."

"Lucy?" I breathed. "Seriously?"

"Where else did she get that mischief that caught you?" said Peasewater.

Where indeed. "And what are *you*?" I asked.

She told me, and I believed her—all that dipping into and out of the water sky-clad made sense now.

"So where do you keep your sealskin?" I said.

"Ach now, that's a secret not even wee Spoongrin knows," said Peasewater, reaching down to scratch between the big tom's black ears. "I don't want him hiding it under your porch, now do I?"

I chuckled. At last, I accepted her as a selkie, the way I did the snarky, snag-haired green-eyed old woman, and the Irish colleen I'd met when she and her son moved next door to Lucy and me. And I accepted the truth of my Lucy as well.

Lucy was here in this cup of her tea warming my fingers. Hell yeah, I missed her. I had to go on, plant new, understand there's growing to do beyond the visible dirt.

"Neither you nor me have ever been, what you call, social to each other, have we, Janet?" I said. "We both let Lucy do that for us. But er —I see now, you were doing your best to keep me shy of the truth. As for me, I was out of line. I warn you, I might get out of line again. Lucy used to say that's inevitable until they plant me six feet down..."

Peasewater snorted. A wide grin split her wrinkled face from grizzled ear to grizzled ear. "Well, then. You can be the cover model for our 'kermudgeonly before' photo, Lewis."

I snorted as she bent to stroke Spoongrin. "So who are we choosing for the 'after' picture?" I said, watching "His Nibs" the devil cat arch his back against Peasewater's hand.

"*Awrawwr, Awwrawn*," said Spoongrin.

He turned that knowing stare on me and transformed. The man standing there now was surely the best "after" you could choose. Arawn—aka Spoongrin—was wearing nary a stitch to his name. Now appeasing the Goddess took on a whole 'nother meaning, and I found myself blushing.

"Oh. My. Sweet. Lorrdd of hell," I said.

ABOUT THE AUTHOR

Brenda Carre writes long and short fiction with a dark, mythic twist. Her short fiction has appeared in the Magazine of Fantasy and Science Fiction, Pulphouse Magazine, and Fiction River, to mention a few. Her indomitable character 'Gret' was the cover story in Pulp Literature Magazine's issue 15. She is currently working on a big book mythic/epic fantasy series she calls: 'Lara Croft meets a Wizard-of-Earthsea in the Pacific Northwest'. She also writes spicy romance under the name Tess Cornwall. Brenda is a visual artist and educator, and teaches a workshop on mapping through story.

Find out more about Brenda at:
brendacarre.com

f facebook.com/carrtell

twitter.com/brenda_carre

g goodreads.com/Brenda_Carre

BB bookbub.com/authors/brenda-carre

EMMA: A FEYLAND DRYAD

DEB LOGAN

I held my breath as Uncle Jim lowered the sim helmet onto my head and adjusted the interface to the grav chair he'd designed specifically for me. He maintained a steady stream of explanations as he worked, while I fought to focus on his words, to stay grounded in reality, to not allow my hopes to soar too high. If the interface didn't perform as he expected, I didn't want to fall too far. I released my breath and concentrated on what he was actually saying...not what I desperately wanted to hear.

"All right, Emma," he said, hands dropping to his sides. "I want you to relax. When you're ready to begin, think very clearly, *Enter Feyland*. When you want to quit, think, *Leave Feyland*. Do you understand?"

I blinked twice, my version of *yes*, and prayed that this new brainchild of Uncle Jim's would work. I tried to relax. It should work. Why wouldn't it? After all, my uncle was the famous James Carter, chief designer of the hottest FullD immersive game on the market.

"Good. I'm switching the interface on...now."

Uncle Jim looked almost as nervous as I felt. His light brown hair was a mess—he kept running his fingers through it and tugging the longer bits on top until they stood nearly straight—and his thick glasses sat slightly askew on the bridge of his nose. Right now he'd make a great mad scientist in a sci-fi vid. A wave of fondness washed over me. He'd always been kind to me, had worked to understand me, and now I watched as he turned the dial that could change my life forever.

He smiled. "Now it's all up to you, Emma."

I closed my eyes, held my hopes and fears tight, and thought, *Enter Feyland*. A black shield slid into place over my eyes, isolating me from the sunny conservatory where I spent my days. A large gold *F* outlined in flames appeared and hauntingly lovely music filled the air. Golden words replaced the *F* and my adventure began.

FEYLAND
A VirtuMax Production

A welcome screen replaced the title, and as the screen changed, the words morphed from gold to scarlet before turning to ash and seeming to blow away. This was better than watching vids with my dad. This was all-encompassing. I was there. I could almost feel the breeze and smell the ash. The game hadn't even started and already it rocked!

As Uncle Jim had explained, my first task was to create a character. After reading through the list of classes, I chose a Dryad. My sense of humor might be warped, but I found a certain poetic fitness in playing a character whose main defense would be to turn into a tree and become immobile.

Trumpets blared, and the screen flared with golden light. Dizzying disorientation seized me, and my stomach lurched as if my chair had suddenly dropped several feet. I closed my eyes and willed myself to calmness. I was no stranger to unpleasant surprises. I could handle this.

Taking a deep breath, I opened my eyes.

I was standing in a woodland clearing, surrounded by white-barked trees. Shock froze me in place, my reality shattered by those three words: *I was standing!*

Not sitting. Not reclining. Not supported by anyone or anything. I was standing in a clearing, on my own two feet, as if it were the most natural thing in the world. As if I were the normal girl I'd always dreamed of being. As if I'd just awakened from a hideous nightmare to find myself here, in this peaceful wooded glade, surrounded by white-barked trees with silvery leaves, under a clear blue sky, with soft moss beneath my leather-booted feet and encircled by a ring of mushrooms.

Laughter bubbled up inside. I wanted to jump for joy! I'd read that phrase a thousand times, but never expected to feel the impulse. Could I actually do it? Could I step over those mushrooms? Their jaunty red caps sprinkled with white spots encouraged me to try.

"Go ahead," they seemed to say. "You can do it. You can do anything. This is Feyland!"

Gathering my courage, I did what all the doctors had said I'd never do. I took a step, and after that, another, and suddenly I was running and jumping and twirling and waving my arms with abandon. I was alive! My body was fully functional!

I laughed and cried and danced and celebrated the enormous gift Uncle Jim had given me. The blessed man had no idea what I felt. How could he? How could anyone whose body behaved the way it was supposed to understand how I felt?

Exhausted by joy, I flopped onto the mossy greenness and rolled, unconcerned about staining my comfortable brown tunic and deep green tights. I closed my eyes and breathed in the goodness of the glade. A cool breeze kissed my face and ruffled my short, dark hair. The air smelled of growing things. Rich dark soil, fragrant flowers, and mossy grass bruised by my frantic exertions.

What a perfect day!

As my heart rate settled, I heard a movement. Booted feet on soft earth? Opening my eyes, I sat up and glanced around. A young man —boy, really, probably a teen like myself—leaned against one of the white-barked trees at the edge of the clearing.

He was dressed in a loose linen shirt, with a dark brown vest laced across his chest, and matching brown pants. His hair was golden brown, and when he smiled at me, it was like the sun emerging from behind a cloud.

"Hello," he said. "You're new here, aren't you?"

I nodded and scrambled to my feet (to my feet! All by myself!), brushing leaves and grass from my clothing and trying to contain the giddy laughter that still wanted to bubble over.

"I've been watching you," he said, and I swore his eyes actually twinkled. "You seem happy to be here."

"I am," I answered. "This is amazing. I never want to *leave Feyland*."

And just like that, my adventure ended. The shield retracted and I found myself blinking at Dad and Uncle Jim. Back in the real world... where I was so terribly afflicted with spastic quadriplegia that I couldn't speak or even sit in a grav chair without straps to hold my body erect.

~

I wanted to scream, to rage at the injustice of that simple phrase pulling me back to a reality I didn't want to acknowledge.

Uncle Jim must have recognized the anger and disappointment on my face. He knelt before my grav chair and, placing his hands on mine where they were strapped in place said, "It's okay, Emma. I can see you have something to say. Let's try the interface's other function."

I frowned. The interface had another function? Something other than allowing me to play the full-D game that Uncle Jim and his company had developed?

"I know it's hard," Uncle Jim continued, "but I want you to relax. Be calm."

When my breathing regulated and my face relaxed as much as it ever did, he nodded.

"Good girl. Now, compose your thoughts. When you're ready, think, *Activate Speech Mode*, then think what you'd like to say. When you want your thoughts to be private again, think, *Deactivate*. Understand?"

I blinked twice.

He grinned and held crossed fingers up where I could see them. "Good luck!"

I closed my eyes and thought about all the things I wanted to say. All the things I'd waited my entire life to express, but not now. Now I just needed to tell Dad and Uncle Jim about the interface...and the magic of Feyland.

Concentrating with my whole being, I thought, *Activate Speech Mode*, and then, *Does this work?*

An oddly mechanical female voice shouted the words.

Dad stumbled forward and dropped to his knees in front of my grav chair. His fingers trembled as he stroked my cheek. "I hear you, baby. I hear you!" Tears brimmed in his eyes, and he turned to Uncle Jim. "Thank you, Jim. I can't..."

Uncle Jim put a hand on Dad's shoulder. "There's no need, Kent. I'm just so pleased it's working."

They both looked at me.

I'd have grinned if I could. Instead, I thought, *Feyland is amazing, Uncle Jim! Dad, you wouldn't believe it. Everything works there. My body works! I can stand and walk and run...and I can talk. It's...it's like a dream come true!*

The voice, my pseudo-voice, had a mechanical twang, but the volume regulated now that I knew it worked and wasn't pushing the thoughts with quite that initial intensity. The voice also sped up and increased in pitch in response to my emotions...and it was nearly instantaneous. A real-time echo of my thoughts. I deactivated it so I could think while I waited for their response.

Uncle Jim beamed. "Emma, that's wonderful." He paused, a little frown creasing his brow. "But why did you come back so soon if everything functioned correctly? Jennet can spend hours in that game."

Jennet. Uncle Jim's daughter. My cousin. The girl who was everything I should've been if life had been kinder. Even though she was only two years older than me, the differences between us were huge. Jennet was perfect, while my difficult and traumatic birth left me with a severe form of cerebral palsy. We should've been best buds. We'd grown up together. Our mothers had been sisters and for most of our lives we'd lived only a few miles apart...but it's hard to get to know someone when you can't communicate. Now, though...maybe we could become real friends at last. Even beyond family ties, we had a lot in common. We'd both lost our mothers a few years ago. We were both motherless girls with overworked, overburdened fathers. Too bad Uncle Jim's work with VirtuMax had caused them to move to Crestview a while back.

But I could think about my family issues later. Right now, I had more pressing matters to discuss. A chill ran through me. I never imagined the word *discuss* would apply to me!

I activated my speech mode and explained what had happened. "Could you please change the exit phrase, Uncle Jim? I was having a great time, and I'd just met another player. We were talking when I said, 'I never want to leave Feyland,' and suddenly the game ended and the interface brought me back here."

Uncle Jim's face cleared, and he laughed. "Of course! I can fix that right now. What would you like it to be? Obviously it needs to be something you can remember easily, but not something that you're likely to say in casual conversation." He grinned and straightened his glasses. "I evidently failed on that last bit."

Dad changed position so he was sitting on the floor by my grav chair instead of kneeling. "I can't believe I can hear you, Emma. After all this time, you can actually tell us what you want." He leaned back on his hands, a thoughtful expression on his face.

"What about *Deactivate Feyland*?" Uncle Jim asked. "That way both of your 'stop program' thoughts will be similar."

Dad nodded. "I like that. What do you think, Emma?"

I wished I could nod too. Of course, I wished I could do a thousand things that my body was incapable of. Right now, I needed to focus on the amazing gift I'd been given. "I can remember that, and I can't imagine that phrase coming up in conversation."

Uncle Jim stepped to the laptop that he'd connected to the interface and began typing. "I'll fix that right now, Emma, and then I'll leave you and your dad alone so you can talk." He glanced up and smiled. "You can continue your game after you've had a chance to catch up."

"Thank you, Uncle Jim," I said, savoring my ability to speak. "For everything!"

Two hours later, I reentered Feyland.

Once again, I stood inside a ring of red-capped mushrooms with cheerful white spots, in a forest clearing surrounded by white-barked trees with silver leaves. The sun shone from high in the prettiest blue sky I had ever seen, and a light breeze played with the ends of my hair. I hopped over the mushrooms, grinning, and twirled. Feyland might be an illusion, but it was one my mind welcomed. I was free! From my chair and the restrictions of my damaged body.

I glanced around the glade and spotted a path leading into the woods. Time to really begin the game. I picked up the oak staff that was part of my costume and fingered the tender twigs and budding leaves that adorned its crown. Magic was awesome. It gave me working arms and legs and let a staff that should be dead wood sprout greenery. How cool was this place?

I marched across the clearing to the mouth of the path, stepped onto its pebbled surface, and called, "Watch out, Feyland. I'm a Dryad and my name is Emma...and I'm free at last!"

My heart beat with joy as I skipped down the path, living staff in hand. I almost started singing—just because I could—but the bird-song and the breeze rustling through the leaves were too pretty to compete with.

I'd just settled down to a quick walk when the path widened into another clearing. Instead of a circle of mushrooms, this one held a low-slung cottage of whitewashed stone and a thatched roof. Window boxes of bright red flowers hung below each of the two windows. A Dutch door stood between them, with the upper portion open. A large oak tree stood just beside and a little behind the cottage, its wide canopy shading the small dwelling.

Stepping into the clearing, I stopped and leaned against my staff, enjoying the peace of the glade. What a charming place to live! I tried to imagine what kind of person lived in such an idyllic cottage. This was Feyland, so the inhabitant would undoubtedly be some race of faerie. Perhaps a dryad? The oak tree certainly seemed to be protecting the place. But I didn't think dryads lived in houses. An elf?

Before I could speculate further, a gnarled old man appeared at the door. His face was as wrinkled as a raisin, and nearly the same deep purple color. The top of his head was bald, but white hair streamed from a half-circle that ran around his scalp from ear to ear. Bushy white eyebrows and a luxurious mustache that flowed into a full beard completed his hairy appearance.

He eyed me from head to toe, then met my gaze. "Who are you

and why are you disturbing the quiet of my glade?" he asked in a rather belligerent tone.

"I, uh, I'm a Dryad," I said, not quite sure how to answer. "I'm just out for a walk, and the path led me here."

"Just out for a walk, heh?" He looked me over again and scowled. "Well, if you want to cross my glade, you'll have to pay my fee. If not, you can just turn around and go back the way you came."

Hmm. This must be the first quest in the game. Since I didn't really want to return to my grav chair in the conservatory, I really had little choice.

"What is your fee, good sir?"

"There's a stream just beyond my oak tree. Bring me a fish for my supper and I'll give you a token that will allow you safe passage through the Forest of Fear."

The Forest of Fear? That sounded ominous. Safe passage would definitely be a good item to add to my inventory. I glanced at the massive tree. I hadn't seen any sign of a stream and hadn't heard the gurgle of flowing water. Maybe it was a bug in the game, but a system so intricate that it could make a quadriplegic girl believe she was walking ought to be able to handle a little thing like the sound of running water. Was this funny-looking little man lying to me?

And that wasn't even the main question. If I managed to find the stream, what would I do? I didn't have any idea how to catch a fish! I mean, I'd listened to enough audiobooks to know people used fishing poles, or rods and reels, but I didn't have any of that stuff. I looked at my staff. Could I use it for a fishing pole? Maybe, but what about a hook and a line? Could I catch one with my bare hands? I'd heard of folks who could, but I usually couldn't use my hands for anything, so I certainly didn't have any experience with such things.

Still, what did it matter? I'd come to Feyland to play a game, so play I would.

"I accept your offer, good sir." A soft chime sounded. Interesting. I hoped that was a good sign. "I'll return with your fish as soon as I can."

"See that you do," he said with a sniff, and disappeared into his home.

I walked past the cottage toward the spreading oak. With every step, the sound of water grew stronger. At first it was a barely detectable gurgle, but by the time I reached the tree, the stream fairly sang. My steps quickened. I could hardly wait to see it, for its melody sang of splashing rivulets, of currents crashing into rocks and then swirling past. It sang of joy and freedom, and my heart sang with it!

My feet skipped across the meadow between the oak and the stream, and I laughed with joy at my unfettered movement. I understood the water's song because my heart was singing the same one.

I ran along the bank until I came to a young willow overhanging the stream. Once upon a time, the current had cut into the bank just beside its roots and then swirled away. Now the willow shaded a deep, quiet pool. A good-sized rock guarded the stream bank, and I sat, trailing my fingers in the water. The movement created soft ripples in the cool, dark water, distorting my reflection.

As the ripples dissipated, another reflection appeared in the water. A golden-haired youth. I turned to see the boy I'd met earlier standing a few feet behind me.

"You came back," he said, smiling. And just like earlier, that smile made the day seem brighter, like the sun had ratcheted up a few notches. "You left so suddenly, I wasn't sure you would return."

My cheeks heated with a blush. "Yes," I said. "That was a mistake. A glitch in my interface. I didn't mean to disappear."

"I'm glad. Your words certainly didn't seem to match your actions!" He grinned, and then his expression sobered. "Will the *glitch* happen again?"

How odd. He almost stumbled over the word *glitch*. As if he'd never heard it before. As if he didn't understand what it meant.

"No. My uncle fixed the problem. I'm all set now." His expression cleared, and he dropped to the grass beside my rock. "I'm new to Feyland," I continued, "but I don't recognize your costume. What class player are you?"

He glanced away, picked up a pebble, and tossed it into the quiet water. The movement caught my attention, and we both watched the ripples as they moved outward, only to be lost in the froth of current in the center of the stream.

"I'm a faerie Knight," he said. "A member of the Bright Court."

I continued to watch the water as it splashed and swirled in the dappled sunlight. Joy personified.

"A faerie Knight? I don't remember that being an option. Do you suppose we're playing different versions of the game?"

"No," he said quietly, his voice so low his words were almost drowned by the noise of the stream. "It is not an option for humans... and I am not playing a game. At least, not the kind you imagine."

My heart pounded so hard that my vision turned gray around the edges. I didn't understand. Something was wrong with what he'd just said. Should I leave? Should I think my safe words and flee the game?

Probably.

But he hadn't done anything to threaten me, and I wanted to understand. If I could.

I turned away from the sparkling water and studied him. Same golden-brown hair. Same linen shirt with dark brown vest and pants. He was the same boy I'd met earlier. I hadn't felt threatened then, and I didn't now. Only his words were strange.

"I don't understand," I said, and he turned his attention back to me. Our gazes met and locked. His eyes fascinated me, green with interesting little flecks of orange. I could get lost studying those eyes, forget all about my questions and concerns. I closed my eyes and shook my head. When I opened them again, I concentrated on his hair instead, the way it waved across his forehead and curled around his ears.

Good Lord! What was it with this guy? Even his hair was mesmerizing!

I licked my lips and dropped my gaze to my own hands. "What do you mean, 'it's not an option for humans'? You're human, aren't you?"

He gave a little bark of laughter, and I glanced up again.

"No. I am not human, but you are safe with me, child of man. I knew what you were the moment I saw you. You think you are playing a game, but you have stumbled into my realm. The true Realm of Faerie."

My eyes widened and my pulse rate soared. "But...but...that's not possible! Faerie doesn't exist!"

His smile was a little sad now. "Oh, I assure you it is, and it does. Others have stumbled across the threshold before you, little one. We, all of us who live in the Realm, have standing orders to bring any humans we find before the Bright King."

"And the little raisin man who sent me to this stream? Does he have those orders too?"

My knight nodded. "He sent you here and alerted me." He paused, studying my face, his own creased with a frown. "But...I cannot say why, but I find myself reluctant to take you to the king. There is something about you that is different from other humans who have wandered into Faerie. Something sad and joyous, innocent and ancient, all at the same time. You perplex me, little human. Will you gift me with your name?"

Alarm bells rang in my brain. I'd heard lots of fairy tales. I'd lived vicariously through the quests and magical encounters recorded in books. I'd always believed them to be fiction, stories conjured from the imaginations of their writers, but now... Now, I didn't know what to think.

But one of the recurring themes in such fantasies was that names had power. And here was a self-professed faerie Knight, a guy who claimed not to be human, asking me to trust him with my name, my essence.

"You first," I said, though how I expected to know if he told the truth, I'd never know.

"In your tongue, my name would be Brendan, but my true name is Bréanainn."

His name sounded something like "Bree-nin," but pronounced like the breeze whispering through the silver leaves of the white-barked trees.

"Thanks," I said, "but I think I'll stick with Brendan. My name is

Emma." There. I'd told him the truth, but not all of it. He didn't need to know my full name.

He rose to his knees before the rock where I sat, took my hand, and bent to kiss it. "It is my very great honor to know you, Emma." Without releasing my hand, he raised his eyes and met my gaze. "Know this: if it is within my power to do so, I will protect you as you journey through Faerie."

My jaw dropped. If the old tales were true, faeries didn't lie. They might withhold information or they might lead you to jump to the wrong conclusion, but they didn't tell outright lies. If he really was a faerie, if this wasn't just another bit of programming in the game—Brendan had just pledged to protect me.

A giddiness to rival discovering that my body worked rose and nearly swamped me. I smiled so broadly that my cheeks hurt.

When my emotions were semi under control, I thanked him, at least, as much as I dared. That was another bit of fairy lore: faeries didn't go in for thanks. "I don't really know what's going on, but I understand what you just said. I'm honored, Brendan."

He nodded and sat back, leaning on his palms. "I hope that someday you will explain the inconsistencies I sense in you," he said. "You fascinate me, Emma...who pretends to be a Dryad in a game that is not a game."

I laughed, stood, and spun around. I spent enough time sitting in my grav chair in the conservatory. I wanted to run and jump and dance while I had a body that could do all those things!

"Do I really have to catch a fish for the little raisin guy?" I asked.

Brendan grinned. "Not if you do not wish to, milady. And you should know, the *little raisin guy* is one of our best gatekeepers. He is a tomten who followed the Vikings from their lands to ours and finally found his way to Faerie. The Bright Court is now his home."

"So," I said, "the Bright Court takes in strangers and wanderers?" A thought so daring I wasn't sure I should allow it to take root pushed its way into my mind. Could I? Would I dare?

Should I even wonder if it would be possible for me to become part of Brendan's Bright Court? It would mean leaving the human world behind, but that wouldn't be so bad. I mean, it wouldn't exactly be a loss to leave my grav chair and my hospital bed and my poor, damaged quadriplegic body behind. But it would also mean leaving Dad...and good people who cared about me, like Uncle Jim.

Besides, I didn't know enough about this place yet to even consider such a question. Better to file it away, somewhere deep and dark, where it wouldn't tempt me to ask. Right now, I should just enjoy the game and Brendan's friendship, and glory in the gift Uncle Jim had given me.

Brendan and I danced to the music of stream and birdsong, away from the water and back up into the meadow. We laughed and twirled and leapt and ran until we fell into an exhausted heap among the sweet green grass and fragrant wildflowers.

I was still catching my breath when Brendan jumped to standing and froze.

"What?" I asked, alarmed, but he waved me to silence as he scanned the horizon.

The next thing I knew, he'd pulled me to my feet. "Your game gives you specific powers, does it not?"

I nodded. "I have something called Wasp Sting and Thorn Bite," I said, "and I can turn into an oak for short periods of time."

"That should suffice," he said, still scanning the sky.

"Brendan, what's wrong?"

"The Wild Hunt is coming. Our friend the tomten must have alerted the Court to your presence."

"What should I do?" I asked, fear making my voice shrill. "Should I leave?"

"That might be best."

I took a deep breath and reached for the calm I always held in reserve for hospital visits and painful tests. When I felt centered, I said, "Deactivate Feyland."

Nothing happened.

I didn't return to my grav chair in the conservatory. I was still in a grassy meadow sprinkled with wildflowers, staring at Brendan.

He tipped his head and cocked an eyebrow at me. "Why do you remain?"

"It didn't work. What do I do now?" Even I could hear the sound of pounding hooves and pack dogs barking.

"They will arrive in mere moments. The Horned One's magic must have trapped you here. Quickly, become a tree."

Oh, wow! Just like that, do something I'd never tried before. I scolded myself for not having used all of my items at least once, so that I knew what they'd do.

No time for if-onlys. I had to act.

I checked my inventory, chose *Be An Oak*, and activated the spell.

My arms and legs snapped together as my body became the trunk of a tree. My hair stood on end, the strands separating and lengthening, reaching for the sky and blossoming into a canopy of limbs, twigs, and glossy green leaves. My toes stretched into the meadow's soil, lengthening and digging, becoming roots that held me firmly in place. My face melted into bark, and while I couldn't exactly see, I perceived all that happened around me.

I was immobile, locked inside a protective barrier of wood and leaf, unable to communicate with Brendan.

Entirely too much like the Emma I'd left behind in the real world.

Panic swamped me, but I fought through it. I'd lived this way my entire life. Only today had I truly been able to communicate in the real world and dance and play in Feyland. I could bear this. I knew this. And, most importantly, I knew this self-imposed immobility would end.

Just like I knew that my silence had ended at home.

Uncle Jim had given me a miracle. I still couldn't dance and play at home, but thanks to the interface, I'd never be a prisoner in my own skull again.

I could endure being a tree in Feyland, and I could endure spastic quadriplegia at home. The interface had freed me.

Brendan's voice filtered through my fevered thoughts. "They come. Do nothing until I say it is safe."

I rustled my leaves in acknowledgement.

Brendan sat at my base, leaning against my trunk. He whistled merrily and was soon surrounded by a pack of milling, snuffling dogs with evil red eyes. A dozen riders on black horses drew up before him. The leader chilled my sap. A massive figure with a dark face and antlers sharp as knives.

"Bréanainn, knight of the Bright Court," said the Horned One. "We seek a mortal who has dared to enter our realm."

Brendan stood and inclined his head. "Lord of the Wild Hunt, good fortune to you."

"Do you know aught of whom we seek?"

"I saw a mortal maiden at the faerie ring this morning," Brendan said, perfectly truthfully, "but she disappeared before I could detain her and drag her to my liege."

The Horned One's steed pawed the earth just beyond the reach of my roots. "She is not here?"

Brendan gazed around the meadow. "I see no mortal maid."

"Indeed." The Horned One studied Brendan for a moment. "Ride on," he commanded his huntsmen. "We'll seek elsewhere for the human." And with that, both pack and riders surged away, riding not across the meadow, but into the sky where they disappeared among the clouds.

Brendan waited for a long moment before turning to my tree. "Return to your natural form, Emma. You are safe now."

I released the oak spell and transformed into my Feyland self.

Brendan caught me when I stumbled and would have fallen. He hugged me tight, then held me at arm's length. "Your departure spell should work now, little one. It would be best for you to return to the mortal realm."

I nodded my agreement, still a bit sluggish from my stint as a tree.

"Dare I hope that you will come again?" he asked.

"Oh, yes," I answered with a smile. "I'll definitely be back." My smile faded. "But how will you know when I come? How will we find each other?"

He pulled a golden chain from beneath his shirt and unclasped it. "Please," he said, "accept my token. As long as you wear this talisman,

I shall find you. Anywhere. Even in the mortal realm, though I have never sought to enter that fell land."

He placed the chain around my neck, and I touched the filigreed pendant that dangled from it before tucking it inside my tunic.

"I'll wear it always."

"Lest you be alarmed," he said with a smile, and again it seemed like the day brightened, "be aware that this talisman will manifest only in the Realm of Faerie. You will not see it in the human world, or even in the game you think you play, but unless you remove it here, it will remain with you and will mark you so that I may find you."

I nodded. "I understand." I didn't, not really, but I could see that Brendan believed his words, so I accepted his belief.

He raised my hand to his lips and kissed my knuckle. "Safe travels, Lady Emma."

I smiled, embarrassed, but incredibly happy. "And to you, Sir Brendan." Withdrawing my hand from his, I murmured, "Deactivate Feyland."

Dad, Uncle Jim, Jennet, and I sat in the conservatory where I could use Uncle Jim's special grav chair and interface that allowed me to speak. We'd finished dinner—a rather tedious affair for me, since I couldn't communicate and my nurse had to feed me—and were discussing Feyland. I raved about the game, praising the interface and Uncle Jim's amazing work. Jennet looked at me a little strangely from time to time, but it was so nice to be able to talk to her at long last that I didn't worry about it.

Finally, Dad and Uncle Jim went to the library so Uncle Jim could use Dad's computer to show him the screenie version of Feyland. Dad was so excited about me being able to use the game that he was thinking about buying a FullD gaming system for himself so we could play together.

That sounded great to me. I wanted Dad to see me as my Feyland self, and I wanted to introduce him to Brendan. Dad wouldn't have to know that Brendan wasn't just another teenager playing a game. Some things were better left unsaid, and I knew Brendan would understand. Faeries were masters of illusion.

Jennet scooted her chair closer to me and said, "Did, uhm, anything unusual happen to you while you were in-game?"

"Unusual?" I asked, hoping my computer voice sounded innocent. "Like what?"

"Well," she said, glancing around to make sure we were still alone. "I couldn't help but notice a certain, well, *glow* about you. I mean, I know you're excited by how realistic the game is, and how it allows you to walk and talk and everything, but still..." She paused, licked her lips, and then blurted, "You just seem, I don't know, different."

I blinked. First she asked if anything unusual had happened in the game, and then she noticed a difference about me, a *glow*? Could it have anything to do with Brendan's talisman?

"Well," I said, "I made a friend. A boy." If I'd been capable of blushing, I was sure I would've turned bright red.

"A boy, huh?" She smiled, relief evident in her expression. How odd. "What character class was he playing?"

"That was kind of strange," I said, watching my cousin for a reaction. Jennet was an expert on Feyland. If there was such a thing as the Realm of Faerie, I was willing to bet she knew about it. "He said he was a faerie Knight, but I didn't see that class when I chose to be a Dryad. Do more choices open up when you get to the higher levels?"

Jennet's face paled, and even though she quickly clasped her hands, I noticed a slight trembling.

"No," she said quietly. "The character classes don't change." She licked her lips again and then asked, "What else did he say?"

"Well, he told me he wasn't human and that he was part of some court, and was supposed to take stray humans to see the king." Jennet's face went paler still, but I kept going. "Honestly, I didn't know what to think, except that he seemed to believe what he was saying. Was it all just part of the game, Jennet?"

My cousin shook her head, took a deep breath, and exhaled slowly, her eyes closed. When she opened them, her color looked better. "No, it's not part of the game. Not at all. The Realm of Faerie is very real, Emma, and it can be dangerous. If your new friend told you he's a faerie Knight, he probably is."

I blinked, gathering my thoughts before willing my mechanical voice to speak. "I guess I should tell you about the talisman, then."

Jennet narrowed her eyes. "What talisman?"

"The necklace. He gave me a necklace and said it would mark me...that as long as I wore it, he'd be able to find me. Anywhere. Even here."

"Oh, Emma." Jennet closed her eyes and almost moaned. "Tell me you didn't accept it."

For the millionth time, I wished I could move my head, wished I could nod my agreement. But, of course, even if I could move, I wouldn't have been able to do that. I *had* accepted the necklace.

"No," I said, my new voice firmer and more confident than I felt. "I accepted it. I'd show it to you, but he said I wouldn't be able to see it in this world...or even in the game."

She reached forward and touched my cheek, staring straight into my eyes. "Promise me you won't go back into the game without me. You can't risk finding yourself back in Faerie without backup."

I hesitated. I wanted to visit Feyland again as soon as possible, even with everything Jennet had said. I'd been frightened when the Wild Hunt appeared, but I'd never felt threatened by Brendan. I really wanted to see him again. But Jennet definitely seemed to understand things I didn't, and much as I wanted to experience a fully functional body again, I wasn't interested in endangering myself.

Unfortunately, Jennet and her dad were just visiting. Her FullD system was at her home in Crestview. I had no idea how long they intended to stay. How long was she asking me to wait?

My cousin seemed to read my mind.

"I know I'm asking a lot," Jennet said, gazing so intently into my eyes that I wondered if she really could read my mind. "I can't imagine what it must be like to finally be free of that chair, to be able to move on your own and talk without assistance. I'm sure you want to go back into the game as soon as possible."

She laid her hand, her strong, capable hand, over my withered one and stroked my fingers. I couldn't feel her touch, but I saw the movement and read the compassion in her eyes.

"We don't know each other as well as we should, Emma," she said quietly. "Stuff has always come between us." Her eyes flicked from the bands holding my upper body in place to the grav chair and back to my face. "But I need you to trust me in this. The Realm of Faerie is a dangerous place. There are things I need to tell you, stuff I need to explain, and it'll be easier if we're in-game when I do it. Will you wait for me, Emma?"

I blinked twice, then remembered I could speak. "I do trust you, Jennet. Your dad has given me a miracle. I can wait a few days to experience more."

She nodded. "Thank you, Emma. I'll message as soon as we're home and we can meet in Feyland." She grinned, and her eyes sparkled with excitement. "I can't wait to see your Dryad character and to have some real girl time, just the two of us. It's going to be mag, playing the game together!"

The next few days were the longest of my life.

Okay. That's not true. I'd endured much longer hospital stays, including ones that had centered on horrifically painful testing. I was no stranger to discomfort. But this wasn't about pain. This was about excitement and anticipation. I longed to return to Feyland, to the freedom I enjoyed there. But I'd promised Jennet I'd wait, so wait I did.

I had long conversations with Dad, my nurse, my physical therapist, anyone who would stand still long enough to hear about the wonders of Feyland and how awesome my uncle was to have made it possible for me to play and, no less importantly, to talk! But I resisted the urge to enter the game alone.

Finally. *Finally*, Jennet messaged, and Dad gave me the time she'd arranged for us to meet in-game. I stared at the clock across the conservatory, and the instant the second hand hit the appointed time, I thought, *Enter Feyland!*

When the opening screens cleared, I stood inside the ring of mushrooms in a familiar clearing surrounded by white-barked trees with silver leaves, and Jennet stood just outside the circle. At least, I thought it was Jennet. She looked a little imposing in her long blue Spellweaver robes, her blonde hair covered by the hood, and leaning on a mage staff.

We stared at each other for a moment, each coming to terms with the changes in the other's appearance. Jennet broke our self-imposed silence.

"Oh my God, Emma! Is that really you?"

I grinned and twirled around inside the circle of mushrooms. "It's me," I cried, "and I can stand and walk and run and dance...and talk with my own mouth and vocal cords! Isn't this the best?"

Her eyes brimmed with tears. "You're beautiful," she whispered. "I mean, you are in the real world too"—she wiped her cheeks as a few tears escaped—"but ..."

"Yeah, I know." My own voice sounded a bit husky. "It's hard to see past the facial tics and grimaces that I can't control and all the straps and stuff holding me in place."

"Oh, Emma!" She stepped across the mushrooms and pulled me into a tight hug. "Your dad is going to flip when he sees you here. You're absolutely glowing with joy."

We parted, and both of us wiped our eyes. I sniffled a bit, then sucked in a breath and, marshaling my emotions, asked, "So what was so important that we had to talk in Feyland?"

Jennet dabbed her eyes one last time with the sleeve of her robe, straightened, and said, "Right. Warnings first, then we can play. First up, take a good look around. Do you see anything different this time? Anything that doesn't look the same as the times you entered the game alone?"

"Besides you being here?"

She cocked an eyebrow at me with a *well, duh* expression on her face.

I grinned, ducked my head, and immediately noticed a difference. "The mushrooms," I cried. "They're brown!"

"They haven't been before?"

"No. Both the other times, I landed in a circle of red mushrooms with little white spots."

She nodded and released the breath she'd been holding. "Okay. That's your trigger. When you play the game on your own, if the mushrooms are red and white, leave immediately and try again later. If they're brown, like these, it's safe to play."

"Seriously?"

"Seriously. The circle of red caps indicates that you've landed in Faerie instead of Feyland."

Jennet stepped out of the circle of innocent brown mushrooms, and I followed. "That's a relief," she said.

"What is?"

"That the mushroom circle holds true. When you went straight to Faerie on both your first two attempts at the game, I was afraid you'd stumbled across a thin spot we weren't aware of."

"Who's 'we,' and what's a thin spot?"

"We're the Feyguard. We've been appointed by the Elder Fey to guard the borders between our world and the Realm and rescue humans who stumble across unaware."

"Like me."

"Exactly like you," Jennet said with a nod. "But no one else has ever been marked so that they could be traced into our world. That talisman you accepted really worries me."

I touched the place Brendan's talisman rested. Even though I couldn't see it, I knew it was there. "He said I was special," I said, half to myself. I looked up at Jennet. "Do you think he meant it?"

"You are special, Emma," she said, her voice full of...I wasn't sure what, but I thought it might be respect. Not something I'd had much experience with. "In so many ways." She gave me a one-armed hug and said, "What can you tell me about your friend?"

"Well, he told me his name..."

"He *what*?" Jennet yelped.

"Yeah," I said with a smile. "I've read enough fairy tales to know that's significant too."

While we talked, we strolled along a path strewn with tiny white flowers, beneath the arching branches of those lovely white-barked trees. Their silver leaves rustled in the breeze, reminding me of the bamboo wind chimes that hung in our garden at home. I told Jennet everything that had happened in my first two visits to Feyland, or rather, as I now knew, to the Realm of Faerie. The only thing I left out was Brendan's name. He'd given that to *me*. If he wanted Jennet to know it, he'd have to tell her himself. She seemed to understand. At least, she didn't press me on that point.

"And he pledged to protect you?" she asked, a frown on her pretty face.

I nodded. "I trust him, Jennet," I said quietly as we stepped into a clearing that led down to a little stream. Very little. Barely more than a trickle of water.

My eyes widened in surprise, and I grabbed Jennet's arm. "There he is!"

Her head whipped up, and she gazed at the trees behind us. "He can't be. We're not in Faerie. We're in the game. I was very careful!"

I pointed, and she turned to look toward the rivulet.

Brendan stood just beyond the trickle of water that barely qualified as a stream. A soft heat haze shimmered around him as he raised a hand, palm out, in greeting.

"Oh!" Jennet exclaimed, as I practically ran to meet him. "Emma! Stop!" she cried. "Don't cross the running water."

I stopped just short of the stream. It was so narrow and shallow that it wasn't much of a barrier, but if Jennet didn't want me to cross, I wouldn't.

"I'm so glad to see you," I said to Brendan. "I wondered if you'd come."

"It is hard for me to enter your game," he said. "It is part of the mortal realm and therefore foreign to me. I cannot stay but a moment. I haven't the strength."

Jennet approached cautiously.

I nodded toward her. "This is my cousin," I told him. "I've been telling her about our adventures, but I haven't mentioned names." I laughed, a bit nervously. "It makes introductions a little awkward."

He smiled and bowed to Jennet. "I recognize you, Guardian," he said. "You need have no fear. I mean your cousin no harm. She has become dear to me."

Jennet returned his bow. "Thank you, sir knight—that relieves my mind. How have you come here?"

Brendan glanced at me. "She carries my talisman. It calls me. But I haven't the strength to remain. Farewell, my friend," he said with a smile. "I look forward to our next meeting."

He vanished, and so did the measly little stream.

Jennet collapsed on the flower-strewn grass. "Okay. That was weird."

"Was it?" I settled beside her. "I'm so glad he came. Now you've seen for yourself that he's not a bad guy."

"No," she said, "he's not a bad guy, and he genuinely seems to like you, maybe even care about you." She shivered, sat a little straighter, and looked me square in the eye. "But you still have to be careful, Emma. Promise me you won't stray beyond Feyland. Not even to see him. Promise me you'll leave immediately if the mushrooms are red."

Her expression was so fierce that I licked my lips. I didn't want to lie to my cousin, and I didn't want to endanger myself or any of her Feyguard friends, but I didn't want to lose Brendan's friendship either. He was, after all, the first friend I'd ever had.

"Emma..."

I buried my hand in my tunic, crossed my fingers, and said, "Fine. Okay. I promise."

And I meant it. Sort of. At least for now. But I had an out if circumstances should ever require me to break that promise.

For now, I'd be content to play the game. To use Feyland to get to know Jennet—and possibly my own father!— better, and I'd be happy with brief glimpses of Brendan. After all, it was more, so much more, than I'd ever had before.

But if a time ever came when Brendan needed my help, I'd act without a second thought. No one had ever needed anything from me before, and I'd never had anything to give, so if the opportunity arose, I promised myself I'd grab it and not let go.

"So." Jennet's voice broke into my slightly rebellious thoughts— something else I'd never had the capacity for, rebellion!—and I turned my attention to the here and now. "Do you want to, you know, actually play the game?"

I grinned and grabbed her hand. "You bet! Lead on, cousin. I want to learn everything there is to know about Feyland."

And maybe Faerie as well, I added to myself. No need to let Jennet know just how rebellious I was prepared to become...

ABOUT THE AUTHOR

Deb Logan specializes in tales for the young – and the young at heart! Author of the popular Dani Erickson series, Deb loves the unknown, whether it's the lure of space or earthbound mythology. She writes about demon hunters, thunderbirds, and everyday life on a space station for children, teens, and anyone who enjoys young adult fiction. Her work has been published in multiple volumes of Fiction River, as well as in *2017 Young Explorer's Adventure Guide, Feyland Tales, Volume 1*, and other popular anthologies.

Find out more about Deb at:
debloganwrites.com

facebook.com/deb.logan.750
goodreads.com/deb_logan
bookbub.com/authors/deb-logan

THE TURNING

LINDA JORDAN

J ade crossed the dark street, pulling up the black leather jacket collar to keep her neck warm. Magic roiled around her, forming an uneasy aura. Spectre, her harlequin Beauceron, padded along beside her, happily breaking all the leash laws.

The large dog looked up at her, his head hip-high, when she glanced down at him. They exchanged emotions. He was alert, but calm. She felt on edge. Something was off. They balanced each other well.

The brutal wind rolled off the Sound. It felt too cold for the end of October. At least Spectre was warm enough in the cold. His short double coat had already bulked up for winter.

Two female Fae got out of a sleek silver sports car parked nearby. They were barely dressed, clad only in slinky short dresses. Rumor was that Fae didn't feel cold like humans did. The blonde's ankle-length hair swirled in the wind as if it had a life of its own, but didn't blow around her face. The other one had dark hair tied back into a long braid, studded with white gems. They walked into Theodore's, a swanky cafe.

Jade let out a breath she hadn't realized she'd been holding. She was pleased to have missed them. She liked to surf beneath the radar of dangerous beings, and her senses identified Fae as potentially dangerous, even though she'd rarely interacted with any of them.

A group of women spilled out of The Lucky Claim, dressed up as ghouls, prostitutes and witches. Two of them held up a third up between them. A couple others staggered behind.

The sweet scent of alcohol and sugary drinks, spilled over the decades, wafted out the doorway at Jade. She was familiar with that smell, but didn't love it. Loud dance music blazed through the air, electrifying it, until the door to the casino shut behind the people leaving.

Jade kept walking, her black boots making clunking noises on the pavement. She moved purposefully, so anyone with half a clue would leave her alone. She never looked for trouble, no matter how often it seemed to find her.

She hoped she could handle whatever was making her feel so

uneasy. It felt like a night she'd be better off at home missing. Sitting and reading a good book. But Jameson niggled at her mind.

She sighed and kept walking.

Main Street was extra busy tonight. Halloween on a Saturday night. People had an entire day to rest up from the week, dress up and get ready to party. It was a full moon tonight, too.

She'd only had a three-hour shift bartending tonight at the Gilded Palace. She'd filled in for one of the other bartenders, who'd ended up in the hospital with the flu.

Port Dare was at the peak of its second prime tourist season: the annual Spook Festival. It had been going on for a week now. The big casinos had costume contests. There were haunted houses, and a large twilight parade with elaborate floats, each group trying to outdo the other. Usually the events happened in the rain, but not this year. This year it had simply been bitter cold.

Jameson hadn't come into the bar as expected, probably because with Halloween and the full moon, there were too many cops about. He wasn't stupid. The crazy man had left a message on her cell saying he'd found something for her, which he must have known would annoy her to no end if she couldn't get hold of him, and he wasn't answering her calls.

He wouldn't be in the Palace, or any of the bars. Not on a crowded night like tonight. Too many partiers and too much competition for all the easy marks.

Jade rubbed her face as she walked. She felt tired. Tired of bartending to make rent money. Tired of this town. Definitely not looking forward to another rainy, dreary winter. Mostly, she felt tired of not knowing what to do with her life, and of drifting.

She continued on down Main Street toward the park. There were people partying down there too, but they were more likely to be locals.

Jade spread out her senses, taking in who and what lay before her.

A group of pagans sat in ritual silence beneath the massive bigleaf maple that must be at least a couple of hundred years old, longer than white folks had lived in the area. They'd lit a fire in a hibachi. The smoke drifted across Jade's path. She smelled the sage smoke they'd used for purification and grounding. They were minding their own business, not a threat to anyone. This was one of their most sacred times and they were using it as such. Communing with their ancestors and delving into the darkness of their own lives. A darkness most people ignored.

They weren't playing at Halloween, like a lot of people did.

Over near the picnic table lurked a bunch of younger teens, clearly avoiding wearing any costumes other than jeans, high tops, and hoodies. They were not very subtly drinking from bottles hidden in paper bags.

They were the kids without access to cars. Those with cars would be somewhere up on the Hill, where cops didn't regularly cruise past.

Along the lighted paved path, at least three couples sat on the metal benches, huddled together and in various states of inebriation. She could hear at least one of them having sex.

The thought of even partial nudity in this weather made her shiver. Why was it so damn cold anyway?

It felt wrong. Unnatural.

Jade spotted Jameson on a bench down near the water, talking to another man that she didn't recognize. Jameson was in his mid-thirties, a couple years older than her. With his brown hair and eyes, and average looks, he was invisible to most people. An everyman. He used that and his charm to steal from the tourists.

The guy he was talking to had long, greasy hair, and kept looking around as if expecting to be attacked at any second. He wore black jeans, and a down jacket which made it clear he was a tourist. It was too rainy here for most people to bother with coats that weren't waterproof.

Jade had rarely seen anyone so nervous. This man could be the sense of her unease.

She and Spectre walked up to the bench where the stranger stood, looking as if he was ready to run.

"Jade, there you are," said Jameson. "This is Ricky. Ricky, Jade. And Spectre."

Ricky nodded at her, keeping his eyes on Spectre.

"Hi. You called me."

"Yeah, just let me finish my business with Ricky and I'll be right with you," said Jameson.

Jade walked down to the water. The shore here was sandy. The gusts whipped strands of long dark hair past her face.

Jade picked up a piece of driftwood and threw it out into the water. She gestured to Spectre and he raced into the water, jumping over the knee-high waves, splashing and dancing with the Sound. Chasing things out in the water was his favorite game. He was still a young dog. Afterwards, they'd go home and she'd get him warmed back up.

She focused on the bench behind her, using her power to hear what was said, beneath the hissing of the whitecaps.

"They're coming," Ricky said. "Tonight. And they mean to take me. They said they'd come back for me at Samhain."

He spoke in an accent she couldn't quite place. It wasn't clipped like an English one, or rolling like an Australian accent. It sounded softer than that.

"I told you, I have a place you can hide. No one will find you."

"They will. They're not human."

"What the hell did you do?" asked Jameson.

"I stole a sword. A magical sword. And sold it to the dealer who I stole it for. They already got the sword back, but they still want to torture and kill me," said Ricky.

Spectre raced back, dripping wet, and brought Jade the hunk of driftwood. He stared at her, his tail wagging. She threw it again and he chased after it, catching the stick midair and then landing in the water. Spectre wrestled with the stick, chewing on it as the waves retreated.

"You stole a magic sword from whom? You still haven't told me who they are."

"The Fae. Faeries. Except they're not flying things, like I thought they'd be. And they're dangerous. The Fae killed him when they took the sword, and they're going to kill me, too."

Faerie had recently been opened to humans. The Fae were supposedly trying to save the earth from all the damage humans had done to it, before it was too late, but no one really understood the Fae. Jade had heard mixed reports from people who'd met Fae traveling around the world. They seemed dangerous at best, gangsters at the worst. She hadn't been able to sort out what was true and which part was bigotry from all the gossip.

"Maybe you should leave here. Get on a plane or something."

"You don't think this happened here, did you?" asked the man. "I'm from Ireland. That's where I stole it. Then I took the money and ran. But I've felt them stalking me. Seen glimpses of them. They're a world-wide organization these days. Worse than the mob."

"Well hell, I don't know how to help you then. If I can't hide you from them, I got nothing."

Jade could see Jameson hold both his hands, palms up. It was a familiar gesture.

Spectre appeared at her side again, but without the stick. She didn't have time to move away before he shook icy water all over her. Now her clothes were as drenched as he was.

"Fair enough," she said to Spectre.

"But Ethan told me you could," the man said to Jameson.

"Well, Ethan was wrong. He didn't help you, did he? One of the most powerful people in this area and he turned you away. What is it you think I can do? I don't have enough magic to go up against the Fae. You stole the sword and they found out who did it. You knew it was stupid going in, so now you pay the price for getting caught."

Ricky stood and spat on the ground. He turned and walked back towards town, hands in his pockets and hunched over.

"Stupid bastard," muttered Jameson. He glanced at Jade. "Ricky, wait! I might have something for you."

Jameson motioned for Jade to come over. Ricky turned back around, hope brightening his face. Jade walked towards the bench, Spectre following her.

"Fae, huh?" she asked.

"That's the last thing we need. Him bringing the Fae down on Port Dare."

"They've never been involved here, have they?"

"Not that I know of. And the word on the street is, they've grown mean. They're angry at us for all the crap humans have done to the planet. They think nothing of thinning the herd. Which probably isn't a bad idea. As long as you're not part of those being thinned."

Jade had heard similar things. She wished the Fae would focus their efforts on the damn politicians and the bloody rich who had the power to change things and wouldn't because it would affect their bottom line. Those people in control of ruining the environment and keeping the rest of humanity under their thumbs. Since she didn't know the Fae agenda, Jade felt confused about where they fit in the world.

Spectre rubbed up against Jameson's legs, and the man rubbed the dog's floppy ears.

"How are ya, buddy? All wet, huh."

Spectre liked Jameson. Knew he was always good for a pet. She sat down on the bench.

"You've got a plan?" Ricky asked.

"Maybe," said Jameson. Then he turned to Jade. "Remember I said I had something for you?"

She nodded. Waiting. Jameson always liked to draw things out.

"Well, a client inherited a collection of magical items. She didn't want most of it. I was able to sell almost everything for her. But this, no one knows what it is, so no one wants it."

Jameson pulled a black silk cloth out of his pocket and gave it to Jade. It felt heavy for a piece of cloth.

She laid it on the bench and unwrapped it. Inside lay a stone. It was gray, smooth and polished from age, or being held by many hands. The stone was small, only about three inches long and an inch wide, but she could feel its power just holding her hand above it.

Jade picked it up. The stone felt warm, not from Jameson, but from the otherworldly warmth of magic it held inside. That power wanted to flow into her, but instinctively, she blocked it. She couldn't tell what sort of energy it held, good or bad, just that it was very powerful.

"She gave me this to try and sell, and it felt like it might have some power. Nothing I could access though. Thought you might be able to." Jameson grabbed the cloth as the wind tried to blow it away, and stuffed the it back in his pocket.

"I'm not sure," said Jade.

Ricky said, "You said you might have a plan. What is it?"

"This. This stone."

"A rock? A stupid rock? That's not going to help me."

Spectre growled.

Jade looked at him, then moved her eyes in the direction his muzzle pointed.

A mass of people moving down Main Street, some riding horses. They sounded like a drunk brass band. There were horns of some sort. And drums. And howling. As they came closer, she saw fog surrounding them. Fog? On a windy night like this? What the hell was happening?

The mad throng continued on into the park.

Beneath the lights near the paved path, Jade could see the brightly colored costumes and trappings of the horses' saddles. Little bells hung everywhere, and some of the riders blew on long brass horns. A group of hounds trotted alongside the horses, baying and barking.

Magic tingled up her spine and the Spectre's hackles raised. These weren't ordinary partiers. Not a drunk trust-fund kid among them.

They were Fae.

Pointed ears stuck out from beneath all that hair. Perfect, luxurious hair that hung down well past the horses' knees.

And the horses weren't ordinary horses. They were tall and graceful like the Fae, but solid instead of spindly, with long manes and thick tails that flowed onto the ground behind them. Blacks, bays, whites, grays, tans, and a mixture of them all. They seemed to snort with annoyance as the Fae drew them up to a stop in front of Jade, Spectre, and the two men.

Jade shivered and stood still, her hand clasping the stone at her side. She could feel its power pushing at her boundaries. Wanting in.

Spectre let out a low growl. He was ready for anything.

Ricky stood on the other side of Jameson, completely frozen with fear.

The Fae in front stood in his stirrups. He was dressed completely in black. Long, dark hair streamed across his chest and shoulders. His angular features were set in anger, and his black eyes focused on Ricky. The Fae pointed at Ricky, but Jade didn't think for a moment that he wasn't aware of her, Spectre, or Jameson.

Oddly, she didn't feel afraid. She knew the threat was aimed at Ricky. But was it right to just give him up to the Fae? He'd done something stupid, yes. Should that mean his death? Over a theft of a magical item which had already been recovered? No.

Whether she was willing to risk defending him was another matter. Even if she could.

Jade didn't know enough about the Fae. They had long swords strapped to their waists, and she felt the aura of powerful magic. How much did they have, and how did it differ from her own?

For what seemed like an eternity, no one moved. The wind whipped through the park and dispersed the Fae's fog, which continued to reform when part of it was blown away.

Jade's patience ended. It was too damn cold to be out here, her clothes were damp from the water Spectre had shaken on to her, and she hated bullies.

She walked forward, followed by Spectre, who continued to growl.

"What seems to be the problem?" she asked, willing Jameson to think of something.

"This man must die," said the Fae.

"And you are?" asked Jade.

He stared down at her, then said, "I am called Niall. You are not known to us."

"I'm Jade. And this is Spectre. Why must this man die?"

"He stole our sacred sword."

Niall glared at Ricky.

"Ricky, do you have a sacred sword?"

"I s-s-sold it," said Ricky.

"We found the sword and killed the one who had it. But this man must pay for his crime."

"By dying? Theft is not a crime for which death is a suitable punishment," said Jade.

"You are not to decide that," said Niall.

"Neither are you," said Jade. "You are here and now. We have courts and a system of law to decide punishments."

"This is beyond your court's understanding. And this theft happened in a different land," said Niall. His cold smile made Jade shiver.

Their horses stomped restlessly, and one of the hounds let out a howl. The other Fae were silent, but menacing. She felt their intimidation and it only made her angrier.

Even though Jade knew it was foolish, she drew an imaginary line in the trampled grass beneath her boots. She would defend this spineless fool, because it was the right thing to do.

"It's not beyond my understanding. There must be another way to solve your problem. For humans, life is sacred. You cannot take his life simply because he stole an object which has since been recovered."

The Fae spat on the ground, and his fury sizzled on the grass near the black horse's feet. It gave Jade an indication of just how much power he had. More than she'd ever seen.

"Life is not sacred to your kind. You kill each other in endless wars. You destroy life with every day you live. This earth would be perfect without humans. We will not bargain with you. He dies."

"No." said Jade, pushing Spectre behind her with a leg. He moved behind her, still growling.

She gathered her power. Felt the stream of energy moving up through her feet from deep within the earth. Pulsing through her feet and legs, centering it in her belly. It flowed down her arms to her hands, waiting.

The Fae narrowed his eyes and Jade felt the first blow. She was ready. Shielded. It knocked her back a bit. Clearly a test.

She let her energy rip. Jade had been focused on the Fae that she'd forgotten the stone in her hand. As she opened her palms to let the magic flow, the stone clung there, as if stuck to her skin. The stone amplified her power.

Niall yelled with rage as her magic hit him, His horse reared, letting out a scream. Niall fought to keep his seat.

Jade stood, unmoving, as he calmed his horse.

The stone clung to her skin. She couldn't feel its energy anymore. It was as if the small rock had attuned its own magic to hers.

Beside her, Jameson was silent, his face white with fear. Ricky still stood frozen. Jade was surprised he hadn't run. The wind off the Sound shrieked around them.

Finally, Niall stared at her and demanded, "Where did you get that?"

"It was given to me."

"You can't use that stone. It belongs to the Fae."

"Apparently, I can use it," Jade said.

Niall rode closer to her. She could feel the hot breath of the horse on her face. The creature gazed into her eyes, looking just like any other horse. It wasn't the threat.

She raised her head and met Niall's eyes.

"You carry Fae blood," he said.

"I do not. I've never been to Faerie. My mother was human."

"Your father, then."

"My father was born long before Faerie was opened."

"Fae have been traveling the human world long before Faerie was closed. And some of them stayed out in your world during the time Faerie removed itself from your kind. Your father must have been one of those Fae."

He sat on top of the tall horse, his eyes challenging her to come up with a better explanation.

But she had none. Jade had no idea who her father was. Mom had always refused to talk about him. And Mom hadn't had any magic. Or if she had, her power had been kept completely hidden. She'd been found murdered, coming home from her graveyard shift job, when Jade was sixteen.

By then, Jade had found others with magic who would teach her. Mentors. For the last ten years Jade had made her way in the world flying beneath most people's radar, and keeping herself safe by being invisible to those who might harm her.

Except for having a large dog. Who made her visible, but mostly to other dog people.

Spectre had moved back beside her and snarled at the group of Fae, horses, and hounds. He would take them all on if she asked. But she wouldn't. She'd just let him growl and intimidate where he could. Did the hounds and horses have magic, too?

"Come with us," said Niall.

"What?"

Jade clenched her jaws to keep her mouth from dropping open. What was Niall's game here?

"Come with us. You are Fae. Join us for our hunt. Meet your kin."

"I don't trust you," said Jade.

"You are Fae. There is no other way you would be able to use that stone like you did. We do not harm our own kin unless they commit terrible crimes against us."

"Humans have magic too," she said.

"Yes, they do. But what you did was not human magic. It was Fae magic."

Jameson leaned over and whispered in her ear. "It's a trap," he said.

Niall sighed and said, "It is not a trap. Any time you ask to be returned to this place and now, we will bring you back. It is a gift we offer you."

"What's the catch? You'll overpower me and take the stone? And kill Ricky?"

"There is no catch, other than you learning more about who you are. We will take you to where the mother of the stone you hold lives. You can speak with her, and decide for yourself whether you should keep that shard."

The stone felt solid in her hand. She wanted to keep it.

"We will remove the sentence on Ricky. Provided he never steals or does us harm again. We Fae take care of each other. You do not know who you are. Until you do, you are in danger of harming others and being harmed. You are more important than he is right now."

"How do I know you'll keep your word?"

Niall put his hands out and looked around as if searching for an answer.

"I can give you nothing if you don't believe me. I speak the truth. I mean you no harm and only wish to enlighten you. Search with your magic. Does that tell you nothing?"

Jade closed her eyes slightly, pretending to send her magic out and search their intentions, although she didn't know how to do such a thing.

She felt Spectre's energy. Wary, but waiting for her command to either back down or attack.

Jameson was anxious. Jumpy. Couldn't stand still. Kept shifting from foot to foot. Putting his hands in his pockets, then taking them out to turn up his coat collar or button it up tighter.

Ricky was even more distracting and anxious. Hyper. Still terrified, but smart enough to remain silent and not move.

Jade searched her own feelings. The desire to learn raced through her veins as if it were blood.

She didn't feel the threat from the Fae that had been there when they'd ridden up. Instead, she sensed a calm waiting.

"If I say no, what happens?"

"We will take Ricky and leave you alone," said Niall. "We only came for him."

She considered that. She could let them have the man. Unfair as it was.

Or she could go with them.

"If I go, so does Spectre." Jade put her hand on the dog's sleek fur.

Niall seemed to be considering that.

"We will need to use magic on him. Otherwise he won't be able to keep up with us."

"I can hold him," said Jade.

"Not riding behind one of us, you can't. Are you a good rider?" asked Niall.

Jade shook her head. She had never been on a horse before.

"I thought not. Your hound will need to keep up with the pack. That will require strong magic. We will be moving faster than humans can see."

"Jade, you can't be considering this," said Jameson.

She didn't reply.

Jade knelt down and put her face next to Spectre's. The dog licked her cheek.

She asked him, "Do you want to go on a run with these hounds and horses while I ride? I don't know where we're going."

"I go where you go."

"All right," said Jade, rising. "We'll go."

"Jade, don't do it. I don't trust them," said Jameson, grabbing her sleeve. "Ricky isn't worth your life."

"I'm not doing it for him," said Jade. "I want to know. I have to know."

Jameson let go and stood back. He glared at Niall.

Niall held out his right hand and took his foot out of the stirrup.

Jade had seen people get up on horses. She could do this. She raised her left foot and put it in the stirrup, took Niall's hand.

"Other foot," he said.

She switched feet and hauled herself up behind him. The horse stood patiently, waiting for her.

Spectre paced alongside, anxious for a command.

"Follow," she said to him.

Then the horse moved forward, quickly.

"Better put your arms around me," said Niall. "We'll be going fast. Don't worry about your hound. I've got him. I'll need the stirrup now. Just wrap your legs softly around Arienne's belly."

Jade put her arms around the Fae, took her foot out of the stirrup, and tightened her legs around the horse's belly. Niall's torso was bulkier than the loose black coat let on. Probably muscle, because his face looked so lean.

The horse picked up speed and began running. Jade glanced back and saw the rest of the Fae and their hounds. Spectre ran at the front of the pack, his gait effortless-looking.

The wind and trees whipped past and soon they were engulfed in fog and cold. The air felt icy. Why the hell hadn't she thought to wear her gloves today when she left the house today?

She could see nothing through the mist. There was only the noise of the horses' hooves and neighing, the hounds baying and barking, and the horns the Fae blew. The jumble of sounds was thunderous, and made her ears ring.

Her mouth felt dry and tasted stale, like the bad coffee she'd drank while bartending earlier that night. She tried not to worry about where they were going. She'd put herself in this situation and just had to trust the Fae. There was nothing else she could do at the present.

The journey seemed to take hours. The horses didn't tire, and when she looked over her shoulder at Spectre, he seemed fine. She tried to connect with him, but couldn't. Perhaps because of the magic the Fae were using to allow him to keep up with the rest of the hounds and horses.

Niall didn't talk to her, not that she could have heard him over the cacophony. At one point she must have fallen asleep, lulled by the motion of the horse. She woke with her cheek on his back, still traveling.

But her face finally felt warm, and her hands were warm too. Not from anything she'd done. The Fae must have some way of warming themselves while they rode like this. None of them wore gloves.

After what felt like an entire day, the horses slowed. Then the sounds around her grew louder as their hooves hit solid earth. Jade hadn't realized they weren't running on the ground before.

The mist cleared, and even though it was still dusk she could see by the light of the half moon the miles upon miles of grassland and rolling hills stretching out before them. The horses ran up the side of one of the tallest hills, then stopped as the land leveled off.

Jade could see in all directions, even though everything was dimly lit. There were no dwellings, only grass, the Fae, and the steaming horses and hounds.

"Time to get down," said Niall, taking his foot out of the stirrup.

Jade felt so stiff she wasn't sure she could move. She put her left foot in the stirrup, clumsily swung her other leg around the horse, and tried to find solid ground. She was able to get a foot down, but while trying to get her other foot out of the stirrup, her right leg collapsed. She ended up in pile on the grass. The horse didn't shift at all, just waited patiently.

Then Spectre was there, licking her face.

"Thanks, buddy."

She untangled herself, and Niall helped her up. Her legs felt all rubbery and weak.

"Here, drink this," he said, holding up an ornate silver flask.

"Is this a trick? I drink it and then can never go home again?"

He laughed.

"If it was, would I tell you the truth? It will restore you. Fae don't operate like that anymore."

She took the flask and sniffed it. It smelled sweet and fruity. Jade sipped the liquid. It tasted of summer berries mixed with herbs. The cool liquid flowed down her throat into the empty stomach. She could feel it warming her, bringing life back to those numb muscles.

"What is it?"

"A concoction we've used for millennia. Made of raspberries and blackberries, thyme, sage and other herbs. The healers don't give out the list of ingredients to others. They control who can make it, so it gets made properly."

She took another sip and handed the flask back to him. He tucked it inside his coat.

"Come," he said.

She followed him across the hill. On the horizon, she could the half moon rising or setting. It looked huge. Spectre followed.

Niall stopped suddenly, and that's when she saw the huge standing stone in the center of the hill. She'd been so busy looking off in the distance that she'd missed it.

"What is that?" she asked.

"That is the mother of the stone you carry. We have brought you back in time to see her when humans first stood her upright and began paying her homage. When she was at her full power, not diminished as in our time."

Jade walked closer to the huge rock. It was about ten feet tall and three feet around. There were no other standing stones in sight. Just the one, at the center of the hill. Smaller rocks surrounded it. They had been arranged to form several circles around the standing stone.

Spectre flopped down in the grass nearby and stared at her for a few minutes. Then he lay down, apparently totally relaxed, and closed his eyes.

She held out her hands and could feel the immense power emanating from the standing stone. It held the same energy as the small stone in her pocket, but magnified a thousand times.

Putting her hand in the pocket, Jade could feel the small stone. It vibrated as if it recognized the standing stone.

She pulled it out of her pocket, laying it on her open palm. She walked closer, moving inside of the small stone rings, until she reached the standing stone. Jade put her empty hand upon the smooth rock. Its voice rang out in her head.

"Welcome, my child."

"Who are you?" Jade asked, silently.

"I am the Stone of Fate."

"What does that mean?"

"I see into the future, past and present."

"Can you see as far into the future as the one I live in?"

"Of course."

"Can you see my fate?"

"Not everyone's path is fully determined. Your path is still undecided."

Jade could feel the massive energy and magic of the standing stone. And, oddly, it did feel female. She wouldn't have been able to explain that to anyone.

Her heart responded to the stone's words in her mind. She felt the open-ended road of her life stretch out before her.

"You have many choices left ahead of you. Soon you will come to a fork in the road. It is your choice which direction to go. There is no right answer. Your life will change no matter which path you take. It has already changed with the knowledge that one of your ancestors was Fae."

"Then how do I decide which road to take?"

"You must go where your magic and your heart lead. Not your head. You've been following your head all your life. It has protected you, but not allowed you to fully live. Now you must choose to follow your heart and embrace the power that was given to you."

That told her nothing. She'd rarely known what her heart wanted.

"Because you don't listen to it," said the stone, answering the question she hadn't asked.

The stone was right.

"Should I return this small stone to you?"

"If you like, you may keep it. But you must take care it does not fall into foolish hands. Much damage could be done with it."

"But Niall said it could only be used by Fae."

"And do you think there are no foolish Fae?"

Jade hadn't given it much thought one way or the other. Fae were new to the human world. At least new in the sense that humanity just found out they existed in the flesh, and not as some tiny winged creature of mythology.

Jade looked at the stone, felt its power, and decided she didn't want that responsibility. She didn't want to protect it, and then to have to find a new home for it at the end of her life.

She took the stone and set it on top of a small ledge-like outcropping far up towards the top of the standing stone that she had to stretch to reach.

The stone said, "Thank you."

Then it absorbed the shard back into itself.

Jade smiled. It felt as if a weight had been lifted from her. She felt lighter and fully alive. And now she knew what direction to head.

She walked back towards the horses. Spectre jumped up and raced ahead of her, his tongue lolling happily. Niall followed as well.

"Where shall we go?" he asked.

"Faerie. I'd like to see Faerie."

"It's a big place. Might take a while."

"I've got time," Jade said.

And she did.

ABOUT THE AUTHOR

Linda Jordan writes fascinating characters, visionary worlds and imaginative fiction. She believes in the powers of healing and transformation.

She's fascinated by nature's peculiarities, mythology and spirituality, what makes humans (and aliens) tick, political systems and the creation of music and art. She loves including all this and more in her stories.

In another lifetime, Linda coordinated the Clarion West Writers Workshop as well as the Reading Series for two years. She also spent four years as Chair of the Board of Directors during Clarion West's formative period. She's worked many other jobs, more than she cares to count. Eventually, she fled the city to live out among the tall cedars.

She lives in the rainy wilds of Washington state with her husband, daughter, four cats, a cluster of koi and an infinite number of slugs and snails.

Find out more about Linda at:
lindajordan.net

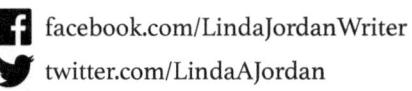

facebook.com/LindaJordanWriter
twitter.com/LindaAJordan
bookbub.com/authors/linda-jordan

TAKE A WALK ON THE WILD SIDE

REBECCA M. SENESE

"Iceland, really? It's the middle of February."

My partner, Trevel, pushed the vacation brochure back across the desk toward me as he made a face.

Considering he was a huge, grey-skinned troll with tusks coming out of the sides of his mouth, the expression was more than a little terrifying.

But I was used to it.

After all, we had been partners in the Spells and Misdeamenours Bureau of the police of Crossroad City for years now.

I picked up the brochure and leaned back in my chair. In the same motion, I swung my boots off the floor and onto my desk, resting my left ankle over my right. My boots were a dark blue leather, almost black but with a sheen that caught the light. I'd fallen in love with them in the store even though they cost almost as much as my upcoming vacation. But I couldn't resist that supple, dark blue leather. Besides they were practical, kind of. They kept my legs warm all the way up to my knees.

It was a cold, grey, and sleeting February day outside the windows of the offices of the Spells and Misdemeanours Bureau. The entire exterior wall of the office was a floor to ceiling set of windows overlooking the downtown core of Crossroad City. A heavy layer of clouds hung in the sky, making it look like it was going to storm, but they'd been hanging there for over a week. Wind made them shift and roll, but hadn't dispersed them.

Things had been slow for the past few weeks. In crappy weather, a lot of people stayed indoors, including any stray magic users that might get up to trouble. Even the Great Tear seemed to be more quiet than usual.

Perfect time for me to take vacation.

The rest of the gang in the Spells and Misdemeanours Bureau could pick up the slack, this lead detective needed a break, especially after the last few months. It had seemed like every magic user had been causing havoc. Even the Great Tear had seemed particularly volatile, not that there was much anyone could do about that but hope for the best.

The Great Tear was a rift that had opened between the dimensions of the normal world and the Nether Realm, and it just happened to slice right through Crossroad City. No one knew what had caused it or how it had happened but we had to live with it—on both sides of the rift.

Now Crossroad City served as a way station between the realms. Magic was heavily regulated in the normal world, the delicate balance of the rift couldn't absorb a lot of magic on this side without catastrophic consequences. To help manage that, the Spells and Misdemeanours Bureau of the police dealt with any and all magical related issues.

Usually landing on this red-haired lead detective called Maeve Hemlock.

But not for the next two weeks.

I sighed. Ahh, vacation, how I'd been looking forward to you.

The brochure was printed on glossy paper, filled with photos of stark, desolate landscapes, barren of trees or other vegetation. Just rock and hard ground as flat and polished as slate. I knew it would be cold and dark at this time of year. Empty of tourists. Quiet. Still. Deserted.

Perfect for a seventh level faerie princess of the North Faerie Court.

"Still think you should go down south, get some sun. You could use some colour," Trevel said. He pushed up from his desk, towering above me. "You want some coffee?"

"No thanks," I said.

He picked up the huge, silver beer stein that he used as a coffee mug. Even as large as it was, it looked like a tiny teacup in his hand. He strolled across the office to the coffee station that sat right outside the captain's office.

We had the best coffee in the station. To prevent the other officers from other bureaus stealing it, Captain Hwon had had the coffee table moved to just outside his office. It allowed him to keep an eye on our precious stash and also encouraged his own officers to chat with him. Even now I heard Trevel's deep voice murmur as he started a new pot.

A moment later, the rich, delicious odour began to drift through the office. From his desk by the window, I noticed Detective Lemmer's head lift from the papers on his desk, like a sunflower searching for light. He picked up his mug and began to wander toward the coffee table.

As I breathed in the scent I was starting to wonder if maybe I shouldn't get a cup after all. A little more caffeine never hurt anyone, even if it was almost three in the afternoon.

A shimmer of movement caught my eye.

I glanced over at the windows.

The same grey clouds hung in the sky, rolling in slow motion as they moved. The buildings below looked shrouded in mist, almost ethereal, or like they had been drawn in broad strokes by some giant artist who had yet to fill in the details. Nothing unusual down there, nothing to catch my attention. The Incantation River, which seemed to flow whichever way it wished, had been quiet for weeks. Even the Magic Circle, a road that shifted and twisted in different ways, sometimes slicing through the centre of the city or along the edge, but never in a full circle, had been quiet.

So why did I feel like something was wrong?

Then I caught it. Movement in the cloud. A darker patch of grey that lashed out and back, stretching forth like a leg before pulling back.

Like the leg of a runner.

No, like the leg of a strange beast.

Running.

But not just running for the sake of running.

A beast on the hunt.

The Wild Hunt.

I shivered even in the heat of the office.

That wasn't possible. It had never happened on this side of the Great Tear, and never in the middle of the afternoon, even a dull, grey afternoon like this one.

The clouds rolled and the image dissipated, like dissolving steam.

Maybe I'd been mistaken. Maybe it had just been the movements of the clouds that made it look like a leg. It wasn't some strange spirit crossing through the rift, leading the Wild Hunt on a rampage through the city.

Just my imagination.

After all, I'd been working hard the past few months, lots of double shifts with corresponding paperwork. I really needed this vacation. Catching a glimpse of an impending disaster was just my overactive, cautious nature. I was just used to looking for any problems with the Great Tear and magic on this side of the rift.

It had just been a cloud. Nothing more.

Except the wings on my back quivered and my heart wouldn't stop pounding.

Ah hell.

There went my vacation.

I picked up the phone to cancel my flight. Although I could fly, I was not going to carry my suitcase all the way to Iceland. Even faeries needed to go through customs.

I hung up the phone as Trevel returned, carrying a steaming beer stein full of coffee. As he sat, his chair creaked under him.

"Don't get too comfortable," I said. "We've got a problem."

He sipped his coffee, swallowed, and set the stein down.

"Oh?" His eyebrows lifted up his forehead, crinkling up the top of his bare head.

"Yeah, the Wild Hunt is coming."

Captain Hwon stood outside his office. He had replaced his usual well-tailored jacket with a bulky, black, bullet-proof vest. Several strands of his black hair hung over his forehead, the rest swept back on his head. He held up one hand and the murmuring of the officers that filled the room faded to silence.

Instead of the usual handful of detectives, the room was stuffed with uniformed officers, all in bullet-proof vests, wearing expressions of tense anxiety.

"Thank you all for coming in for this special shift. I'm sorry for the short notice. I wouldn't have called you in if we didn't think this had the potential for being a major problem. I know many of you have had dealings with the Spells and Misdeamours Bureau before but a few of you haven't. You will be divided up into squads with a detective from SAMD leading. Follow their directions precisely. Do not go off on your own. We could be dealing with strange forces that may cause you harm if you're alone. Stick together and follow directions. Understood?"

He paused, sweeping his gaze over the officers that filled the room. A few shifted from side to side but no one spoke.

"I'm now going to have Lead Detective Maeve Hemlock brief you. Pay attention to what she says. She's the expert here."

Hwon nodded to me.

Expert. Great.

Just because I was a faerie from the North Court, had witnessed the Wild Hunt in my years growing up at court, and had learned all about it at the knee of several of the more advanced fae wizards in the North.

I guess that did make me the expert on this side of the Tear.

Just great.

Why hadn't I taken my vacation a week earlier?

I stepped out from beside the coffee station. I could feel the officers' attention shift to me. Some of them I knew, others I had seen around the station, and others still were completely new. Maybe even pulled in from other precincts.

I could tell from some of the expressions what they were thinking: who was this short woman with long red hair, wearing a long black leather coat and knee-high boots? What did she know about anything?

With a shrug of my shoulders, I flexed my back muscles. My vibrant blue fae wings unfolded. With a single flap, I floated into the air, hovering above the officers until I almost reached the ceiling. My leather coat hung open, revealing my holstered wand.

Eyes widened. Several mouths dropped open. All suspicious looks vanished.

Good.

I allowed myself to float back down to the floor. No sense expending more energy than I had to.

As my boots touched the tile floor, I opened my mouth.

"Our job tonight is simple," I said. "Keep all citizens safe and off the streets if possible. You are going to witness one of the most astonishing and frightening events you'll ever see in your life, but you will be safe if you stay out of the way. Do not try to interact or affect the event. Let it pass by. You are only to stop any humans from joining in. That's all."

I took a breath. Several officers in front of me swallowed. The scent of sweat intensified.

"I am expecting the Wild Hunt to pass through tonight," I said. "It is one of the most mystical, magical events, even in the Nether Realm. You can not contain it, you can not stop it, you can only survive it. The only way we can affect it is to not allow anyone to join in. The longer we can stop any human on this side of the Great Tear from joining in, the shorter of duration we expect the Wild Hunt to be. It may even discourage it from happening on this side again. But only if we do our job and keep everyone away from it. Any questions?"

Hands flew up, just as I expected.

Were soft, rubber batons really the best thing to have? Why weren't we carrying our guns? Did we know the route the Wild Hunt would take?

The words washed over me and I answered as many questions as I could.

We had to try to avoid any deaths tonight. They would only give more fuel to the Wild Hunt as any freshly dead spirit would give it new and vital energy.

I suspected the Hunt might follow either the path of the Incantation River or the Magic Circle as both of those were the most magically affected areas of the city, but I couldn't be sure. There really was no way to tell where the Hunt would travel. I was stationing officers at central cross streets so they could respond in whichever direction was necessary.

Finally, the questions were exhausted. In front of me, the officers looked even more uncertain and tense. I didn't blame them. It was going to be a hell of a night.

I glanced over at Captain Hwon who nodded. He stepped forward to stand by my side.

"You've been given your assignments," he said. "Let's get out there and keep our city safe. Be careful and remember to stay out of the way of the Wild Hunt."

Murmuring voices filled the room as the officers began to flow through the door, following the detectives of SAMD out. Before he left, Trevel raised his hand to me in a wave, then gestured at several obviously fresh recruits who stared up at him with wide eyes. They stumbled after him through the door.

"Tell me this is going to work, Maeve," Hwon said to me as the last of the officers filed out of the door.

"Damned if I know," I said. "It's the Wild Hunt. I have no idea why it's coming through the Great Tear in the middle of February."

Hwon sighed. His normally calm, bland expression creased with worry.

"Great. If you don't know, how are we going to deal with it?"

"I'm just a lowly detective, sir," I said. "But even in my former life at the North Court, the fae did the same thing we're doing now. Hunkering down and waiting for it to be over."

"Will it be over?" he asked.

"Eventually, sir," I said. "Eventually."

The Hunt hit just after seven that night.

In mid-February, seven o'clock was as dark as midnight. Wet, slushy snow had started falling just after sundown and turned the street and sidewalks into a wet, slippery mess. One good effect of the horrible weather, people stayed indoors. No one wanted to venture out into the mucky night.

I flew through the cold, moist air, checking on as many of the officers positioned around the city as I could. I had enchanted myself with a drying spell that kept the worst of the wet snow from adhering to me, but after hours in the air, it was starting to wane. I could feel the occasional dribble of water trickle under the collar of my coat and slide down my back.

My muscles were sore from flying for hours. The vibrant blue of my wings had faded to a slate blue, another sign of fatigue. I had tied my long red hair back into a bun to keep it out of the way, but it was now starting to unravel. Stray strands clung to my cheeks.

It was going to be a long night.

I'd prepared myself by having a stash of enchanted adlaberries in one pocket and chocolate-covered cocoa beans in another. Imported from the North Court, the purplish berries acted like caffeine on humans, but boosted magical abilities in fae. They would help fortify my magic and the cocoa beans would help fortify my caffeine levels. Together, they should help me survive this.

So I thought.

Until I hear the first trumpet blast announcing the arrival of the Wild Hunt.

It was by no means a sedate, disciplined tone. Instead, it was a wild shriek of noise that sounded like the cross between a howl and a braying banshee wail.

Around me, the air seemed to crystalize. The wet snow froze, turning to hail. The clouds thickened, rolling and grey.

I dove as fast as I could, dodging hail pellets as I descended. I broke through the bottom of the clouds and found myself hovering over top of the Crossroad City Secondary School. It was an old, grey brick building that looked almost like a castle, with turrets on the street-facing side of the building. An empty parking lot extended off the back, empty except for one car parked under a lit light.

An old man appeared, exiting from the back of the school,

hurrying toward the car. He was bundled in a heavy woolen coat, a hat pulled down over his ears.

What the hell was he doing at the school?

I didn't have time to ask him. The Hunt was already upon me.

It emerged from the swirling clouds. At first, it appeared to be more of the same, just thicker and darker, a dense black of smoke that seemed to twist and turn in on itself. It was at least two blocks wide and double that in height as it stretched upward into the night sky.

The howling shriek grew louder. Then the black smoke seemed to break apart, and the Wild Hunt emerged.

Spirits of little form or substance flowed forth. In fae lore, we believed they were the souls of the damned, cursed to ride across the earth, hunting for release. They could appear in any form, but usually took the form of those you knew. It was a way for the Wild Hunt to draw others to the chase. A way to trick you to join.

Swirls of smoke formed into figures riding atop beasts. Some of the beasts looked like horses with manes of flame streaming from their necks. Others looked like craven beasts with claws that sliced at the air. And the figures atop...

I spun away, diving down, heading for the parking lot. I didn't want to see the faces and forms that the figure took. They could look like my family or friends, colleagues from work or even errant magic users that I had arrested for misusing spells. That was how the Hunt caught you and pulled you in.

But they weren't pulling me, nor would be pull anyone else in. Not on my watch.

The man had reached his car but instead of unlocking the door and climbing in, he stood at the driver's side. His head tilted back, glasses glinting from the parking lot light as he looked up into the sky.

Looking toward the Wild Hunt.

The shrieking wails had caught his attention. It was only a matter of time before it sucked him up for the hunt.

I dove straight for him, managing to pull up for a landing just before I slammed into him. My heart pounded from the strain. I gulped in air. I could feel my wings sagging on my back.

On any other night, I would have astonished the man standing before me, but tonight he ignored me completely. His face was lifted toward the Hunt.

"Hey, mister," I shouted.

He continued to ignore me. Even as I watched all expression started to drain from his face.

I had only moments before he was completely enthralled.

I hauled back and slapped him.

Hard.

The effort whipped his face to the left. His glasses stayed on, but hung crooked on the bridge of his nose. For a moment, the unfocused, hazy look remained on his face, then the pain and shock of the slap caught up to him. He righted his glasses, lifted a mittened hand to his right cheek which had started to redden.

"Hey," he said.

I opened the left side of my coat, revealing the badge affixed to my shirt.

"What are you doing out of your home?" I asked. "We've been blasting emergency messages all over the city all afternoon. No one is supposed to leave their homes until further notice."

"I was working," he said. "I'm a custodian in the school. They asked me to come in early. I just finished my shift."

Damn typical. We'd enforced closures of schools, businesses, and government offices, telling everyone to go home, yet so many places didn't bother to place any value on cleaners and other labourers.

The mark from my slap was already fading. Fortunately he kept his gaze fixed on me. Worry lines were etched in his skin. The bottoms of his glasses fogged with his breath.

But how long would he be able to resist the call of the Hunt? I had to make sure he could get home safely.

I pulled an adlaberry from my pocket and popped it into my mouth. The first crunch sent sweet and sour flavour flooding my taste buds. It faded within a second as the berry dissolved. I felt my wings perk up. Magical energy flowed through me. The howling shriek that had been tugging at the back of my mind receded to almost nothing.

Not gone, not by a long shot, but so much easier to ignore.

I unholstered my wand but kept it down at my side.

"You need to drive straight home, sir," I said. "No stopping. Do not look up into the sky. Do not go to a store or restaurant. Straight home. Do you understand?"

He swallowed. Nodded.

"I'm going to give you some help to get home safely," I said.

Alarm tightened his face.

"Wait a minute, I don't consent to any spell."

"Too bad, this is a public emergency."

Before he could protest again, I lifted my wand and spoke a simple focus spell. I then repeated my instructions for him to drive straight home and go inside without looking at the sky or stopping anywhere else.

As the spell settled in, he got the dreamy look of a man enchanted. Then he turned away from me, back to the car. He unlocked the door and got in. Without even glancing at me, he turned the car on and headed off. The back wheels spun in the slush but gained traction as he aimed for the exit.

I could see how he kept looking straight ahead. No glance upward even as the howling increased in volume.

That spell should last long enough to let the man get home safely.

Now I just had to make sure no one else fell prey to the call of the Wild Hunt.

I set my wings ablur and rocketed into the sky, skimming the rooftops as I flew. The howling and wailing of the Wild Hunt followed, close on my heels.

As the street I followed swung east, it hit the Incantation River flowing west. I followed the street for half a block, then spun and headed for the river.

Flying above the Incantation River was tricky at the best of times. Affected by the Great Tear, it magically shifted position and directions, seemly at whim, if a river could have a whim. Sometimes at night it sparkled with a golden glow. Other times it shimmered in silver. I had even seen it ripple in multicoloured waves, like a flowing rainbow.

But tonight, with the Wild Hunt at my back, the river flared and boiled beneath me. Waves reached up as if trying to grab me, forcing me to fly higher than I wanted. After each reaching wave, the water dipped back down. I followed it lower, trying to stay within five feet of the churning water without letting it touch me.

Maybe, if I was lucky, the Wild Hunt would be drawn to the magic of the Incantation River. My magic would be puny and minuscule in comparison. I should then be able to veer off and the Hunt would continue following the river's path. Maybe it would even start to follow the Magic Circle.

That was the plan anyway.

Ahead I spotted where the river veered to the left, passing several old warehouses on the right. They reared up from the water like black blocks against the darkness.

I put on a burst of speed. I could feel my wings straining in the frigid air. Hail pellets struck at my face, barely missing by a fraction of an inch. My hair was soggy on my head. My coat felt heavy with water.

My drying spell couldn't keep up with my speed.

Just a few yards.

A few seconds.

The river bent under me.

Turning left.

I darted right.

A concrete wall loomed in front of me. I nudged right.

And slipped into the crevice between the two buildings.

The shrieking howl of the Wild Hunt increased. I could feel it vibrating in my bones. I clenched my teeth to stop from calling out to it. The urge was so strong. I clung to the wall of one of the buildings, feeling the rough, frigid surface of brick and ice under my fingers. My wings fluttered too fast for just hovering. Every part of me felt the pull of the Hunt.

Let it follow the river. Please let it follow the river.

The shrieking howl seemed to lessen. It felt more distant.

The Wild Hunt had turned left, following the path of the river.

I had evaded it.

I sagged, letting my wings slow so I drifted down to the ground. Ice crunched under my boots. At least they had kept my legs warm and dry. My coat and hair was a sodden mess.

In one smooth motion, I unholstered my wand and murmured a quick drying spell. Nothing fancy. Just enough to pull the moisture from my clothes and hair. A delicate, mild spell.

But it was enough.

Beyond the opening of the crevice, I saw the swirling cloud of the Hunt pause. The howling increased in pitch. A call to the pack, to rally, to turn.

To Hunt.

Oh crap.

I'd sparked magic. I'd given it a target.

Me.

I shot upward, out from between the two buildings. A quick glance showed me that the Hunt was already roaring toward me. Beasts of flame and smoke. Horses of cloud and fire. Souls that looked like skeletons reaching with bony fingers. Others of unspeakable shapes. Vaguely familiar faces twisting and shifting.

All focused on the game. On the target. On the rabbit.

On me.

I flew faster than I'd ever flown before. Darting between buildings, flashing past trees.

The Hunt stayed right on my tail. Gaining with every mile.

If they were going to catch me, I couldn't let them do it in a populated area. Who knew what the magical effect would be?

I angled north, heading for the Black Forrest Park.

Like the Incantation River, the park had absorbed a lot of magic with the opening of the Great Tear. This caused it to act in strange and unpredictable ways. The park now flexed its boundaries in an arbitrary fashion. Sometimes the trees pressed right up against the southern most road of Forrest Valley, branches reaching almost all the way across the asphalt to the other side, spooking people driving past as the branches seemed to grab for the cars. Other times the trees retreated, sometimes as far as half a mile, leaving empty earth, scourged by deep ruts as if some giant god had scratched deep furrows in the land with his claws. My theory was that the trees ripped their roots up from the soil and shuffled their way across the damaged earth.

As winter came, the forest's activities lessened, as if hibernation affected the magical forces within.

Better for me for flying into the forest. Not so good if I wanted it to act as a distraction.

But at least in this cold, desolate night there would be no one else around. No one else to be captured by the Wild Hunt.

Just me.

I reached the southern edge of the forest and plunged in. The empty, frozen branches seemed to sparkle in the darkness, alerting me when I got too close. The ice that crystalized on the trucks and branches coated the roughness in smooth, clear ice, giving it a bluish sheen.

As I darted through the trees, it reminded me of home in the North Faerie Court. The forests there dwelt in an almost unending sleep. Thick branches sheered of foliage or bud. As a child, my cousins and I made it a game of climbing as high as we could without the use of wings. The one to last the longest and get the highest won.

Being the youngest and lightest, I always won. Until my cousins had taken to knocking me out of the trees.

I'd blasted a wakening spell through the lot of them, enveloping the closest trees. Jolted from their hibernation, the trees had lashed out at the fae closest to them. Leaving my cousins with numerous welts and bruises from the swinging branches.

My mother had given me a stern lecture about the expected behaviour of a seventh level princess, but my cousins never knocked me out of a tree again.

I wondered if the same principle would apply here.

Would the forest, disturbed by the Hunt, rise up to vanquish it?

Maybe I'd been going about this all wrong. Not that I'd had much chance to plan anything.

I darted behind a huge oak. The trunk was even wider than Trevel's waist. As I drew closer to the trunk I could feel the slumber within. A dimming of the tree's life.

Sleeping. Still. Quiet.

I gulped several adlaberries, felt them buzzing through me. My magic seemed to shimmer around me. I lifted my wand.

Wakey wakey.

I cast a heat spell.

The ice that coated the trunk thawed instantly. Water splashed to the ground. Huge, brown branches lifted outward. I felt the sap begin to flow, jolted at first, then raging like a river.

It was as if I'd shot the tree full of adrenaline.

I could almost feel the trunk expand and creak, as if it were taking a breath. Tiny green buds appeared on the branches but the cold air and sleeting snow made them shudder. A deep rumble sounded from the ground, almost like an annoyed growl.

It was awake, but I needed more than just one tree for backup.

I swiveled, facing away from the tree, and raised my wand.

Something whacked me across the back, sending me rolling through the air.

The oak was not pleased to be awake in the middle of winter.

I managed to right myself before I smashed into another tree and stayed there, hovering out of reach.

"Look, I'm sorry," I said. "We've got a big problem. The Wild Hunt is rampaging through this realm. I know you want to be asleep but it feeds on magic and it's only a matter of time before it starts feeding on you, and the Incantation River, and the Magic Circle, and every other piece of errant magic in this city. I caught its eye and it's after me now but it'll start absorbing you."

My heart was pounding and I felt like I was talking a million miles a minute. My wand shook in my hand. Or maybe it was my hand shaking the wand.

I couldn't tell. I was more hyped than I'd ever been.

Maybe too many adlaberries.

The shrieking howl began, a little distant. The Wild Hunt must have lost my magical scent when I reached the forest, but the reprieve wouldn't last long. It would catch it soon enough and the Hunt would be back on.

I needed reinforcements. Now.

"That's it, the Wild Hunt," I said. "What do you say? Will you help me?"

The green buds on the branches shriveled but I didn't get the sense that the tree was falling asleep again. The branches reached out, brushed against the branches of the closest trees.

A low hum started underground. Ice began dripping from the other trees, soon falling in clumps. Branches creaked. Trunks seemed to expand and contract.

The tree I had awoken was waking others.

Maybe my crazy idea wasn't so crazy.

But it was only a few trees. I needed the whole forest if this was going to work.

I lifted my wand, preparing to cast a wider heat spell.

A branch whacked me in the side, sending me spinning. Before I could right myself, another branch lashed out.

I had to dive to avoid it.

Maybe I hadn't been as convincing as I'd thought.

Instead of the tree deciding to help me, it was waking others to punish me.

Another branch lashed at me. I reared back.

Into the path of another swinging branch.

It caught me on the side of the head.

I spun away. My vision swirled. Darkened.

I felt like I was falling. My wings fluttered, kept me alight.

But I lost my grip on my wand.

It fell, swallowed by the muck and cold and wet.

I shook my head. I couldn't fall unconscious, not now. Not missing my wand with the Wild Hunt on my tail, surrounded by disgruntled trees.

The shrieking howl drew closer and louder. More confident. The Hunt had picked up my magical scent again.

So much for the masking ability of the forest.

I didn't want to leave without my wand. I didn't exactly need it for magic, I'd learned to cast spells without it at home, but in this realm it helped focus the magic. Without it, my spells would be weaker, more scattered.

As if I needed another disadvantage against the Hunt.

But from the sound of it, I would never outrace it.

If I was going down, at least I wanted to go down fighting as best I could.

I dove for the ground. Slush and muddy earth squished under my boots as I landed, splashing up.

Great, with everything else my new boots were covered in filth.

If I got out of this I'd find out if the extra weather proofing I'd paid for was worth it.

I dropped to my knees and held out my hands in front of me. Even opening my senses a little, I could feel magic crackling in the air around me. It heightened the earthy smell of the mud, the wet damp of the melting ice, the frigid cold of the air. The ground squished under my knees, soaking past the edges of my boots and into my pants. My leather coat felt heavy and soaked on my shoulders. Even my wings felt heavy, fatigue weighing them down. Even in the dimness, I could tell they had faded to a pale, almost translucent, blue.

Without my wand to help me, I'd never be able to focus a spell in this condition. And it was way too soon to eat more adlaberries. Instead of helping, it would burn me out faster.

I had to find my wand.

I breathed out, feeling my heart beat slow. Through the crackling energies that swirled around me, I sent out a singular call to my wand. *Come, come to me.*

I waited. Staying still. Trying to focus through the swirling, crackling power. As the shrieking howls drew closer.

Come.

I felt a tingle of response.

The tiniest of tingle. Hardly anything. If I had been just a little less focused, I would have missed it. Even now I couldn't be completely sure of it. I called again.

A moment later, the tingle came again. A little stronger.

In front of me. To the left.

I moved my hands forward, reaching, sending out the call.

The tingle came again, even stronger.

Almost there.

A wall of energy blasted over, sending me flying through the air. I slammed into a tree trunk. Breath whooshed out of me.

I dropped into the muck.

Magic and energy swirled and crackled above me. The sky was lit with flashes of light, like a psychotic lightning storm. Sparks of red raced across the sky, visible through the trees. Swirls of clouds appeared, descending from above and emerging from it, the Wild Hunt itself.

And I didn't even have my wand.

My body felt like one gigantic aching bruise. I could just lie here and let them take me. As the smoke figures descended, it was an attractive thought. Then I heard my mother's voice in my head, disdainful and filled with wrath.

How dare I, Maevelyndaria, seventh level of the House Hemlock of the North Faerie Court give up so easily?

Nothing like your mother's voice in your head guilt-tripping you while you faced a living horror.

With a groan, I pushed up onto my knees. Another groan, louder than the first, and I managed to get to my feet.

At least if it was going to kill me, I would die standing.

I lifted my hands, holding them apart, and began to murmur the chant for a blasting heat spell. Without my wand, it would dissipate quickly, but if I held it back until the last second, I might be able to give them a good roasting before I fell.

The howling and screeching filled the air. Smoke covered the sky now, hiding the flashing of light. It floated down through the trees. As I watched, the branches shivered and seemed to turn black like ash. A rumbling sounded from beneath my feet. The trees waking up to the danger, realizing that I'd spoken the truth.

A little late, fellas.

Creaking sounded. Branches began to sway above me. Several swiped at the smoke but they passed harmlessly through, not even disturbing the images as they appeared.

Beasts with claws that sank into the earth stepped in front of me. Huge muzzles filled with ragged teeth. Spikes protruding from some of the heads, long, flowing coarse hair from others. Skeletons wearing rags and bits of flesh rode atop them. Snarling, roaring, whining. They hoisted swords and spears, waving them in triumph.

But they didn't throw them or swing them at me.

Instead they drew closer. Six feet. Five feet.

I held my hands at the ready, feeling the invisible ball of fire I had conjured swirl between my palms. At three feet, I would throw it. It was a little close for comfort at that distance, I'd probably also be burned, but it was the best chance for my magic to hold together long enough to do some damage.

Four feet.

The Hunt stopped. Holding fast at four feet away.

Did I have enough focus to cast it and maintain it at that distance?

I had to try.

I took a breath.

The Hunt parted.

A black horse stepped forward, wings of charcoal grey sprouting from its sides. A white stripe showed on its forehead, flowing down toward the nose where it veered off onto the right side of its face.

Wait a minute.

I knew that stripe.

Sitting atop the steed was an armoured figure in dark grey. The helmet was fashioned like some strange muzzled beast, with great, huge teeth. One hand reached up and I spotted a lever on the side. The top of the helmet flipped up.

And a familiar red-haired head poked up. A grin broke across the pale face.

"How goes, cousin?" said the man. "You gave us a right good hunt."

Somehow I managed to keep my mouth shut, although in my head, my jaw dropped.

My cousin, Tiranial, of the Eighth Level of the House of Hemlock. The first of my cousins to knock me out of the trees at home when we were children.

"Tiranial, what are you doing riding with the Wild Hunt?" I asked. "Do you realize how dangerous that is?"

"Oh this?" He waved a gloved hand around at the beasts surrounding him. "It's not so dangerous as you might think."

He gave a snap of his fingers. The smoke images began to dissipate, dissolving and drifting away.

Revealing four other armoured fae on winged horseback.

Helmets lifted, revealing grinning members of my family, all looking quite delighted with themselves.

A trick. A hoax. One that had almost shut down the city.

I murmured a quick incantation, shifting the composition of the spell I'd cast that still swirled between my hands. My cousins, meanwhile, sat on their steeds, chuckling at the joke they'd pulled on me.

This revenge was gonna be sweet.

Two large steps and I let loose the spell.

It washed over them, shifted now from a burning heat to a freezing cold that locked them into place. As fae of the North Faerie Court, the cold wouldn't hold them for long, but I'd added a little twist of my own design.

Paralysis that depended on me saying the unlocking phrase.

Tiranial gurgled. His hand was still raised, fingers snapped together. Frozen in place.

I smiled as I stepped forward.

"I'm sorry, cousin, but I'm going to have to arrest you for unauthorized magic in the normal world. Didn't you all remember that I'm a detective here?"

All I got in response were strangled gurgles from my frozen cousins.

"Best not say anything," I said. "Anything you say can be used against you in the court of law."

I could see Tiranial straining to move but my spell held him fast.

This should teach him to toss me out of a tree or try to trick me with the Wild Hunt.

"Just hold that thought," I said. "I dropped my wand and have to find it. Shouldn't take me longer than an hour."

The gurgles sounded even more strangled, if that was possible.

I grinned and stepped back, turning away to find my wand. Now where had it gotten to?

A creaking sounded above my head. A thick branch from the closest tree swung and whacked Tiranial on the side. Unable to duck, he toppled from his mount, landing on his right in the muck. Mud squished onto his face, almost covering his nostrils.

I supposed it wouldn't do to let my cousin drown in mud.

I bent over and turned his head a little, clearing the worst from his nose.

"Didn't you know that the Black Forrest Park is one of the more magical places here? Seems like trees just aren't your thing, Tiranial."

I stepped away to find my wand. It wouldn't really take me that long, a few minutes once I opened myself up to it. But my troublesome cousins didn't know that. They needed to stew a bit before the North Court intervened and requested extradition. It would be granted, of course, although my cousins would need to pay damages.

That was nothing compared to the wrath they would face at home, especially from my mother.

Poor idiots, they would have been better off facing the real Wild Hunt.

A few creaking branches moved above my head. The trees were getting ready to return to their slumber. Soon even their magic would fade as they fell asleep, making it even easier to find my wayward wand.

But I was in no hurry. After the wild race through the city, walking through the trees and breathing the crisp, fresh air was relaxing.

It occurred to me that after considering Iceland, walking among trees wasn't half bad either.

Maybe it *would* take me an hour to retrieve my wand after all.

I grinned as I tilted my head back to take in the dark beauty of the night sky.

What the hell, maybe it would take me two.

ABOUT THE AUTHOR

Based in Toronto, Canada, Rebecca M. Senese survives the frigid blasts of winter and boiling steams of summer by weaving words of horror, mystery, science fiction and contemporary fantasy.

She is the author of the contemporary fantasy series, the *Noel Kringle Chronicles* featuring the son of Santa Claus working as a private detective in Toronto. Garnering an Honorable Mention in "The Year's Best Science Fiction" and nominated for numerous Aurora Awards, she has a story in the upcoming *Obsessions Anthology*. Her work has appeared in *Fiction River: Superpowers, Fiction River: Visions of the Apocalypse, Fiction River: Sparks, Fiction River: Recycled Pulp, Tesseracts 16: Parnassus Unbound, Imaginarium 2012, Tesseracts 15: A Case of Quite Curious Tales, TransVersions, Future Syndicate,* and *Story-teller,* amongst others.

Find out more about Rebecca at:
rebeccasenese.com

f facebook.com/Rebecca.M.Senese
🐦 twitter.com/RebeccaSenese
g goodreads.com/Rebecca_Senese
BB bookbub.com/authors/rebecca-m-senese

OF EARTH AND FAE

SHANNON LAWRENCE

Mary chipped the ice covering the stream away once more in order to draw water from it. Her hands were red and raw from so long in the cold, but the welcome scent of the chimney smoke assured her she'd warm quickly once inside the cabin. She wrapped her hands in her deerskin dress long enough to dim the pain before picking up the full water bucket and heading back.

A stag stepped out from behind the cabin. It froze and stared at her as she stopped. They studied each other for a moment, both fearless, but respectful. Finally, Mary nodded her head slightly, and turned away from the antlered beauty to go inside. His hooves crunched through the frozen grass, telling her he'd also moved on.

Inside, the warmth enveloped her. A sigh escaped, a shiver running up her spine as the heat forced the cold out. She poured the water into the kettle over the fire, and warmed her hands before returning to the job of chopping the root vegetables for the stew. Conor would be home from town soon, and he'd be hungry, cold, and weary. It was a long ride in for supplies, especially this time of year.

The vegetables done, she removed a portion of the now boiling water and set it aside in a smaller pot. She added the vegetables, rabbit meat from last night's catch, dried herbs, and wild onion paste to the kettle. Into the smaller pot she put bits of the inner bark she'd pulled from a ponderosa. This she settled next to the fire. By the time Conor got home, there would be a nice healing tea awaiting him.

As a Ute woman, she had never expected to marry outside her band, but the moment she'd met Conor during a stop in town for trade, she'd known they were meant to be with each other. Love had come later, after fate repeatedly brought them together between her band's travels. His light skin, blue eyes, and red hair had been a stunning contrast to the men she'd grown up around, and it had taken her some time to get used to the difference, though she had been attracted to him from the beginning. His small stature was also different than the wiry thickness of the Ute men. He had a hidden strength underneath his diminutive exterior.

More than physical attraction, there was a spiritual pull. Mary had grown up attuned to the earth and its spirits. Conor had a shimmer about him that spoke of a power most wouldn't be able to see. Most white men, anyway. Through many nights they had discussed each other's beliefs, and she had discovered Conor was of the race of Aos Si. Fae, as some called them. Driven into hiding long ago by invaders, most of his people had perished. Some had fled to the Americas, where Mary's people faced a similar fate, something he felt great guilt about, though his people were few and kept to themselves.

They'd both made changes to create their union. She'd taken the name Mary to sound more European. He'd agreed to live in the foothills, though farming was better on the prairie.

The sound of a horse and wagon crunching across the frozen ground pulled her from her reverie. Conor was home. Warmth coursed through her, and she smiled. She always missed him so when he was gone, even though she also appreciated having the time to herself. She pulled her thick, black hair back into a knot, then stoked the fire to ensure warmth for him when he came inside. It would be a while yet before he finished unloading the wagon and taking care of the horse.

Mary dragged his chair over nearer the fire and bustled about the one room cabin, clearing the scraps from her dinner preparation. His people liked a tidy space, and she knew it would draw him inside all the quicker. She lit a lantern to defeat the dying light outside. The cabin became a warm, amber color, filled with the scents of cooking meat and herbs.

Just as she settled into her chair, a sharp cry drew her attention. She ran to the door and stepped out onto the porch.

"Conor?"

A small, dark shape darted out of the barn, followed closely by Conor, who clutched a hand to his chest. He shook his head. "It's nothing. He just startled me, is all."

The dark shape came into the light, and Mary recognized the coyote. She clicked her tongue and shook a finger at it. "You know better than to come around here like that, little brother."

The animal lowered its head, then trotted off into the shadows. A moment later her brother stepped back around the building, his dark hair hanging loose, a coyote pelt across his shoulders. "My apologies. I've come to warn you. A strange energy has settled around us, and father sent me out to discover the source. I met a stag as it left, and it told me to clear away from here, and to let you know. Something is coming. Something not known to us." He looked at Conor. "It may have to do with you."

"What's that?" Conor came up onto the porch and wrapped an arm around Mary. "What does it have to do with me?"

"I felt it when I neared the barn. Your energy is different. You feel like a wounded animal."

Mary closed her eyes and let her energy combine with Conor's. Sure enough, something simmered below her usual awareness of him. It poked at her skin as if she'd walked through a thicket of nettles. Beyond that, an ominous energy ate away at her, making her feel tired and frightened. She felt like prey, a rabbit with a snare closing around it.

She'd been inside her own head, distracted by her thoughts and duties. How long had this been creeping up on her? Her cheeks warmed that it had taken someone else to alert her to an incoming threat.

She turned to Conor. "Reach out. Do you feel it?"

His brow narrowed, and concern flickered over his face. His eyes became distant, unfocused. After a moment, he shook his head. "I should have known this was coming. I thought we'd be safe here."

"What is it?"

"The Wild Hunt comes. No wonder Sean and Niall weren't in town. We need to prepare."

"How? What is the Wild Hunt?"

"There's no time to explain it. I think the Fomorians are coming for those of us who fled Ireland." He turned to Coyote. "We'll need help. Any who can fight evil. The Hunt's arrival will bring chaos and death to all around."

Coyote nodded, turned, and ran, his form changing in the distance from tall and striding to long and loping.

"Are these hunters like you?" Mary asked Conor, her heart pounding in anticipation and fear.

He drew his lip between his teeth in thought. "They're similar, but not the same. They can be hurt by the same things I can. The stream will keep them out on the west side; they won't cross it. Get your box from the woods. We're going to need it."

Mary ran to get the box. When they had decided to homestead together, Mary had buried a box of items harmful to Conor off in the woods where she had access to them, but they wouldn't be near enough to hurt him. In it were various items made of iron, plus a dress made with bells, shells, and elk teeth she used for ceremonies and gatherings. The noise of the ceremonial garb irritated him. Luckily, he was only part Fae, so he could stand it, but she didn't like to irritate him. True Fae would have trouble getting past the cacophony it caused.

By the time she got back from the woods, changed into her dress, and plaited her hair, Conor had strapped the horse's tack on and added a variety of noisy metal objects, such as cups and pans. This made the horse restless, but it didn't appear scared.

They went into the house and settled down to eat. Conor brought in the thick pair of deer skin gloves she'd made for him. "I'll need to be able to touch iron to get through tonight."

As they ate, she and Conor each carved a thick branch about leg-length, and tied iron knives to the tip with hide and yucca rope to ensure they were well affixed. Around her thigh she used hide to tie on her last iron knife. She had no idea what was coming or how many, but she certainly didn't feel well armed against a hoard of Fae hunters.

Outside, the horse let out a frightened whinny. Seconds later, a loud rumble filled the air, accompanied by high-pitched screams and deep shouts. Mary's blood quickened, and her wide eyes met Conor's. They didn't need to speak to know that the threat had arrived ahead of any aid that might be coming.

"Stay in here," Conor said, pulling his gloves on. He grabbed his makeshift spear and crossed quickly to the door.

Mary stood up and followed him, her own spear in hand. She ignored his huff upon arriving next to him on the porch, the fog from his warm breath dissipating into the frigid air. He knew her well enough that he wasn't surprised to see her there. She'd never been one to cower. They would face this together, no matter what end came.

Off in the distance, a deeper darkness stood out against the night shades of the foothills. Even with limited visibility it appeared ominous, like a dangerous storm on the horizon. The air felt charged and on the brink of explosion. Conor's hair stood out in a glowing red halo against the meager light flowing from their cabin door. Lightning flashed out from the dark mass, disappearing into the ground around it with a loud clap of thunder.

The wood of the porch vibrated with the approach of the hunters. Mary could feel it in her chest, a savage drum beating against the rhythm of her heart. Her breath caught.

They came closer, and now Mary could make out the figures. Tattered and skeletal, their eyes flashed with red lightning. Their horses were black, with the same flickering lightning where their eyes should have been. The riders held aloft swords, spears, and other weapons, and the stench of death preceded them.

At the lead was a larger figure, more flesh than bone, unlike his riders. His horse shone white against the black of the others. The leader wore a long beard and flowing white hair.

"Woden," breathed her husband beside her. Awe and fear intermingled in his voice.

Mary braced herself, aware once again of their woefully small defense.

The riders stopped on the opposite side of the stream. Now she could see Woden's eyes. Unlike the dark pits filled with flashes of light she'd noticed on the others, his eyes were pure white, with a single black pinprick in the center. Knowing that meeting a Fae's eyes could sometimes bring them under one's control, she stared directly into his. He didn't blink, flinch, or look away.

Woden didn't speak a word. Instead, he gestured with his spear to left and to right. The Fae riders around him split up, probably trying to seek a way past the stream. Woden remained alone, his gaze locked with Mary's.

Conor stepped forward. "Why are you here?"

Woden reached behind him and brought forth two objects. At first, Mary couldn't make them out, then she recognized them as human heads. Conor must have recognized them at the same moment, for he gasped.

"No!"

The heads, bloodied though they were, were recognizable as Sean and Niall, the two men Conor had migrated with to the Americas. Their open eyes rolled, and their mouths gaped in silent, continuous screams, even though they made no sound. Mary's stomach turned at the sight.

Woden's face held no expression. He sat calmly astride his horse, which pawed at the ground before it.

From either side of the property came the approaching sound of horses. They'd found a way around the stream, which meant they'd discovered the pond where the stream ended. Mary had hoped it would take them longer to find a way around. Her palms sweated despite the freezing air, and she had trouble catching her breath. If help didn't arrive soon, she and Conor didn't stand a chance against the horde.

Conor squeezed her hand. They waited for the riders to draw within sight of them. Shadows came with the riders, gathered from the surroundings, and announcing them before they were visible.

Then there they were, two armies of the dead streaming toward the cabin from north and south.

Mary turned to the left, Conor to the right. She held her spear before her and issued a war cry that would have made her father proud. The embellishments on her dress tinkled and rang, making the riders nearest her draw up short. Thinking of her ancestors gave her strength, and she stood tall and proud, prepared to meet her death if that was what it would take.

She ran at them, using the full force of the garment by creating a clatter. Their horses reared. Some of them turned back.

Out of the corner of her eye, she saw Conor dash toward the barn.

She pointed the spear forward and lunged toward one of the remaining horsemen. The tip held true, plunging the iron into his chest. His eyes dimmed, and he burst into black sand. His horse did the same.

The clatter of her dress had stopped as soon as she did, and the riders returned. This time they held their ground when she ran forward. So much for that weapon. At least she still had her spear. She would take as many of them with her as she could.

From the barn burst their horse, the metal objects on him making far more noise than her dress had. The riders covered their ears and screamed. They bent in the opposite direction from the racket, but they still didn't flee. One of them stood in the horse's path. It reared up and struck out with its iron-shod hooves, obliterating the rider.

A rumble filled the air, and it took Mary a moment to realize that it came from behind her, from the one direction the riders hadn't yet approached by. She hadn't considered a rear attack. She, Conor, and their horse were already vastly outnumbered.

Desperate, she kept her body toward the riders she could already see, and darted quick glances behind her to gauge what came at them now. Nothing showed itself. They were still too far away, to the east of the property.

The riders in front of her drew nearer. One broke from the pack in her direction.

Off to her side, Conor yelled, "Bring on your swords and spears. We will fight you to the end!"

Emboldened by his cry, she slashed at another of the nearby riders. He drew back before she could land the blow, then struck out at her with his sword, which elongated as it swung. She just barely managed to duck beneath it. Its passage singed her back with an icy heat that both burned and chilled as it slashed through the air above her.

She rolled and came up beneath the horse, shoving her spear up through its breast. The spear went through its back and into the rider, turning them both to sand. Another hunter darted toward her, and she stabbed him. Interconnected somehow, both he and his steed turned to sand like the others had.

The riders charged at her all at once, no longer willing to attack one at a time. They surrounded her and closed in.

Rather than blindly swing at them, she calculated their approaches, jabbing first toward the closest, then sweeping the weapon behind her toward one that came from that direction. The sound of sand spilling to the ground told her she'd gotten the creature.

Most of her energy now went into blocking the blows coming from the riders surrounding her. Her hands vibrated painfully with each hit the spear took.

The rumble grew louder. Her and Conor's fates were sealed.

With a desperate, forceful swing, she sliced into one of the riders and another's horse. Both riders and horses fell and became sand.

Before the remaining riders could close in, a tree-shaking snarl came from behind her.

A surge of hope filled her breast. These weren't more riders. These were her people!

A large bear crashed into the fight, sending riders flying as it swept them from their horses with a giant paw. A pair of black wolves leapt into the fray, taking down two more riders. A puma screamed and took out several riders on its own, ripping them apart.

Coyote snuck in behind one of the riders, jumped up, and swatted him playfully with a paw. The rider drew its horse around, only to find one of its fellow hunters behind it.

Mary left her brother to his play.

More of her people had joined Conor, bringing the fight to the riders and forcing them back.

Woden sat atop his horse and watched. He still grasped the heads of Sean and Niall by the hair, dangling them at his side.

Heat and ice shot through Mary's abdomen. One of the blackened blades of the riders briefly showed through her clothing, then pulled back out. She dropped her spear and fell to the ground, clutching her stomach. The pain spread outward in seeking tendrils, clawing its way through her insides like an infection. Blood roared in her ears.

She screamed once, but refused to stay down. Tears of pain blurred her eyes as she struggled to stand. Her brother's wet nose nudged at her cheek.

"I'm getting up, Coyote. Let me be." She grasped his thick fur and used it to pull herself up.

With a yip, Coyote rejoined the battle, dancing lightly on his paws.

"I'm not that easy to defeat," she called to them. Reaching beneath her dress, she pulled out her knife. This time when she screamed, it was a cry of battle, not of pain. This was the earth and air of her ancestors. These creatures from Ireland, dead though they might be, had no place here.

As soon as she thought this the ground beneath her moved, but did not crack. She held her position while it continued to shift. The bright forms of her ancestors rose from the dirt. Their vaporous forms solidified, and they surrounded the riders, pulling them down from their horses, and attacking them with weapons now made real. Flint-tipped arrows flew true from bows of cedar and sheep horn. Spears punctured the air, as well as the hapless enemy riders.

Mary and Conor switched from fight to finish, using their iron blades to kill the riders felled by her people. Without that final blow, the riders merely climbed back upon their horses and continued to fight. Her people were powerful, but they did not have weapons of iron. The only exception was Bear, who had found her now broken spear on the ground, and used it to finish off his own victims as they tried to pull themselves together.

Many of her people were wounded. Furred bodies fell, some switching back to human. Through it all, Coyote continued to count his version of coup, something he'd learned from the Plains Indians. He played tricks on those fighting, causing them to turn on one another. Even in a battle such as this, his playful nature couldn't be dimmed. He was, however, also a warrior, and he took as many lives as he spared, leaving the struggling riders for one of those with iron to finish off.

The sun sent its first morning rays across the prairie to the east. The light appeared to weaken the riders. Even Woden, still on his perch on the other side of the stream, appeared diminished in size and power. The bright white of his skin and hair had turned a pasty yellow, like that of paper.

Conor appeared beside her, panting and covered with wounds that stood out stark against his pale skin. "We have to get to Woden, or this entire battle will have been for naught. He'll return on the next Hunt with more of his riders."

Nodding, Mary went with Conor toward the stream. Wherever pain from the spear hadn't yet penetrated, she felt sore. Exhaustion filled her, but she knew she had to keep going. Each step caused the sand in her legs to become heavier. Soon she would become like the ponderosa, rooted deep into the ground and unable to move.

Mary shifted a log across the frozen stream to allow their passage. The closer Conor got to the water, the weaker he would get. If they were lucky, it would weaken Woden more. She crossed over first, Conor close behind. He kept up with her better than she'd expected. Perhaps the water didn't bother him as much as she'd thought.

Woden had watched their approach. Now he dropped the heads of Conor's friends on the ground with a set of hollow thumps and climbed down from his horse. He held his spear at the ready and studied Mary and Conor.

Conor still held his spear. Mary only had her knife left, so she'd have to get in close to do any damage. She put some distance between herself and Conor, waiting for him to take action. His people were not warriors like hers, but he had survived this long for a reason.

Conor ran forward, tapped Woden on the side with the spear, and rolled away from Woden's return jab.

Puzzled, Mary braced herself to move in as soon as Conor truly attacked. He wasn't the sort to play around this way.

Conor danced beyond the reach of Woden's spear, but made no move to attack. He tossed his spear, but it went far to the left of

Woden, who drove forward with his own spear. Conor deflected the blow enough that the spear went into his shoulder instead of his chest. He gripped it, holding Woden in place long enough to give Mary a chance.

Mary darted toward Woden and sliced across his throat with her knife. A gash opened up, dark sand pouring from it.

Woden pulled the spear out of Conor's shoulder and swept it toward Mary.

She was too close. The point of the spear missed her, but it knocked her to the ground next to where Conor had fallen when Woden pulled the spear out.

Conor looked up at her and grinned, blood in his teeth. His form melted before her eyes, and there was her brother Coyote, looking smug as ever.

The real Conor appeared behind Woden, spear raised. Time froze as the point of his spear burst through Woden's chest.

Mouth open in surprise, Woden's eyes turned black. He clutched at the spear head.

Conor used his knee to break the wood of the spear, leaving the iron knife inside Woden.

Woden's hands and chest turned to black sand.

The rest of him followed.

The white horse reared back and screamed as it, too, turned to sand and disappeared into the soil.

Sean and Niall's heads remained, but they no longer showed signs of life, released from the agony and torment they'd been in.

A cry went up behind them. With a great sense of relief, Mary turned in time to see the remaining riders turn into sand. She joined in with her people as they cheered their victory with yells and yelps and growls, her own elation swelling in her chest. Her ancestors disappeared back into the ground. She owed them more than she'd be able to repay in one life.

She helped Coyote across the stream. He turned once more into his animal form, licked her hand, and limped away.

Conor pulled her into his arms. They clung to each other, blood, dirt, and sweat mingling. Her energy evaporated, and she sank to the slush covered ground, pulling him down with her.

Together they watched her people make their way back into the mountains where they belonged. Where part of her would always belong. This cabin in the foothills was her home now. Conor's, too. They'd built this as a team, a sign of their love for each other. Mary knew now that they would defend their home, no matter the price. They weren't meant to be together solely in this life, but in all those to come. She snuggled more deeply into his arms, and sighed happily in response to his whispered words of love.

ABOUT THE AUTHOR

A fan of all things fantastical and frightening, Shannon Lawrence writes in her dungeon when her minions allow, often accompanied by her familiars. She writes primarily horror and fantasy. Her stories can be found in several anthologies and magazines, including Space and Time Magazine and The Literary Hatchet, and her short story collection *Blue Sludge Blues & Other Abominations* is now available. When she's not writing, she's hiking through the wilds of Colorado and photographing her magnificent surroundings. Though she often misses the ocean, the majestic and rugged Rockies are a sight she could never part with. Besides, in Colorado there's always a place to hide a body or birth a monster. What more could she ask for?

Find out more about Shannon at:
thewarriormuse.blogspot.com

goodreads.com/shannondkl

facebook.com/thewarriormuse

twitter.com/thewarriormuse

instagram.com/thewarriormuse

pinterest.com/thewarriormuse

bookbub.com/authors/shannon-lawrence

THE LAST PRIVATE IN THE GRAY HOODIE AND BLUE JEANS BRIGADE

DEANNA KNIPPLING

T here was a trick to the walking trails that connected behind James's back yard.

The trails weren't even real trails. They were sidewalks, smooth enough for fat little girls in pink roller skates, stinky awful bubblegum perfume, and sequinned short-alls with UNICORN POWER shirts. The sidewalk ran through some green space between one backyard and the next.

There was always some guy jogging. Not the same guy, not anybody James ever recognized, just some guy with a face so boring he might have been a spy. The only thing other than the joggers' absolute forgetability that they shared was their taste in technologically advanced running shoes, with weird 3D-printed soles and blue gel bags for extra impact absorption. In the winters a guy on a small four-wheeled tractor with an orange-and-blue Broncos stocking cap would plow the cement trails, then scatter sand on top of the leftover sludge so none of the anonymous joggers slipped. Nobody made eye contact unless they had dogs. Joggers didn't have time for eye contact with mopey teenagers. Little girls on roller skates glared at you like something out of a movie trailer. LITTLE GIRLS ON ROLLER SKATES 4: THIS TIME IT'S PERSONAL. People with dogs, though, they always had time to look at you.

I have a dog do you want to pet it?

People with dogs were either genuinely friendly or genuinely insecure. James hadn't actually decided which. Either way, they were nicer than the joggers. Today his opinion was that people with dogs started out as insecure, but the dogs fixed them. If you had a dog for long enough, it made you genuinely friendly. Dog owners probably thought that everybody would be a better person if they had a dog. James's parents didn't have a dog, and wouldn't let him have a dog. They weren't dog people. They were joggers.

James himself was part of the small, unnoticeable gray hoodie and blue jeans brigade. He used to have two other friends in the brigade, Christian and Mark. There was a line in Shakespeare they'd had to read in *Hamlet* the year before for English class: "Faith, her privates we." They had joked about their privates...a lot. And corporal punishment. But James was the only one left now. Mark had killed himself a year ago, near the end of their junior year, after someone called him gay and the bullies came out, an unending swarm of them, on the phone, sending emails, messages, texts, notes in his locker. There was no end to it—until Mark ended it for them. In a supposedly unrelated coincidence, Christian's family had moved away right after that. Now there was just James left. You could have replaced James with any of a hundred other guys and nobody would have noticed, not even their parents. James refused to wear jogging shoes. He wore Vans Winston DX Men's Skate Shoes in Black Dachshund. He knew he was supposed to appreciate the subtle cool details, but didn't. It felt like marketers were making a cult of bland clothing just for him, a subtle signal that meant: *Don't bully me, I'm not even gay, so just chill.*

It worked. James's look was so non-intimidating that women didn't switch over to walk on the other side of the street when they saw him. Little kids looked at him like he was an NPC in a video game. Joggers barely swerved.

James wasn't anything in particular. He wasn't a nerd, he wasn't a jock, he wasn't a goth, he wasn't a stoner. He was going to the University of Chicago in the fall. People wanted to know what he was going to major in.

He didn't have an answer.

At least he had the walking trails.

Other walking trails ran between houses, leading from schools to parks along little streams. The ones in James's neighborhood looped around and across each other in a crazy non-pattern that seemed to change every few days. It was a real labyrinth, one that didn't go anywhere in particular, just around and around, except in a few places where it led across the street to the next block. Every intersection of was a compass rose of the American dream, dotted with engine oil and roadkill.

In other words, boring. Like everything else.

But the walking trails in James's neighborhood were different. There was a trick to them, which was this: if he practiced hard at being unremarkable and unnoticeable for long enough, the trails got seriously weird.

There was a small stream running through sort of the middle of his block. There, the green area widened to what was officially "open space," which meant the grass was longer and the trail wider, enough for two joggers to pass each other without having to wave. Signs were posted everywhere: *COYOTES ACTIVE IN THIS AREA! Keep pets on a short leash. Do not run or turn your back. If attacked, fight back!* James always imagined the coyotes lurking in the shadows, waiting for an unguarded, pink-clad little girl on her chunky slow roller skates to pass.

When the open space area was behaving more or less normal, the stream at the bottom reflected the same sky that lay above it, and the green space was filled with fruitless crabapple trees, scrub oaks, and fluffy pines that leaned across the water, keeping it in shadow. But on weirder days, the stream reflected stars at noon, or the slimy flesh of some enormous monster, or flocks of tiny hummingbirds made of diamonds.

Either way, it was a bad idea to wade in the stream. The stream wasn't deep or fast but it was a pain in the ass to work your way down the crumbling, naked banks. In the summers everything smelled like half-cooked mushrooms and pond scum. On the weird days, it could smell even worse than that, like dead bodies mixed with rotten teeth. Sometimes there were fireflies.

But that wasn't the important part.

The important part was that if James followed the stream long enough on a weird day, it was possible to get lost.

Not just lost but lost-lost, like, *pack your backpack with protein bars and bottled water because you're going to need it* lost.

Reality? Dreams? Madness? Migraine?

Whatever. It was kind of cool. An escape.

~

I t had snowed the night before, a light sprinkling that didn't stick on the ground, so the guy in the Broncos cap didn't have to plow that morning, It was the very end of April and it wasn't supposed to snow—that's what people said every year, and it still snowed. This year, the buds on the crabapple trees had just opened and the snow made a lot of the petals fall, leaving splatters of rotting pink petals on the sidewalks.

James was supposed to be waiting for the school bus. But he could feel the words *Fuck it* rising him like vomit. He was trying not to think about what day it was. He was trying to stay focused. The words bubbled up again: *Fuck it*. He tried to choke them down, making barfing cat noises in the back of his throat. The elementary and middle-school kids on the recycled plastic swings in the tiny play area near the bus stop gave him funny looks.

He let a long, steady *fffffff*, then spat on the sidewalk and started walking away from it all.

Today, of all days, he needed to be lost.

It was Mark's Death Day Anniversary. One whole year, no Mark, and no Christian, either, except over voice chat during a video game. Not the same.

James pulled out his phone and plugged in his headphones. He had a whole playlist of songs that Mark used to like that he hadn't listened to in a year. The fact that the list would never change sucked ass, but it wasn't like he could just delete it, either. It was cold, but not cold enough to make him go home for a heavier coat. A rattling noise caught his attention. Behind him on the play equipment, a boy in light-up shoes dangled upside down from a bar, slapping his soles to make the lights light up. He waved at James.

Bye.

James slipped away. It wasn't hard. He was good at being invisible. He was okay in all his classes. He showed up on time and didn't make waves. He was only going to college because his parents were making him. He didn't know what he wanted to be when he grew up. He wasn't sure he wanted to know.

James followed the trails as they went from tacky, half-frozen wet pink gum, to cobblestone, to copper strips in a grid pattern. The trees got tired of being crabapples and pines and scrub oaks and turned into postmodern art made of tin soup cans with a woman's face on them, then to regular trees covered in knitting, then to thickets of paper dolls, the kind you cut out of folded paper. The stream hissed along its banks, throwing up clouds of steam that smelled like dog breath.

Suddenly James saw something walking beside him, between him and the stream. It seemed to be avoiding the sidewalk itself. James could just catch it out of the corner of his eye. He was afraid of it disappearing if he looked directly at it.

It was made out of stone or old cement, walked on two feet like a man, and had long, swinging arms that reached down past its knees. Even though it was made of cement it looked old and saggy. Its face was a bear's face, long and narrow with a snout at the end. Its hands and feet ended in claws. But it wasn't a bear. Bears didn't look graceful walking on their hind legs.

James risked taking a better look at it. It had pointed ears and part of its stony skin was peeling off, showing stony bones underneath. It didn't have lips.

Hello, mortal.

The creature's voice wasn't just a sound in his head, but a voice like the stone giant from *The Neverending Story,* like rocks grinding together.

"Hey," James said. "What's up?"

The creature didn't answer immediately, though somehow the situation wasn't awkward. It smelled like mud and rock and left dark footprints in the bits of snow that were still stuck to the grass.

Are you here for a reason? Or just traveling?

"I wanted to be lost for a while," James said. "You?"

I like to walk here and think. It's nice to be able to think without thinking too much about it, the creature said. *There's a trick to it.*

"I know what you mean. I mean, I think I know what you mean."

James shook his head. "Actually, I don't know what the fuck I mean. I'm supposed to be deciding what to do with my future."

Oh?

"I mean, I don't have any plans or anything. I'm just doing what I'm supposed to do."

The creature didn't ask his major.

I could give you something that might help.

"What?"

Almost anything you could want. Ecstasy. Forgetfulness. Women. Power. The ability to play a lute like a banshee. Whatever it is that mortals want these days.

James thought about it. "I don't think people have changed much, but nah."

You don't want anything?

"I want something. I just don't know what it is."

Ah. I think mortals ask for those other things because they think it will make that feeling stop.

James laughed. "Yeah, I can see that. What about you? What do you want?"

I want another year.

"Are you dying?"

Not quite. But I am running out of time. The creature scratched at a piece of flaking cement on one cheek.

"I'm at one end of a life, and you're at the other," said James. "Both falling apart."

They walked in silence.

Mortals generally want a purpose, said the creature. *Something that makes them special.*

"Yeah, okay," admitted James. "That *is* what I want. But everything that I'm supposed to want seems pointless. I'd kill myself, but that sounds boring, too."

I might have just the thing, the creature said.

"What?"

I can change you.

"Change me? How? Like, a new haircut? You're gonna make me ten feet tall?"

It's the kind of change you can't see in yourself, said the creature. *You won't be able to see it if you look at yourself in the mirror, for example. But you'll feel it. Everything will be different.*

Whatever it was, it sounded better than what he had now. In fact, too good to be true.

James let out a breath, his shoulders sinking. "You're just screwing with me, aren't you?"

No, said the creature. *It's not like a children's story where the boy gets a magic amulet and then loses it and a magic fairy appears, saying, "The real magic was inside you all along." This is a real thing.*

"And what do you get out of it?"

If all goes well, the creature said, *I get another year.*

"You're not going to take my soul, are you? You're not a devil?"

The creature had to think about this for a moment. *I'm older than the devils. I'll give you something that makes you special, something that gives you a purpose. Something to do for the rest of your life—something that you'll be very, very good at, I hope.*

"What, dying?" James said bitterly.

I don't want you to die, said the creature. *I want you to live. As long as possible.*

Without thinking too much about it—that *was* what this place was good for—James decided to accept. "Okay. Whatever. Yes, I mean. Do it."

Thank you, said the creature.

"Is it going to hurt?"

It's already done.

Whatever it was, just like the creature said, James couldn't see it.

The creature had given James a nod, then wandered deeper into a stretch of trees made out of silver wire, disappearing in the shadows.

James walked along the pathways on his own until he got bored, then started working his way back to the more normal parts of the trails, until he was walking on sidewalks covered with melting snow and crabapple petals.

A jogger passed him, barely swerving, leaving dark, technologically advanced tracks behind him that sank into wet slush.

That night, James played *Call of Duty* with Christian for a couple of hours. They didn't talk about Mark. James told his mom that he was going to eat junk food for supper.

She rolled her eyes. "Boys."

He curled up in bed, ate Doritos and caramel popcorn from a bowl all mixed together, and listened to Mark's playlist while watching old movies on his laptop with the sound off. He was watching something about a couple of guys and their mules in a desert or something. Then he woke up and suddenly a bunch of women in long dresses were dancing around a bald dude. It was morning.

He got up and went to school. The words *Fuck this* were still trying to vomit themselves out of his mouth, but it was easier to keep them down.

In second period, English, they were reading some collection of short stories about a guy who'd been in the Vietnam War. James hated it. The whole thing was about a guy who gets drafted to have to fight in the war, tries to escape the draft by running away to Canada, doesn't make it, then gives up and goes home and gets drafted anyway. It was all out of order and the stories were pointless and depressing. The main character wasn't a hero, either, just a nobody like James.

It felt like the teacher was deliberately taunting him. James was exactly the same kind of loser as the narrator in the book. The teacher was just rubbing in the fact that he, James, was going to end up as disposable trash, good for nothing but shooting people in jungles.

The teacher droned on and on about the book. It was his favorite book of all time.

James put his head on his hands, balancing his elbows on the top of the desk, and tried to fall asleep.

Finally the teacher asked, "So...what did all of *you* think about the book?"

Which was a question he should have asked half an hour ago, if he wanted anyone to answer without drooling.

The teacher's dull blue eyes fixed on James. "James? What about you? What do you think?"

For the first time in over a year, James said what he really thought. He didn't bother to take his chin off his hands. It wasn't like anyone would listen. "I didn't like it. It didn't mean anything. O'Brien went to war and made some friends, most of them died, it was pointless. The end."

It was 9:29 a.m. Outside the window the sky was gray but not dark, just gray, like it wasn't even there. A few crabapple petals drifted past the glass. The bell rang.

And then the thing happened, the thing that the dying cement creature had promised.

Suddenly James was special. Every eye in the room turned toward him. They were beyond pissed. James, the nobody, had just insulted the teacher's favorite book.

James felt the rush of air, clean and cold, fill the room. His breath fogged up in front of him.

I think he's gay, someone whispered.

The other students were changing, twisting, sprouting horns, growing hooves—becoming monsters. The teacher became the biggest monster of all, an enormous spider-creature that threw spiderwebs across the windows and doors to trap James in the room and eat him.

The old cement creature had wanted a year.

James had wanted a purpose for the rest of his life.

He just hadn't asked how long the rest of his life was supposed to be.

Had Mark had tried to make the same deal a year ago, a deal to find a way out of being nobody? His mom and dad had said he'd killed himself.

But maybe what had really happened was weirder than that.

Monstrous voices roared outside in the schoolyard, hungry animals sniffing out prey, eager for the chase.

I want you to live, the creature had said.

James tore his way through the spiderwebs across the classroom door and ran, heading for the outside and for the walking trails that ran behind the school. The ones near the school had never gotten weird before, but maybe today would be different, with all those monsters after him.

The trick to the walking trail was to be a nobody.

And James was good at that.

ABOUT THE AUTHOR

DeAnna Knippling is always tempted to lie on her bios. Her favorite musician is Tom Waits, and her favorite author is Lewis Carroll. Her favorite monster is zombies. Her life goal is to remake her house in the image of the House on the Rock, or at least Ripley's Believe It Or Not. You should buy her books. She promises that she'll use the money wisely on bookshelves and secret doors. She lives in Colorado and is the author of *The House Without a Summer: A Gothic Novel*, and other books like *The Clockwork Alice*, *A Murder of Crows: Seventeen Tales of Monsters & the Macabre*, and more.

As always, this story is dedicated to Ray,
without whose love none of this would be possible.

Find out more about DeAnna at:
wonderlandpress.com

f facebook.com/deanna.knippling

🐦 twitter.com/dknippling

📷 instagram.com/deanna.knippling

g goodreads.com/goodreadscomdeannaknippling

BB bookbub.com/authors/deanna-knippling

@ pinterest.com/dknippling

SCRAGGLES GOES HUNTING

LOUISA SWANN

The night started like every other night—chasing an uncooperative mouse through the bushes, dodging roots and weaving around thorns. The roots and thorns were almost as uncooperative as the mouse, not a surprise when you're operating with only one eye.

Not that the eye was actually gone. Scraggles just couldn't see anything worthwhile with it. Made life rather challenging at times, especially for a cat who relied on successful hunts to keep himself alive.

Wet weather had kept him inside for two turns of the sun. A *little* rain was tolerable. Rivers falling from the sky were not. All warm-blooded life had sought shelter—if they'd had any sense, that is.

The rain had finally stopped as day slid into night, leaving the world a sparkling mess of wet earth smelling of soggy dirt and leaves that dumped a despicable amount of water if a cat so much as sneezed. Clouds blew away, shredded by a crisp wind that spoke of the winter to come.

Anyone with half a brain knew that dirt has many smells—dry and dusty, warm and growing, ice and snow—but not everyone knew the stench that fills the air and plugs the nose after the earth is turned to water and struggles to become earth again is a unique combination of rotting vegetation, wet soil, decaying bodies—insect, furry, feathered, and shelled—ancient urine from a myriad of creatures, and dissolving dung from those same creatures.

Scraggles pulled to a stop after negotiating a particularly snarly bush. He lifted his paws in disgust at the combination of soggy grass and mud dirtying his paws. He snorted. The rotting stench would be interesting any other time, but not under the current circumstances. He inhaled the enticing scent of warm mouse, hot and fresh and somewhere close by—

The mouse leapt from its hiding place beneath a branch, scrambled onto a pile of rocks, and disappeared into a sky blurred with blue and green.

Blasted eye.

The mouse vanished back into the brush without a whisper, but

Scraggles didn't follow. His entire coat—knots, burrs, and all—inexplicably stood on end, something that generally happened during storms that lit the night sky with bolts that could fry a cat on impact, not because colors ebbed and flowed across the stars like shadows in the wind.

He hissed in annoyance. His meal was so close he could smell the hot blood pumping beneath the delicious aroma of mousy terror. No time to dwell on dancing-sky anomalies or worry about rebellious fur. He scrambled over a pile of slick rocks and darted into the extra-thorny, extra-wet, brush.

And was rewarded with a cascade of trapped rainwater just waiting to be released. He ignored the soaking, focusing instead on the mouse's nose quivering in the air beneath a low-hanging branch of thorns.

Did the stupid creature think a few thorns would deter Scraggles the Glorious Hunter?

He crouched, wriggled his haunches, and readied himself to pounce as an overlarge drop plopped heavily on his brow.

"To the stars, minion," a voice screamed. A light touch tickled his skull directly behind his right ear.

"Fly, minion, fly," the voice cried. "Together we shall ride to Eternity and Beyond!"

Mouse forgotten, Scraggles twisted and bit at the air, trying to dislodge the pest that had attached itself to him. Larger than a tick, but just as tenacious, the tiny imp whooped and screeched.

But it didn't let go.

What manner of creature was this?

He couldn't catch sight of the creature to determine what it might be and snapping at it proved pointless. The cat had gotten used to hunting with one fang (having donated a fang to the hide of a grizzly and lived to tell the tale), but successful hunting depended on the prey being in *front* of him, not attached to his head.

"Enough playing," the over-sized tick creature said. "It's time to hunt."

Hunting was something Scraggles understood. He stopped trying to rid himself of the strange pest and glanced around, studying the undergrowth for signs of the mouse he'd been chasing. Perhaps the creature wanted to share his kill. The cat growled, keeping the sound low in his throat. He'd get the mouse, then get the pest when it came down to feed—

A sharp pain stabbed his skull.

"It's time to hunt," the little pest insisted. "Leap to the sky, minion. Eternity awaits."

Scraggles screeched, infuriated by the pain and the pesky creature parked on his skull. He was a cat. Cats didn't *do* sky or eternity. Cats did sunshine and mice.

There were other ways to rid oneself of pests. Biting them off was only one option.

Scraggles yowled and hissed, dropped to the ground and rolled. When that didn't work, he dashed toward the thorniest bush in sight—

:*This will not do,*: a voice said *inside* his skull, a voice he'd never heard before, so deep and low he felt rather than heard it. :*There is no time for such persuasion.*:

And everything vanished...

He was floating in a black void, empty of all senses. No sounds of scratching mice or howling wind. No scent of hot blood or rotting leaves. No tastes tripping across his tongue.

What in blazes is happening to me? Am I dead? Or—

An odd sensation twisted his gut. Fear, perhaps, though he didn't really feel afraid.

Then, Scraggles *expanded.*

His physical body didn't grow, it simply felt as though *he* were growing, especially his skull—or was it his mind?

Pain blazed through his body, a searing, ripping agony that culminated somewhere between his eyes. He screamed, the sound tearing at his throat. The stench of rotten bird eggs stung his nose...

Sound erupted around him—howling wind, growling thunder, moaning trees, and other noises he'd never heard before. Colors chased the sounds, attacking from all sides—brilliant greens and blues and yellows, followed by colors he had no name for. The coppery taste of blood coated his tongue.

"Well, that was unexpected," said the tiny pest on his head. "Guess he *was* impatient. Now can we get going? We'll be left behind."

Who was 'he'?

"Left behind?" another voice asked.

Scraggles leaped sideways, fur standing out from his body as though lightning had struck mere inches away. He peered suspiciously at the bushes around him.

"That was you, idiot," the pest said.

"Me?"

This time the cat managed to stay in one place. What did the pest mean, 'it was you'?

"That was *you* talking to *me*. It appears he's granted you enlightenment—enough to converse, anyway."

"Impossible," Scraggles said, listening intently as the word came out of his mouth.

He *was* talking, not just uttering cat sounds.

He promptly sat and began washing his fur, his default mode when life became too confusing.

"No!" the pest screamed. "I am fairly certain you weren't granted this modicum of enlightenment so you can sit around cleaning yourself."

"I'm a cat," Scraggles said. "That's what we do."

"Cats hunt!" the pest insisted. "That's why I chose you. And now we're missing the Hunt!"

The cat stood. He stretched. He studied his surroundings. "That mouse has long since vanished, you fool."

"Forget the mouse! We have much bigger prey to catch!"

Bigger prey?

Exactly how this ability to speak a foreign language was going to help when it came to catching larger prey remained a mystery. Speaking had never been a problem while hunting in the past (though not everyone was privileged to speak Cat). Scraggles was willing to give it a go—as long as hunting was involved.

"And where is this prey?" he asked. He sneezed and cleaned his paw with a disinterested air.

"Up there!" the pest screeched. "Among the stars!"

"Precisely how is one supposed to get up *there*?" Feigning a yawn, Scraggles glanced at the sky, ignoring the pest's anxious tugging on his ear—

And immediately leaped backward, ducking beneath the closest bush and snagging his coat on a myriad of thorns.

Before today and his new "enlightenment" Scraggles had lived in the moment—as all cats do. Dwelling on memories of the past didn't catch supper. More than a bit irritating that his enlightenment brought memories raining down on him with the intensity of the recent storm.

It was the human's fault, he remembered. The human had started all the craziness.

Descended from a long line of hunters, Scraggles' ancestors had hunted rats on ships filled with stinky humans. Their kits had kept wagons, tents, and cabins free of rats and mice for decades, before his great-grandparents went with their chosen human to live in the mountains. The human built something called a cabin that stank of smoke and sweat and lived by himself—except for his cats. The human was shrewd enough to realize cats were the best of company.

The human lived years longer than a normal human—or so Scraggles' parents had claimed.

After Scraggles' birth, the human had moved from the cabin into a cave he'd discovered high in the mountains. Something in the cave had made Scraggles' skin itch all the time and it hadn't been bugs.

That same something drove the human crazy.

Instead of living a quiet life, the human began creating strange creatures, creatures that should have been familiar, yet had been changed in odd ways. Giant lizards with teeth that could tear a horse limb from limb. Flying rabbits.

Furry pigs with claws instead of hooves.

All created by that crazy, claw-pulling, fur-shredding human.

Then Scraggles' parents disappeared.

And Scraggles fled.

He'd been but a kit at the time.

So long as he maintained a distance from the crazy human and the strange power the human had somehow released life had been his—calm and mostly predictable.

Until now.

"There they go," the pest on his back screeched.

Scraggles snarled low in his throat.

Though not in human form, the craziness was back.

Energy billowed through the air, a gust of tingling power that swelled into churning wind, tearing leaves from the bushes, digging stones from the ground and hurling them into the sky.

The cat breathed deeply of the soggy earth, relishing the stench. The stench was normal. Expected.

What was happening around him was as unnatural as the strange creatures the crazy human had created.

"Up, up, up and away!" the pest cried.

"Not going anywhere, particularly with you," Scraggles said. He peered upward...

And hissed in alarm.

The stars had been replaced by the dancing colors, both familiar and unfamiliar. That much he had expected.

He had *not* expected to see figures milling within the colors. Most had a human-like appearance, some almost skeletal, others so muscular their clothing had practically ripped from their bodies. There were other beings mixed in—a handful that looked like humans who had been squished beneath a giant boulder; others with humanoid shapes and the heads of ravens or other creatures.

And they were all riding mounts almost as fantastical as the riders—

:*You must go with them*,: the new voice said, the voice *inside* his head. :*Lives depend upon you participating in this Hunt*.:

"Who are you and why should I listen to anything you say?" Scraggles asked the voice.

"My name is Tinder," the pest on Scraggles' head said. "I'm a fairy. Now get your tail in gear and let's join the Hunt!"

"You are *not* a fairy," said another voice, this one also new, though —fortunately—outside his head.

Scraggles leapt from his hiding place, certain the voice came from directly behind him. A quick look confirmed his suspicion—to a degree.

A woman hovered above and behind the bush he'd used as partial cover. With flowing black hair and skin as pale as death, the creature was human in appearance but not in fact, judging by her scent. She seemed substantial enough, even though her gown shimmered and flowed like a contained river.

"*I* am fae," the woman said. She glared at Scraggles, though he got the distinct impression she was actually glaring at his passenger. "*You* are a pixie."

"Same thing," the pest said.

"You're a pest," Scraggles grumbled. The woman shifted her glare and Scraggles felt himself wither beneath her gaze.

"Not you," Scraggles added. "Him."

He pointed a paw at his head.

The woman nodded and seemed to relax. "Agreed."

Scraggles felt as though he'd just escaped execution.

The woman glanced over her shoulder. "Come along, then, pixie. If that is your ride. The Huntmaster has arrived."

"We're coming," the pest said. "Be there in a flash."

Scraggles was a bit more pragmatic. "You might be there in a flash, but how is a cat supposed to do that?"

He snarled at the beings milling overhead.

The woman smiled, revealing teeth as sharp and pointed as his.

Unfair, Scraggles thought. She still has *both* her fangs.

"Have you tried to join them?" the woman asked. She seemed to be growing smaller, then Scraggles realized she was moving away—without moving.

Something tiny drummed against Scraggles' skull.

"Let's. Go," the pixie pest said.

"Fine." The only way to get rid of this pest was to do as it asked, Scraggles was sure of that. As sure as he was that he'd be inviting epic failure as soon as he took a leap.

:*You must have faith*,: the voice said.

Faith in a voice. Right.

He shook all over, spraying water in all directions.

And failed to dislodge the pest.

Oh well. Might as well give it a go. Wouldn't be the first time he'd failed. Or the last.

He gathered his paws beneath him, crouched as if preparing to spring on a mouse, and bounded into the air.

Extending his front paws, Scraggles prepared to land as he'd landed thousands of times before.

Instead his paws clawed at empty air.

"Yeehaw!" the pixie crowed. "Make way for Tinder and Company."

Scraggles was too busy figuring out what to do with his paws to take offense at being called *Company*. He was airborne, though he had no idea how to stay that way or how to direct his movement. There was nothing firm to push against, after all.

One glance back at the ground and he almost panicked. He'd jumped down from some pretty high places—boulders, trees, and the like.

But he'd never jumped from the sky.

The crowd surged around him, yanking him into the center of a seething storm, with branches and debris flying in every direction. The air stank of rotten eggs and death and blood and bones and other things he'd never smelled before.

He had thought the crazy human's creations unnatural and monstrous, but those creations were nothing compared to the beings seething around him, bumping and jostling against him and each other like a nest of angry snakes. He caught flashes of antlers and fangs, fur and scales—

The sound of a horn split the air, filling the night sky with haunting tones that made Scraggles' fur stand on end. If this nightmare continued, standing-on-end would become the normal state of his fur.

"Follow that horn," the pixie cried.

Claws and tails, how did the pest expect him to move? Without solid ground beneath his feet, there was nothing to push off from. What would happen if he fell? What if whatever was keeping him in the air, just...quit?

Wind tickled Scraggles' tail as the power surged. Mounts and riders alike swept forward, following what appeared to be a deer with enormous antlers. The horn's call was replaced by the thunderous sound of pounding hooves so intense the cat's ears began to hurt.

Odd there was any sound at all, considering hooves, claws, and feet were running on nothing but air.

He tried to relax and let himself be swept along, still uncertain how this running-on-air thing worked. The movement of the others gave him some momentum but did not add to his speed.

"We're going to be left behind," the pixie insisted. "You have to keep up."

Exasperated, Scraggles moved his legs like he was walking and his speed picked up. A little. "What is this all about anyway?"

He broke into a trot and moved a little faster. Instead of falling behind, he was actually keeping up.

With the rear of the pack.

Never one to come in last, he broke into a gallop.

And slowly moved up to the middle of the pack.

Once again, Scraggles found himself surrounded by heaving bodies. He sucked in his breath and flattened his fur, trying to make himself smaller, and fought to maintain a straight path as riders and mounts seethed around him.

His ears—even the one that had been ripped from his head—ached from the cacophony created by all the pounding, grinding, and screaming.

The riders must be the hunters, he surmised, snarling under his breath at the injustice. He was a predator, not a beast of burden. He should have his own mount. Should be riding to the Hunt, not be ridden.

"Now we're moving!" the pixie cried. "Yeehaw!"

A creature that resembled a living mummy—human-style—moved up on the cat's left.

Riding a monstrous lizard.

With a spiked tail.

Scraggles fought down an urge to leap away from the creature and forced himself to keep moving forward. When he'd been a kit, he'd witnessed an enormous herd of great furry beasts trample an unfortunate rabbit. Nothing left but fur and bones when the herd finally passed.

He did not want to become that rabbit.

The pixie shifted position, and for a moment Scraggles thought the little pest had fallen off. The sense of relief following that thought was cut shorter than one of his nine lives when a question popped into the cat's mind: Would he lose his ability to run in the sky without the little pest messing up his fur?

"Yippee," the pixie yelled. "Head 'em up and move 'em out!"

Looked like the pest was still there.

Worse than a tick in summer, Scraggles grumped to himself.

"Showoff," grumbled one of the squished human-types. It was mounted on what looked like a pig made out of rocks, clinging to the rocks like it expected to fall off at any moment. The pair ran so close Scraggles could practically feel dust from the rocks sifting into his fur.

"You could stand on your mount, too," the pixie crowed. "If you'd stop strangling it. Tinder!!!!!!"

"I think you mean 'Timber'," Scraggles said. He dodged sideways to avoid a flying talon as an enormous bird raced by.

Pain stabbed through Scraggles' skull, pain fierce enough to make him stumble. It took several strides before he regained his balance.

"Enough of that," the pixie said.

The pain vanished almost as quickly as it had struck.

"Enough of what?" Scraggles asked, adding an indignant meow for emphasis.

"I *meant* 'Tinder'," the pest said. "That's my name. Why would I say 'Timber'? Sounds ridiculous."

"What did you do to me?" Scraggles demanded. "Why did my head hurt so bad?"

"We're a team," Tinder said primly. "Each member of the team has to do his part. Part of being a good teammate is to make sure the other team members do their jobs."

"Making my head feel like it's splitting open is being a good teammate?"

"If that's what it takes."

Scraggles swallowed his anger and decided to change the subject. "What are we hunting?"

"Humans!" Tinder cried.

"Humans?" Scraggles asked. Had he heard correctly?

"Humans!" Tinder screamed.

Scraggles wondered if the little pest ever lost his voice. Then again, judging by the feather-light touch on his head, the pixie probably needed to yell just to be heard by anything other than another pixie.

"Any particular humans?" he asked. Why would anyone want to hunt humans? Far as he knew, they weren't nearly as juicy as mice.

Then again, he'd never tried to munch on a human.

"Hunters bear a great responsibility."

Scraggles glanced sideways to find the woman—the fae—once again by his side. She smiled, baring her lovely teeth. He idly wondered if she'd consider parting with one of her fangs.

"Yes, we do," he agreed. "Not only are we responsible for catching our prey, we are responsible for eating it as well."

"*Eating* them?" Tinder screeched. "What kind of barbarian are you?"

"The most barbarous kind," Scraggles said. "I'm a cat."

The woman's smile disappeared. "We are not barbarians. We are

Hunters. Responsible for protecting spirits on their way to the next realm."

"You hunt dying humans?" Scraggles asked, unsure he'd heard right. "Or their spirits?"

The woman nodded.

He hissed in frustration. "Which is it—humans or their spirits?"

Again, the woman nodded. "We find the humans when their physical bodies give out, then escort the spirit back home."

Scraggles twitched his tail. How had he managed to get involved with this convoluted human business? Until he'd been catnapped by a pixie pest, a wild hunt meant chasing an uncooperative mouse through thorny brush.

He wriggled his whiskers at the beings seething around him. "This is the first time I've seen a Hunt. What happens to all the humans who die during the day or when the Hunters aren't around? Their spirits have to go someplace, don't they?"

"The beings we hunt aren't your typical humans," the woman said. "They are of the gods and have chosen to live in the physical realm for reasons known only to them, just as you have chosen to live as a cat. When their time in the physical realm comes to an end, they must be returned to the place they belong."

The Hunt surged left, carrying Scraggles along with it. The galloping, seething mass blurred into a river of madness. Different from the human's craziness, this was a madness he could feel creeping into his bones.

He had used cunning and strength to stay alive after leaving his own crazy human, honing his hunting skills until only the fox was stealthier than he. After a brawl that left the fox with a ripped ear and a limp, Scraggles had graciously allowed the fox to live in his territory.

Wild creatures trembled when Scraggles the cat stalked the land.

The wildness of this Hunt, however, was different from anything Scraggles had known. The power and energy surging through the pack or horde or whatever they called themselves felt limitless. Living wild came with rules—unless you were a wolverine or weasel. Wolverines were savages. Weasels, simply bloodthirsty. Wolverines were crazy, weasels insane. All creatures—Scraggles included—kept to their dens when wolverines and weasels were on the prowl.

The Hunt was more like a wolverine, moving as if rules and boundaries had simply ceased to exist.

Both crazy and insane.

And yet somehow...*normal.*

"What do you mean I *chose* to live as a cat?" he suddenly asked.

The fae woman gave him a flat look that made him want to find a tree and climb it.

"Tinder will explain it to you," she finally said. "Or he won't."

And then she was gone.

:*Sheer arrogance,*: the voice said. :*You are cat. Nothing complicated about it. Now pay attention. Time to earn your enlightenment.*:

Earn his enlightenment? "Never asked to be enlightened," Scraggles grumped.

"Below us!" Tinder said, his voice quivering, though the cat couldn't decide if the quiver came from excitement or fear.

They swooped low over what appeared to be a set of ruins cloaked in a light mist. His "enlightenment" told him the ruins had once been wooden buildings where humans had lived, what humans called "a town."

The town nestled in a narrow valley surrounded by raw mountains that erupted from the earth like enormous teeth. Heaps of charred, broken wood lay along either side of a large road stretching from one end of the valley to the other. Whole buildings appeared to have been ripped from the ground, then mangled and wrenched apart like carcasses ravaged by scavengers.

Dark mounds—oozing with the sickly-sweet scent of burned meat and death—dotted the scene as if someone had scattered giant flakes of black pepper throughout the devastation. A large moon was just cresting the eastern mountains, creating a silvery backdrop for the dancing colors of the Hunt.

The stench of burned wood tickled his nose and he sneezed.

:*There*.: One word. A word that carried so much more. Fondness. Desolation. Worry.

Scraggles peered at the ground. One of the buildings had two upright walls and part of a third. A section of the roof remained, canted at a precarious angle, partially sheltering a figure so tiny he almost thought it another cat.

That was their prey? Hard to believe it took the entire Hunt to round up something so small—

"Poor little thing," Tinder said. "She's barely begun her time in this life."

Of one accord, the Hunt switched direction, wrapping around the town in a giant circle. Swooping toward the ground—

"What happened to your ear?" Tinder asked, drawing the cat's attention away from the Hunt. "It's rather rude of you not to have two ears to hold on to."

"Wolverine got it," Scraggles said. "It was either the ear or my life. Sorry if that offends you, little pest."

"Pixie," Tinder corrected. "We're not pests. We're—"

:*Prepare yourself*,: the voice ordered.

The entire atmosphere shifted.

"Something's wrong," Tinder screeched.

"Ya think?" This whole experience was *wrong*. The cat wanted nothing more than to find a good bush—not a tree, he'd had enough of heights for a time—and go to ground. His eyes felt stretched like a mouse between two cats. Any more stretching and he might finally lose the eyeball he couldn't see out of. Might lose both the good and bad eye if things got any stranger.

And if this *noise* kept up, he just might tear out his other ear.

Not that he'd lost his hearing along with the ear itself. Sound just wasn't as...sharp...without a decent cat ear to funnel it.

The sound around him suddenly morphed from general cacophony to a nerve-shredding dissonance.

And then the noise stopped.

Scraggles felt as though he'd gone stone-cold deaf or been wrapped in a cocoon. He stared in fascination as a small light—not a star or anything connected to the Hunt—circled through the town, hovered around the child, then rose, getting closer and closer until it gently came to rest on Scraggles' brow, wrapping him in an otherworldly glow.

:*It is done.*:

"What is done?" Scraggles asked. Awareness of the Hunt returned in full force. They all seemed as confused as he.

:*It works.*:

What worked?

"Run!" Tinder yelled.

Startled, Scraggles realized the attention of the entire Hunt was focused on *him*. Maybe they were after the pest, he decided. That fae woman hadn't liked the little pixie at all.

Didn't matter. The Hunt was headed his way. And they didn't look happy.

The cat tried to retrace his steps—moving backwards. Walking backwards didn't seem to be one of the modes of locomotion when one wasn't on the ground, however. He floundered, paws and legs paddling as if trying to swim (he never had been a good swimmer).

A cat in the wild learns to evade those who think creatures smaller than themselves to be easy prey. He had plenty of experience with escaping.

He spun on his haunches—a maneuver that seemed absurdly simple considering their location and the difficulty he'd had walking backward—and dashed off. His effort was rewarded with a burst of speed and he pulled slightly ahead of the Hunt. He had no idea where the Hunt took the ones they were "returning" and had no desire to find out.

The sky and the stars were the Hunt's turf. Cats preferred all four paws on the ground, though not necessarily at the same time.

So Scraggles took to the ground, the Hunt hot on his tail.

They drew so close he could hear their heavy snuffling beneath the unholy screeching threatening to deafen his ears, could feel their hot breaths scorching his fur. His nose twitched at the overwhelming stench of sulfur, rotting flesh, and putrid fruit. A claw—twice as long as his tail—whooshed past his face.

Time to stop playing around.

Cats are fast and sneaky, able to turn on a dime. He utilized all those skills and more, ducking beneath half-burned beams, and dodging around doors still standing in the frames even though the walls around them were gone.

He leaped over sticks and branches, plunging through leaf debris that had somehow been trapped between remnants of shattered boards that hadn't burned.

And everywhere was ash—drifting through the air, fogging his vision and clogging his nose.

What had happened here?

No time to spend wondering. No time to satisfy his growing curiosity.

A plank rattled beneath his paws, half burned and covered with designs—words—made by human hands.

Welcome to Fallen Rock

Hunters howled and something snagged his tail, almost dragging him to a stop. In one quick move that would have knocked a mouse silly the cat spun, lashed out with his claws, and bounded on.

The tip of his tail snapped, sending pain exploding from his tail to his skull, but the hold on him vanished.

:I come. Be calm.:

Something enormous and black blotted out the stars and colors overhead and settled on the ground before him. A black shadow—Scraggles didn't know what else to call it—shaped like a winged lizard of tremendous portion.

The cat instinctively made an abrupt turn—though logically a shadow would do him less harm than the creatures that made up the Hunt. He took three enormous strides, gathered his paws beneath him, leaped as though he were striving to reach the middle of a huge tree—

And was immediately snatched from the sky.

Not really snatched. More like the shadow simply opened its maw and swallowed Scraggles whole.

:*Be calm!*: the voice thundered.

Two thoughts blasted through his mind at the same time—this shadow was also the *voice*, and how on earth could he 'be calm'?

Tinder screamed—a tinny sound that made Scraggles grind his teeth. He was plunged into blackness so intense he was certain he had gone completely blind. The stench of things long dead set his teeth on edge.

He splashed down in a puddle of something he didn't want to identify, landing on all four paws, of course, though how he managed to retain an upright position was a bit of a mystery considering he couldn't see a thing. The cat shook, trying to rid himself of the stinking wetness. When that failed, he shook each paw, one at a time.

And had to put them back into whatever he was standing in.

"Are we dead?" Tinder asked, sounding more like an extremely small being than an arrogant pixie.

"Takes more than being swallowed to kill a cat," Scraggles said, repeatedly shaking his paws. Apparently, it also took more than being swallowed alive to dislodge a pixie pest. "But we've definitely gone to the dark side of...something."

"Well, aren't you the epitome of cheerfulness."

"And you are annoying as a prickle burr."

"You can't keep a good pixie down," Tinder crowed.

Furballs and catweed. If they were somehow stuck in eternity or wherever this place might be, he had the pest's cheerful demeanor to look forward to. If the pest ventured anywhere near his mouth, Scraggles was going to eat him, hungry or not.

:*Keeping you in my gullet would prove my demise,*: the shadow voice rumbled. :*The Hunt is not convinced I have claimed you, however. It might take a moment for them to move on.*:

Claimed him? Whatever was the shadow on about?

:*I had to act quickly, hence your part in this small deception.*:

The explanation confused more than clarified.

:*Be calm. It will soon be over.*:

197

There was a sensation of movement though the cat hadn't done more than lift a paw. He was thrown abruptly off his feet and tossed one way, then the other. Tinder screeched in his ear.

And the world exploded.

Scraggles flew upward, tumbling amid a fountain of stinking liquid. Stars reappeared, followed by treetops and small bushes. It appeared whatever swallowed him had discovered just how unpalatable a cat can be.

Served it right.

He had a brief moment of satisfaction before he splatted ignominiously on the ground.

Splat being the most appropriate word. He'd landed in a mud puddle that softened his landing but left him covered in more stinky muck.

At least this muck was natural. That other stuff had been...he didn't know what it had been.

Scraggles rolled onto his belly, embarrassed to find he had *not* landed on his paws.

"Probably because we were just upchucked by a dragon," Tinder said. It sounded like the pest had something in his mouth. The cat took perverse satisfaction knowing the pixie had suffered the dunking as well.

A glance around the area confirmed the cat's suspicion—he was home.

How he'd gotten here was another mystery.

"Wave goodbye," Tinder called.

Scraggles peered around in confusion. Just who was he supposed to wave goodbye to?

He glanced at the enormous black shadow obliterating the starry expanse, a shadow with the shape of a lizard. With wings.

:*The little one lives. Thank you for your assistance.*:

One beat of the enormous wings and the creature was gone. The stars reappeared, twinkling like jewels in the night sky.

Colors no longer danced among the stars and the only things

flying were bats, moving in silence except for the beeps they emitted from time to time.

Had it all been a catnip-induced dream? Had he inadvertently chewed on something stronger than mere grass?

"That was rather exciting," Tinder said.

Scraggles' heart skipped a beat. "I was hoping you were just a nightmare; gone as soon as I woke."

"Well, aren't you grumpy as a werewolf on a bad hair day." Tinder rapped on the cat's head.

No pain this time. Just an annoying *thud thud* that made the cat twitch his tail.

"Perhaps you would deign to explain things to me," he said. *Before I scratch you off my skull.*

"There was this dragon, see," the pest said, sounding like he was trying to explain the facts of life to a young kit. "And then there was the Hunt. We flew with the Hunt and got eaten by a dragon. Easy peasy. What's so hard to understand?"

"Why did the Hunt turn on us?" Scraggles demanded. "Or do they always do that—decide to eat their fellow hunters if they can't find prey."

"First of all, the dragon wasn't part of the Hunt. I've never seen it before. Second, we'd found the prey, just as I told you. That little human was ready to go home."

:Pay no attention to the flea.:

Scraggles glanced at the sky. Was the dragon back? But no shadowy form blotted out the stars.

:The fact you cannot see me means nothing,: the shadow voice grumbled. *:The flea is wrong. The child has work to do. That's all you need know.:*

Right. Why did he get the impression there was a lot more going on?

The puddle shivered and splashed around the cat's paws. He spotted a rock off to one side and leapt onto it, shaking water from his fur as he went.

"Why did the Hunt turn on me?" he repeated.

"The Hunt didn't turn on you," the pest said.

Scraggles growled deep in his throat. "Of course, it did."

:*I guess you could say I pulled the fur over their eyes and made the Hunt believe you to be its prey. That's why I had to claim you. They believe you still deep in my belly. Unless you call them back, the Hunt will leave you be.*:

"The only thing I'll die from is starvation," the cat grumbled. "You and your Hunt chased off all the mice."

Life would be different now, Scraggles realized. Was he still even supposed to hunt now that he'd been *enlightened*?

"Of course, you are." The pest was being pesky again. "You're a cat. That hasn't changed."

"Not talking to you."

That shut the pest up. For a heartbeat or two.

"Can you take back this enlightenment thing?" Scraggles asked.

:*Enlightenment is a way of being,*: the voice said. :*Once achieved, it cannot be undone, not easily.*:

Of course.

"You *want* to go back to existing as a stupid beast?" the pest asked.

Scraggles growled deep in his throat. Cats were not stupid. Still...

"Do you have anything that gets rid of pests?" the cat finally asked, directing his question at the voice. If the shadow dragon could solve a young girl's problems, perhaps it could solve this particular issue.

"What pests?" the pixie demanded. "I don't see any pests."

:*You can always call the Hunt.*:

Not funny.

Scraggles growled and twitched his tail as he glared at the stars.

Not funny at all.

ABOUT THE AUTHOR

Growing up in the wilds of the Sierra Nevada mountains, surrounded by deer and beaver, muskrat and bear, Louisa Swann found ample fodder for her equally wild imagination. As an adult, she interweaves her experiences with that imagination, creating tales of fantasy and science fiction, mystery and thrillers, steampunk and historical fiction. Her short stories have appeared in Fiction River anthologies, including Reader's Choice; Mercedes Lackey's *Elementary Magic* and Valdemar anthologies; and Esther Friesner's *Chicks and Balances*. Novels include light-hearted mysteries (*It Ain't No Bull, The Trouble with Bulldogs*) and her new steampunk/weird west series, *Abby Crumb and Myrtle Creek* (with Brandon Swann).

Find out more about Louisa at:
louisaswann.com

 facebook.com/swanngang
twitter.com/LouisaSwann
bookbub.com/authors/louisa-swann

OF BLOOD AND BONE,
EARTH AND AIR

KIM MAY

I sat on the roof of the park's enchanted castle and watched the sun sink below the treetops. The leaves, which had just begun to turn red and gold, reflected the sun's amber rays, spreading summer's farewell embrace across the land. The air had finally acquired the bite of winter. Soon the park would close and for a short time I would be able to roam the full extent of my domain.

Below, a girl tugged on her mother's sleeve and pointed at me. I dispersed before the mother caught sight of me as well. It was better for them to think that they imagined me. The last thing I wanted to do was to make modern mortals ask questions. Questions led to investigations, which brought scientists, spiritualists, activists, preservationists, and too many other ists. It was bad enough that I had to surrender this corner of my forest to humans for half the year. I didn't want a horde of intellectuals trampling my thickets, leaving devices in my forest, and distressing the wildlife. Genius loci like myself couldn't be too careful. Any being or thing that threatened the health of my forest threatened my life, and I had no intention of dying.

Suddenly the land shuddered and roiled as an icy foulness slid across me like an invisible wave. The birds took to the sky, and creatures of the field bolted from their dens and copses. This time of day they should be hunting for their evening meal and bedding down for the night, not fleeing in terror.

No hunter would have instilled this much fear and no fire was this frigid. There was however an intense hunger. It felt as if the intruder hadn't fed in a century.

Oh, no! The prisoner is loose!

I didn't know what the Unseelie Fey had imprisoned in the mountain on the furthest edge of my territory, but I had known the cell wouldn't hold forever. I told them. They didn't listen. Now their carelessness threatened the delicate balance I'd maintained for millennia.

As much as I wanted to rush over and take care of the prisoner, I couldn't leave the park until I was certain that the guests were safe. The tremor caused a few of the more intelligent patrons to run for the parking lot, but most of them were too frozen with fear and confusion to do more than breathe. For a species at the top of the food chain they certainly didn't possess as much common sense as the wildlife.

To my relief, Nathanial—the park's winter guard and the first man of Multnomah decent I'd seen in many years—rallied the staff around the witch's candy cottage. He quickly set them to clearing the park of guests. As soon as the staff dispersed, he ran in the direction of the prisoner.

I sailed by him on a passing breeze, wanting to reach the site before him. Nathanial might be simply doing his job, but his actions were enough to earn my protection—something I wouldn't be able to do until I knew what we faced.

I stopped at the fence behind the dwarves' mine roller coaster. The animals loved to forage here, since the children always left crumbs behind. This was usually the noisiest corner of my lush forest. Only now it was completely silent. Not the silence of a wolf on the hunt or the silence of snowfall. This was the silence of death.

Nothing stirred. Nothing breathed. Even the wind changed directions to avoid the prisoner's notice. If I had had a physical form this would have sent a shiver down my spine. The wind was an unstoppable force of nature. What was so powerful and terrible that even the wind would fear to cross its path?

Nathanial carefully climbed over the fence. His green uniform and brown skin made it easy for him to blend in with the trees. He moved through the forest with caution, and I followed by his side.

Though faint rays still shone through the canopy, a palpable darkness slid its moist tendrils over the land. Terror crippled my movements. I commanded the noble firs to swat the tendrils aside with their branches. They didn't respond. The firs were so coated with murk that they weren't able to hear me. I dropped low to the ground, hoping the tendrils would pass right over me; Nathanial swiped his arms through the air like he'd just stepped through a giant spider web.

A shrill laugh that slashed through the woods faster than a chainsaw made both of us jump. The tendrils retreated to the source of the laugh. However the source didn't wait for the tendrils. Instead it darted from tree to tree with a speed that baffled me. What in creation moved that fast?

As soon as I finished that thought I knew the answer. The chill that passed through me froze the grass I rested on.

A slim female stepped out of the shadows. The sight of her nearly made Nathanial retch. The revulsion I felt before increased a thousandfold. This *thing* shouldn't exist.

Her carnelian eyes glowed softly, making her pale face look like a hot ember. Blood, black and thick and older than any tree in my forest, writhed across her curves like a second skin. The blood seemed to sense our presence, because it shifted into the form of several screaming faces across her body. Whether it was a warning or a plea I didn't know. Considering that the dark Fey liked to mix messages, it was likely both.

"That's far enough." Nathanial said. His voice shook like the last leaf on a tree in winter.

She laughed. "I think not. You see if I come closer," she took another step forward, "then your heart beats faster."

Nathanial stepped back. She matched him step for step. "Pit pat, pit pat, pit pat...faster and faster 'til your heart gives out." With each repetition she increased the pace to match his heartbeat. It sent a shiver through me that the nearby branches echoed.

"It would be a shame if that happened," the Unseelie continued. "I have such fun planned for you. It starts with you running for your life."

No, Nathanial! Don't play her games.

His feet twitched as if they wanted to run, and I could tell it took every bit of will he possessed to hold his ground. I swirled in front of him, and projected the warmth and strength of a boulder in the sun to give him my support.

She pulled three sticky strands of blood from the mass that swirled across her stomach and tossed them to the ground in front of her. The strands oozed toward Nathanial, consuming the plant matter in their path. Each death sent a pang through me. The blood grew and expanded until each strand became a slick, human-shaped blob a foot taller than Nathanial. Their faces were frozen in the soundless screams they would never be able to voice.

This time Nathanial ran.

The blood men chased after him. I threw fallen trees into their path, but the trunks passed right through them. Nathanial was in such a panic that he strayed from the path and stumbled through the brush. Branches snapped, and the jagged edges tore his clothing, while hidden roots tripped his feet.

I parted the canopy so that a ribbon of twilight could guide him along the safe, clear path. I closed the canopy behind him and swung fallen branches and blackberry vines into the path of the blood men. Trees along the path joined in the effort by swinging their low-lying branches into the blood men's path. Those whose branches were too high severed their strongest limbs so I would have more with which to fight.

The prisoner laughed and scampered in the wake of her creations. With each step I felt her power grow. She was feeding off his fear. I had to stop this wild hunt. If this continued, soon she would be beyond my power to contain.

I altered the path so that it brought Nathanial to the field where the park often staged joust reenactments. The field adjoined the parking lot, which still contained a few bewildered guests. Nathanial ran for the lot. From his wide eyes and pale complexion, I had a sinking feeling he sought to escape rather than to expedite the evacuation.

I raced ahead of him, and used my own fear to freeze a patch of bare ground moments before his foot connected with it. His foot slid underneath him and he fell hard. I held him there while the blood men encircled him.

Spotting a young blackberry vine at the foot of one of the blood men, I seized it. If there was one thing wild blackberry was good at it, it was growing quickly. At my command it wrapped around the blood man at an alarming rate. More shoots burst from the ground at the feet of the other two and swiftly did the same.

The blood men tried to ooze through the briars, but there were too many. As soon as one of them passed through a layer, more vines arose and blocked the blood's path. The vines turned brown as the blood sucked the life from them, but even that proved useless. The blood men didn't possess the physical strength to break through, and without a gap big enough for them to pass through they were effectively trapped.

I released Nathanial. With the blood men immobilized he had calmed down somewhat. The Unseelie was too dumbfounded to move, which bolstered my confidence. I shifted so that one of the thorn tombs hid me from her sight, and coalesced into a human-like shape so Nathanial could see me. *Let me in.* I whispered to him. *Lend me your body so I can fight her.*

Nathanial didn't react right away. Had he heard me? It had been so long since I'd addressed a mortal. I'd assumed that his people would have remembered me, but perhaps I'd made an error. This also could have been one shock too many, but I didn't have much of a choice. I could only do so much in this form. If I was going to have any chance of defeating her, I needed all to have all of my faculties at hand.

His reply came like the first flower of spring. At first it was small and hesitant, but grew bolder and more assertive. *I don't know what the hell you are, but if you can stop this thing then use me as your meat puppet.*

It wasn't the response I'd expected but it was enough to satisfy the Great Mother. I quickly entered his body before he could reconsider. Every muscle in his body stiffened. I didn't let that deter me. With the sureness of a river I flowed into his mind, and coursed through every muscle and vein. His consciousness retreated. I could feel his apprehension, mingled with a touch of fear and hope.

Be calm. I silently told him. *Allow me to do my duty.*

I stood, taking a moment to stretch, reveling in the sensation. The Fey had regained her senses and had moved out from behind one of the thorn prisons that held her blood men. She cocked her head, staring at us for a moment.

I drew energy from deep in the earth until Nathanial's body

almost quivered from the strain of containing it. Remembering her probing, I sent out tendrils of my own; smooth, white, and glowing like the full moon above us. They circled her bare feet, slapped her hands, and tugged on her hair.

Not a speck of annoyance showed on her face. Looking into her eyes, I could see the wheels turning. She was too busy figuring out what I was to be riled.

Her mouth turned up into a smile that almost reached her eyebrows. "I've never eaten a genius loci before. This will be —"

A bright flash cut her off. Two men, one a foot shorter than the other, stood at the edge of the meadow. Behind them two women stood by a truck, their expressions worried. The taller man took pictures with one those small handheld devices humans favored.

The Unseelie laughed. "Appetizers."

She leapt across the distance and seized the shorter of the two by the hair. I tried to awaken the blackberry again, but she was too fast. The Unseelie clamped her jaw onto the human's mouth. He tried to scream but very little sound came out. The Unseelie sucked in hard. With each draw the man's skin lost its healthy color.

"What the hell?" the tall man asked. He turned his back to them and ran, almost dropping his device in the process.

The Unseelie flicked a piece of her blood suit at him. Her aim was perfect. It hit him on the back of his head and spread across his shoulders. He fell to his knees screaming. The blood drained the life from him as fast as the Unseelie sucked the life from her victim. When the blood finished it flew back to its mistress to offer its bounty.

The men's companions climbed into the truck and drove away, nearly hitting other vehicles in their haste. The Unseelie raised an eyebrow—part question, part dare. She took a knife from the short man's belt and used it to slit his throat. The blood that issued forth filled the gaps in her suit. Red swirled with the black, making the distorted faces on the suit even more macabre.

With a slash of my hand the earth parted, offering the bones of a hundred dead. Men, deer, birds, all were proffered for my use, and I gratefully accepted every one. I gathered the bones with a gust of wind. They took to the air in a graceful arc that passed over my head and landed on an even patch of ground behind me. The jumbled bones assembled into a twenty-foot tall beast. Finger bones formed claws on the bear paw like hands and feet. The long narrow snout, formed of an amalgamation of femurs, had a double row of wolf's teeth. Skulls, some many centuries old, stared out from the body, and two great antlers protruded from its head. Earth covered the bone and filled in the gaps, giving my construct solidity and strength, but I needed one more element to give it power.

I turned to the thorn prisons and addressed the blood men. "You have intelligence and therefore have will. Attune your will to mine and you will have the revenge you desire."

The blood men stilled for a moment before sighing as one. "Yes."

With a loud crack the thorn prisons burst. The Unseelie's wicked laugh echoed across the field. "Save yourself the effort, guardian. You'll never win."

"This isn't about winning," I said. I spread my arms wide. At the command new vines sprouted forth. The blood men seeped into these and shot forth to wrap around the bones, providing the sinew, lifeforce, and discernment my construct needed.

The construct stepped forward. With each step a loud boom reverberated through the broken ground. When it reached me it stooped down so I could mount. I took position between the antlers.

The construct rose and I had to hold on tight. The rush of sensations coursing through Nathanial's body was disorienting. His consciousness trembled in the back of his skull. Apparently he didn't like heights.

She bared her teeth at me and hissed. I sneered at her. She sprang into the air, twisting a strand of her blood suit into a whip, which she immediately put to use. The whip wrapped around the construct's right forearm. Within the vines the turncoat blood men shivered.

I quickly made the same offer to the blood in the whip as I'd made to the blood men. There was dissention in the ranks. The drops within the whip that wanted to join separated themselves from the rest, worming their way to the top.

The handle of the whip fell limp in her hands. She growled in frustration as she landed gracefully on one of the empty thorn prisons. The thin horizontal gaps in the ragged maw of brambles made it look like she was standing on a seven-foot tall human ribcage. She stood with the poise of a queen on a pedestal, but I could see the cracks in her armor. When she sent more blood to strengthen her whip there was a bare spot in the blood suit over her left hip. She was running out of resources.

Seeing an opportunity, I told the construct to attack. It swiped a paw across her midriff. Its claws left deep furrows in her flesh widened the gap in the blood suit. The blood that served me didn't waste time convincing their brethren to join. Her whip dissolved in her hands and joined my construct.

A dark light that shimmered with iridescence like a raven's wing seeped from her wound. She pressed a hand to the wound, not that it did much good. With a snarl she leaped again. This time she didn't form a weapon. She used more direct methods.

She landed on the construct's shoulder and grabbed Nathanial's leg. She bit down and sucked hard. Nathanial and I screamed. I felt his life force and mine leave his body with each suck. Nathanial writhed and clawed his way to the forefront. I withdrew myself from Nathanial's legs. Since I was no longer controlling his legs, they crumpled beneath me. The construct shifted bones and brambles aside so we landed on soft earth. I curled up my own legs in Nathanial's chest and pressed against his ribcage, forcing his mind to retreat.

"Calm down and let me work!" I shouted at Nathanial. He whimpered and curled up in a ball in the back of his mind.

The Unseelie lifted her head to grin at me. I pulled a femur free from the construct's head and bashed her over the head with it. I must have cracked her skull because more of that iridescent light leaked through her hair. The Unseelie had released Nathanial's legs but she still held fast to the construct. I had hoped to knock her to the ground so Nathanial and I would have a few moments to collect ourselves. The Unseelie shook her head to clear it and reached for Nathanial's legs again. I swung the bone at her, this time aiming for her hand. The femur shattered on impact, but so did her hand. Even though I hadn't heard the telltale crack, her cry of pain made it clear.

"You'll pay for this!" she screamed.

"No," I said calmly. "It is only the first installment on your debt to me."

I dropped the broken femur and partially emerged from Nathanial's body. My head and torso rose above his. I rested one hand on the crown of Nathanial's head and the other on one of the construct's antlers. In the moonlight my translucent body shimmered like a dragonfly's wings.

"You defiled my forest and harmed those under my protection. For that you will pay with your life. I am witness, judge, and executioner. I am the life that brings death, and you are a poor imitation."

I slipped back inside Nathanial's body. His consciousness had calmed down now that she wasn't draining him anymore, but he was weak. There was still a lot of life in him. It was a weakness of will. There was no fight left in him.

"Be strong," I said softly. "I won't let her kill you."

I felt him nod, but he remained curled in a tight ball.

She leaped at me, her good hand reaching out, ready to claw his flesh. The blood that served me rose, pushing mud and brambles up to form a barricade between her and me. She landed on the barricade hard enough to knock the air from her lungs. The barricade gave a little, but held. She grabbed onto anything that would give her purchase. Mud fell off in great chunks as she dug her fingers in and climbed to the top of the barricade.

The blood shied away, terrified of getting sucked back into her suit. The construct grabbed her and pulled her off. She held on with her good hand, pulling brambles and fistfuls of mud with her. The vines snapped and the construct threw her across the field. Her body left a deep furrow in the ground. She lay face up, unmoving.

We charged before she could get to her feet. The construct lunged and speared her in the belly with one of its claws. But instead of shock or a howl of pain she merely laughed. The blood in her suit raced up the construct's arm.

At my command the blood loyal to me withdrew and the vines holding that arm to the body severed themselves. The arm, invading blood suit, and the Fey fell to the ground. The claw impaled the ground, pinning her to the earth. She pushed against the severed arm but her one good hand wasn't enough to even budge the massive limb. She screamed and pounded her feet against earth. Unless she was willing to cut herself in half or be crushed by the weight of the arm, there was no way for her to escape.

I had the construct walk over to the park's front gates. A six-foot tall wrought iron fence with spiked heads on each bar was embedded in a four-foot concrete wall. The construct pulled a four-bar section free of the concrete and brought it with us back to the Unseelie.

She had withdrawn her blood suit from the arm. Now it spread around her like a pool of midnight on the earth. The grass within a foot of the suit had withered and died.

"You're not going to get enough life force from this field to save you."

The construct knelt on the ground. It laid the fence section flat on the grass and started rolling it like a cigarette, first at the blunt end, then the middle, and finally at the point. It worked the metal efficiently with its one remaining limb.

When the Unseelie saw the spiked cold iron she started clawing and kicking the earth, trying to dig herself free. Her carnelian eyes were larger than the park's candy apples and her pale skin had turned pure white.

"No! Let me go! I swear I'll never return!"

Her plea sounded sincere but I couldn't banish the doubts in my mind. A creature that delighted in torture and pain usually couldn't be trusted.

"As tempting as that is, I don't trust you. In fact, I don't trust any Fey. They said that your prison would last and we both know how truthful that statement was."

I climbed down from the construct's head and sat on its shoulder so I'd have a better view.

"I could rebuild your prison. I'm sure the Seelie court would prefer this option. However since I owe them no fealty I fail to see how going to those lengths to curry their favor is in my best interest."

The ring of dead grass around the Unseelie had grown while I talked. That was all the confirmation I needed that my doubts were well founded.

"There is only one solution that will satisfy me."

My construct thrust the spiked end of the rolled fence into the Unseelie's chest. Her body seized as one of the points pierced her heart. More of her dark iridescent blood seeped from her wounds and leaked from the corners of her mouth. Her cheeks sunk in and cobalt smoke rose from both eye sockets. I expected her blood suit to try to attack us, but it didn't. The pool seemed to sigh. The expressions of the faces that appeared in the swirls turned from grimaces and screams to peace and relief. The pool sunk into the ground and disappeared from view.

The construct gently deposited me on the ground. I shook Nathanial's head to clear his vision. Eventually the spots faded so I could see the star-strewn sky. With a wave of my hand I created a rent in the earth beneath her body, going deeper and deeper until lava welled into the gap. The wrought iron melted and fused with her remains, ensuring that she would never rise again. I watched her remains burn until there was nothing but ash swirling on the magma's surface.

I turned to the construct. "Thank you for your service."

The construct fell into the searing maw. I put the ruined thorn prisons and the two men's bodies there as well. I watched the three bodies burn and sink into the lava. When the ashes of all three had burned out of existence I closed the gap with more earth than was probably necessary. I used the extra earth to form a small burial mound.

A sigh of relief issued from both of us as I drifted out of Nathanial's body.

Nathanial fell to his knees. His shoulders slumped forward and his breathing was slightly ragged. The poor man looked ten years older than he had an hour ago. His dark hair was lightly streaked with white. He wasn't going to have an easy time explaining his sudden aging, and unfortunately it also put me in a tricky situation.

I couldn't control what he might say about tonight's events. Given his appearance questions were unavoidable, and I knew all too well what questions led to. I didn't want to deal with that, not after tonight's ordeal.

An idea came to mind. It wasn't a perfect solution. I couldn't stop the investigation—the two men she'd killed would be missed—but this would make the duration of that investigation brief.

I solidified my form a little so he could see me better. "Nathanial, I'd like to repay you for your generosity. Do you accept my gift?"

He didn't answer right away. I remained silent. This choice needed to be made without any interference from me. As the silence stretched I felt the wildlife return to the woods and their dens to sleep off the trauma.

"All right. I accept."

I laid my hands on his head. My fingertips sank into his skull, melding with his spirit. The white streaks in his hair darkened and the wrinkles around his eyes smoothed. When I pulled my hands back my fingers were an inch shorter.

"I have imparted on you some of my life to replace what you lost in the battle. I cannot do anything for the wounds to your psyche and I am sorry for that."

Nathanial nodded.

"I must also apologize for a minor side affect to this. I was born of and am eternally tied to this forest. Because a part of me is now a part of you, I regret that you will always feel a pull to this forest. Whether you return here or not is entirely up to you."

Nathanial stood up. His legs were shaky but he didn't fall. "I understand. Thank you." He forced a laugh. "The elders aren't going to believe this. I can tell the elders, right?"

I nodded. "Only them. The more who know the greater danger I'll be in from human malefactors."

Nathanial nodded. "Is it okay if I go home now?"

I chuckled. "Yes. I'm eternally grateful for your assistance. If I don't see you again, I hope your life is full of happiness."

Nathanial walked back into the park to shut everything down for the night before heading home. I turned to leave, but an uneasy feeling made me hesitate. It wasn't the uneasiness that preceded a threat. It was the uneasiness of not feeling whole, and it came from the burial mound.

I waved my hand over the mound. Grass and wild iris sprouted from the ground.

It wasn't in my nature to leave grave markers, but if it made the land more content I wasn't going to object. I'm only its guardian, after all.

ABOUT THE AUTHOR

Kim May has always been a storyteller—just ask her mother. On second thought don't. She knows too much. Kim writes fantasy, sci-fi, thrillers, historical fiction, steampunk, and a bit of poetry because she collects genres like a cat lady collects strays. Kim lives in Oregon where she works at an independent bookstore and watches a lot of anime. She's a retired stage actor and has a penchant for fast cars, high heels, and loose screws.

Find out more about Kim at:
ninjakeyboard.blogspot.com

GETTING GOOD

BRIGID COLLINS

S telli was running late.

She thundered down the basement stairs, her backpack thudding against her tailbone. In her rush, she'd forgotten to drop it in her bedroom, but she couldn't stop or slow down now. Instead, she wriggled her arms out of the straps and tossed it aside at the bottom of the stairs. The motion sensitive lights flicked on, bathing the walls and plush carpet in a soft light designed to feel soothing, but which today looked accusatory.

"They're waiting for you," it said in its warm tones. *"You're keeping them waiting."*

Stelli dashed across the wide, wide expanse of the entertainment room to the raised section at the far end, where the family's two FullD systems waited. Stelli would swear the one on the right, her customary system, had a reproachful air to the angle of its plasleather-covered chair.

But she didn't have time or breath to apologize to it, nor to consider how ridiculous apologizing to an inanimate gaming system would be. She scooped up the simming helmet, jammed her hands into the gloves, and slammed herself down onto the chair hard enough to elicit a squeal of resistance from the supports. It would be fine, though. VirtuMax made resilient products.

A flick of her gloved fingers darkened the screen within the helmet. She panted and gulped and focused on the golden *F* logo of Feyland as the game logged her in slowly, slowly, slowly.

Come on, they're waiting!

Finally, after long enough that her breathing had nearly evened back out, Feyland loaded. Stelli selected her Spellcaster character—easy and quick, as it was her only character—and let the game whisk her away to the place where she and her friends had last played together.

Daylight blinded her as she appeared in the center of a ring of mushrooms in an open, rocky pass. Stelli and her friends had reached a higher level of play, and as such, had left the more familiar forested areas of the early game. With no trees besides a few stunted and gnarled, hardy scrub to block out the simulated sunlight overhead, Stelli's vision danced with spots as she stepped out of the faerie ring to greet her friends. The air was hot and dry, but a sage-scented breeze rippled Stelli's white caster's robes about her body.

"I'm here," she said. "I'm here. Just give me a moment to sort out my notifications."

"Oh, we didn't think you were coming," said Genna.

Stelli's login notifications menu appeared before she could get a real look at her friend, but she caught glimpses of Genna's new Dryad character's leafy dress fluttering beyond the menu's edges as she sorted through the pile of mildly interesting dev announcements.

"Yeah, sorry about that. Had to pick my grandma up from her doctor's appointment on my way home from school. Traffic was pretty tweaked, too, and— Hey, did you guys get this updated Midnight Huntsmen quest?"

Normally, the new quests that got automatically added to her quest list upon login didn't interest Stelli, but the old Midnight Huntsmen quest—a super-early game quest that set player characters to defend an NPC village against a horde of wicked fey hunters—was one of her favorites. She'd played it many times with her friends and with her grandmother, until she'd gotten so good at it that playing it now felt like wrapping herself in an old blanket whose every hole and fray she knew and treasured. In a funny way, she felt like her best version of herself whenever she went up against the Midnight Huntsmen.

Almost unconsciously, Stelli gestured to open the quest.

"Ride with the Midnight Huntsmen and learn your true strength," she read aloud. "Oh, that sounds so awesome. Kinda weird, too, riding with the baddies. Do you guys want to—"

"Why don't you go play it by yourself?" said Deshawna, her voice quick and overfull of smiles. "I don't think any of us got that quest anyway, right?"

Stelli laughed. "What are you talking about? We always play together. This seems like a good opportunity to gain some extra XP before we tackle this new dungeon. 'Learn your true strength,' it says. I bet it's worth a lot."

"Maybe your grandmother will play it with you," said Genna. Her tone curled, as if she were wrinkling her nose.

"Nah, she doesn't like to sim as often as we do." Stelli dismissed her quest menu with a twitch of her finger and found her three friends all looking at her with expressions of pity and exasperation. "What?"

Genna shot a glare at Deshawna, while Ray rolled his eyes.

"Deshawna was *supposed* to talk to you about this in biology today," said Genna.

"I didn't get a chance! We had a pop quiz."

Stelli's throat tightened as the realization hit her. "Oh my God. You're cutting me out, aren't you?"

Another look passed between Genna and Deshawna, and then the two girls looked at Ray.

He sighed. "It's not that we don't like playing with you, Stelli. It's just... Well, honestly? With your simming performance lately, it's not really worth our effort to convince you to play the levels we want to play, anyway. You always end up getting wiped out."

VirtuMax certainly didn't make shoddy products. Even in the simulated world of Feyland, Stelli felt her stomach drop. "You think I'm no good."

"We think you're making dumb moves you never did before. We used to be able to rely on you, you know? I don't know if you're losing your touch or if you just can't handle the higher levels, but I know you got KO'd in the last three dungeons, and we had to overburden ourselves to carry all your stuff out for you."

"Well, I'm a Spellcaster—you can't expect me to survive a direct hit from an enraged ogre." Her voice squeaked through the anger tightening her throat. "We're fragile."

"You charged into that den of Red Caps last week before we had a chance to set up a defense. The three of us basically played without you the whole time."

Ray gestured at the rocky pass behind him, his armor clanking. "We've been gearing up to play the Rock Troll's Dungeon for weeks now. We've got plenty of XP. I don't want to go back to the low-level quest lines *one more time*, and I'm getting sick of having to drag you away from playing them over and over again."

Stelli gaped. "I just thought— I mean, it sounds like fun..."

"And I'm sure you'll have tons of fun playing it without us grumbling along the way," Deshawna said.

Getting cut out hurt, but that placating tone added a cruel twist to the dagger Stelli's supposed best friends had stabbed into her gut. The tears prickling behind her eyes turned hot with humiliation. Her blood roared in her ears.

Irritatingly, her friends' voices still managed to carry through the roar.

"Maybe if the devs implemented an easy mode, she could play with us on the higher levels."

"Aw, come on, D, don't start up that 'easy mode' crap again. Games are supposed to be challenging."

"But if Stelli could put the Rock Troll's Dungeon on the same difficulty level as the Midnight Huntsmen quest, she could handle it no problem."

"Yeah, she beats that level with her eyes closed at this point."

"We can *all* beat it with our eyes closed, guys. At some point, she's gotta move on to the next level."

"I'm right here," Stelli said around the ball of rage in her throat. "Don't talk about me like I'm elsewhere."

Genna and Deshawna fidgeted, but Ray put his hands on his hips. "Sorry, Stelli, but it's true. We're ready for this dungeon. You're not. Go play the new version of the Midnight Huntsmen and maybe try to focus on getting good enough for this level. We really do like playing with you when you're able to carry your own weight."

He gave a curt nod and a lopsided smile, as if his proclamation hadn't deepened the fresh cracks in their friendship, and then strode down the pass toward the dark maw of the dungeon. His steel boots crunched against loose rock.

Deshawna avoided Stelli's gaze and trotted after him. "I'm just saying, she wouldn't have to spend time getting good if she could play on easy mode."

At least Genna gave an awkward shrug before sidling away from Stelli.

And then the three of them were gone, swallowed up by the darkness of the dungeon's entrance.

Stelli stood alone. Her throat felt as if she'd been screaming for hours, and she'd dug her nails into her palms hard enough to feel them even beyond her sim avatar. The sage smell of the dry breeze made her want to puke.

She logged out.

The familiar exit animation played. Funny how she used to find the annoying little pixie such a temptation to log right back in.

She tore the helmet off and struggled out of the FullD chair, her skin sticking to the plasleather. She was drenched in sweat. That always happened when she got angry.

Damn it, now she'd have to take a shower before dinner.

Standing, she held the sim helmet between her still-gloved palms and trembled.

"Oh, good, you haven't started yet," said Grandma Marylan from the stairwell. "I thought I would be too slow to catch you today. Will your friends mind if I tag along today?"

Stelli figured her friends would be ecstatic to have her former professional gamer grandma with them for the Rock Troll's Dungeon. Grandma Marylan was so beyond needing the theoretical "easy mode" that Ray and Deshawna argued about.

Grandma Marylan never got KO'd. She hardly ever broke a sweat.

Stelli gripped at the sim helmet tight enough to make the plasmetal creak.

"Stelli, honey? Are you okay?"

Stelli blinked, as much to avoid looking straight at Grandma Marylan's concerned face as to keep the burning tears from spilling over. Her friends were such total jerks, she couldn't believe it. Now she couldn't even look at her own grandmother without fighting back sobs.

"Not gonna sim today. Just remembered I've got a math quiz tomorrow. Really should study."

She let the helmet fall onto the FullD chair with a dull thud.

"What happened, honey?"

"Nothing," Stelli said, making for the stairs. "Absolutely nothing."

Instead of studying, Stelli took her shower and had a good cry under the warm spray. The shower was the best place to have a cry you didn't want anyone to know about, with the hiss of the water to cover your hitching breaths and the steam to soothe your puffy cheeks afterward. And when you'd finished your cry and turned the water off, any lingering redness could be covered with a fresh coat of makeup.

As she rubbed at her hair with the towel—like she was going to spend the effort to blow it dry before dinner, right?—she met her own gaze in the misted mirror. Her eyes were a little puffy, but she'd let all her frustration run down the drain. All that remained was determination.

Ride with the Midnight Huntsmen and discover your true strength, the new quest had read.

The problem, she'd realized, was that her friends had changed the game without telling her. They used to play Feyland in order to have fun together, on whatever level they wanted to play. But now the others wanted to play to win, to get good. They wanted to *be* good.

They hadn't ditched her. They just didn't see that Stelli missed the memo.

But that was fine, she decided as she brushed a little foundation under her eyes. She'd got it now, and she knew what to do.

From this point forward, Feyland was no longer a game. The new Midnight Huntsmen quest wasn't a chance to discover more interesting lore, or a fun level to mess around in.

It was a chance to get so good she'd make Ray's head spin the next time they met in-game.

S he'd meant to wait until tomorrow's after school simming session. Really, she had. But the longer Stelli lay in bed staring at the ceiling and envisioning meeting her friends in first-period history, the less she could stand the idea of doing so without having made some progress toward showing them her improved skills.

So she snuck downstairs, careful not to wake her parents or especially her brother, and settled herself into her FullD chair.

She willed the golden *F* logo of Feyland to spin faster, ready to jump in right *now*.

But she hesitated at the character-select screen.

Something about the memory of Ray's face in his Paladin's helmet as he told her she wasn't good enough to play with them sparked at the embers of her anger. She didn't want to just get good enough; she wanted to get *better* than him.

She skipped over her Spellcaster's profile and created a new character.

She didn't spend too long customizing it. The point was to *get* good, not *look* good. But she did modify the armor choice from clanky metal to something a little more moveable, a little more suitable for riding in a hunt.

Satisfied, she sent her new Mercenary character in-game. A swirl of light and a rush like the roar of wind in her ears later, she stood in a circle of red and white mushrooms in a night-dark forest. In fact, the darkness seemed deeper than usual for this early area of the game.

A quick glance upward showed the virtual sky clouded over. Not even a sparkle of starlight dripped through to shine off the silvery bark of the birch trees that surrounded her.

If Stelli had chosen to play her Spellcaster, she could have given herself a light easily enough.

But no. It was bad enough the familiar foresty aromas already had her feeling at ease when she wanted to remain alert. She shook off the wish for her more familiar character, too. Besides, she could handle these early levels even with a brand-new character build.

With a deep breath to fan the coals of her resolve, she slunk into the darkness.

At least, she tried to slink. Dried leaves crackled under her heavy Mercenary's boots. Her sword clanked and dangled awkwardly from her left hip. The leather armor she'd chosen for mobility creaked.

She paused at the edge of a small clearing. With the moon still obscured, she could barely make out the outline of a jagged boulder jutting from the middle of a circle of grass, but the longer she stared at it, the more certain she became that a faint glow emanated from the stone, as if the moss that coated it were bioluminescent.

No signs of life filtered through the deep dark of the forest, neither fey nor simple beast. Either she'd frightened off every creature with her clumsy racket, or something dangerous lurked nearby.

The glow of the stone grew a little stronger.

She let her hand drift to the hilt of her sword.

"Halt, mortal."

The voice came from behind her. Stelli spun to find herself flanked by three grimacing faeries, all of them tall and pale, yet dark enough to seem to be disappearing into the shadows as she looked on. Two of them held their bows drawn with arrows pointed for her head. The one who had spoken stood in the middle and bore no obvious weapon, but a pair of thick black ram's horns curled from his forehead down around his ears.

The leader of the Midnight Huntsmen. Stelli smirked.

The leader snarled. "The Huntsmen suffer no outsider to look upon the source of our power."

He lifted one clawed hand, and the two archers pulled their bowstrings back further.

Stelli gave a bow, but maintained eye contact with the leader. "It is lucky, then, that I come to you seeking no longer to remain an outsider to your people. I come in answer to your summons."

She may be here in order to get good, but that didn't mean she'd abandon *all* role playing.

One of the bowmen bared his teeth. "We sent out no summons,

mortal. Give us the signal, Huntmaster. We'll fill this wretch with holes."

The leader narrowed his eyes until they were slits of glowing red. His nostrils flared, and Stelli suppressed a shudder at the sensation of being smelled.

"Indeed we sent no summons, but I do not deny we have need of the power this mortal brings. She could be the one to solve our little problem, if her devotion is true," he said. He lowered his hand, and the two bowmen likewise relaxed their weapons. "You truly come to bind yourself to the Huntsmen, to become one with Midnight?"

Stelli hesitated, though she tried to make herself look unconcerned. Talking with the fey NPCs was tricky, and a good player thought carefully before agreeing to anything the fey asked for. These things tended to have permanent effects on one's character progression.

But then, Stelli had created this character solely for this purpose, hadn't she? She meant to use this Merc to practice, to get good, and then use those skills with her real characters. She hadn't even given it a custom name, but had simply allowed the system to fill in a random one for her.

This character was disposable.

"I come seeking my true strength, and would ride alongside the Midnight Huntsmen in order to find it."

The leader held her gaze for a heartbeat more, just long enough to send a bead of sweat down Stelli's spine. Did he think she was lying? Would he have his archers shoot her after all? It didn't matter that her body was virtual. Arrows in the face sucked.

Then he snapped his fingers. From the murky shadows beyond the trees, four black horses emerged, their eyes glowing just as red as the fey folk's. Smoky wisps of steam rose from their flanks and their nostrils as they stamped and snorted, but they quieted under the hands of their masters.

The leader vaulted astride his mount and waved a hand toward the remaining horse. "The night's prey awaits our chase. All things live only to be killed eventually, after all."

The two archers laughed and spurred their horses off into the night. The leader waited, but even he couldn't contain his horse's wild readiness to sprint. Stelli had only this moment left to decide once and for all. She didn't need it.

She mounted up.

～

A curl of blood flowed across the flat surface of the pond, distorting the image of horse and rider and shaking Sealgaire's already tenuous grip on the scrying spell loose. He tried to hold on, grunted with the effort, and then let the frayed magic slip away. He panted. The muscles in his legs had cramped from too long crouching at the pond's edge. He'd used too much of his meager magic this morning baiting his trap. But at least he'd managed a clear enough view to confirm the bait had been taken.

Slowly but surely, his power was returning to its old strength.

As the magic dripped from his mind, the revelry around him filtered back into his senses. The hunt had been successful tonight, and his people sang eerie songs in praise of death and pain and the spice of fear as they cleaned their kills. The blood that had ruined his spell had seeped deeply into the earth at the bank and stained the blades of river grass that grew there. The sharp aroma made his mouth water.

He'd killed a water nymph himself this evening, his cleanest kill since returning home from his ordeal. He hoped his brothers and sisters remembered to save her skin for him. He needed a new cloak, and even a nymph's scant power would be a boon with his current weakness. But he had to take this opportunity to peer into that between place, the game world called Feyland, to see if his plan was working.

"You're taking a dangerous risk, Sealgaire," said another hunter lounging on the bank. A strip of raw goblin meat dangled from her fingers, and blood stained her skin up to her elbows. "Our master is already furious about the mess you left behind in that place. This could make things worse."

"I am doing what I can to set things right. Whatever solution I work, I have to keep my promise in mind."

His sister huntress snorted and tore a chunk from her strip with her teeth. "The fey folk ought never to make promises to mortals."

Sealgaire would have agreed with her if he could. Strange situations bred strange partnerships, and having been trapped in that horrifying between place for so long...his fey essence was only now beginning to return. Hence, his slaying of the nymph, normally a simple thing, was such a milestone.

But it would take more kills than that, and more complex ones, to convince his brothers and sisters he was still worthy of riding with the Wild Hunt. He was lucky enough that the master had allowed him to tag along despite his weakness, despite his mistakes and the sloppy magic he'd worked in the mortal game Feyland.

Well, he'd fix his mess and show the whole of the Wild Hunt he could be just as good as the rest of them, if not the best of them all. The promise he'd made to the elderly mortal woman who helped him escape was merely an extra hurdle for him to twist his strengthening fey magic around. It was an opportunity to get better.

He'd done what he could this night. Further work would have to wait until later, when his grasp of the magic returned. For now, he was forced to trust that the trap he'd set would close the way he meant it to, now that it had been triggered.

He stood from his crouch and brushed bits of grass from his clothes. He had a skin to collect.

⁓

"It's been a while since we simmed together," Grandma Marylan said from the passenger seat. "I'd be up for a little Feyland when we get home, if you want."

Stelli drummed her fingers on the steering wheel, watching as another grav-car took the extra space she'd left between herself and the person in front of her. She hit the brake.

"Uh," she said once she could concentrate on conversation again. "I'm kind of in the middle of a pretty involved solo quest line right now."

"Pretty involved" was an understatement. She'd simmed twice a day for the past five days, once at her normal afterschool time, and again in the dead of night while everyone else slept. It just felt right, practicing her newly learned skills in the day session, then moving up in the ranks of the Midnight Huntsmen under the cover of darkness. She was making progress, but hadn't yet been allowed another look at the glowing stone in the clearing, the obvious goal of the quest. Maybe tonight's session would get her there. Maybe she needed only a little more practice to be good enough.

But man, was she tired. Her eyes burned as she forced herself to keep watching traffic. Her shoulders and butt whined from the long hours put in with the FullD chair.

It was all worth it, though. She felt good when she played now, in a different way than she used to. Like she was close to mastering muscles she'd never used before. It was fine; she was young. She didn't need sleep.

What she needed was for this super-tweaked traffic to clear up so she could get simming faster.

"A solo quest? I thought you'd been playing with your friends."

Her friends. Right. She'd barely even spoken to them since they'd cut her out of the Rock Troll's Dungeon run, though she'd seen them retelling stories at lunch.

"They're doing their own thing," Stelli said.

"Let me know when you meet back up with them, then. I miss playing with you."

"I'm sure they won't mind if you join them. They could use your Kitsune character on the team."

Grandma Marylan looked at her, but Stelli was too busy pulling into their driveway—finally—to meet her gaze. Strange, but the anger she'd felt a week ago, the humiliation that her freaking grandmother was better at simming than she was, had melted away. She just didn't have the energy to keep up the embarrassment.

Stifling a yawn, Stelli reached into the back seat and grabbed her backpack. She got out and slammed her door, hoping the sound would jar the bits of sleepy cobwebs from her eyes, and marched around to the other side.

Grandma Marylan got out without Stelli's help this time, and she shut her door much more gently.

Stelli held her wrist up to the pad to unlock the house door.

"Is your solo quest line fun?" Grandma Marylan said.

Stelli shrugged. "Sure."

The door clicked open.

The Midnight Huntsmen pursued all manner of prey during their nightly rides. Animals, humans, even other fey; no NPC was unattractive to the bloodthirsty huntsmen.

And every quarry Stelli helped chase down gave her more experience, both the game mechanic variety and the true strength-building variety. Her muscles learned the way to swing a heavy sword or to pull a bowstring taut so the arrow would fly silent and sure.

She learned to be fearless and remorseless in her kills, to ignore the pleas of each NPC they chased down. She learned to dodge and parry attacks flung at her by fey NPCs willing to put up a fight for their digital lives.

She learned to clean blood out of leather, and then she learned instead to let the blood linger and dry into a growing pattern of power. She had only to glance down at herself, to breathe in that coppery tang, in order to feel invigorated to ride hard and long.

But she wasn't good enough yet. The power she felt on those rides was only temporary, and when she used her Spellcaster character during her daytime sessions, her actions didn't flow right. It didn't matter that the quests she played after school were more fun. She felt rubbery and stupid by day, to the point where she knew she was getting worse.

She needed the power in that stone.

During a rest in the hunt one night, while the other huntsmen worked to prepare their first kills of the evening by silver moonlight and pale fey fire, Stelli nudged her lathered horse alongside the ram-horned Huntmaster's.

"I have ridden with you for"—she paused, unable to recall how many nights now she'd snuck out of her bedroom to improve her skills—"for many moons. When I joined you, you spoke of a problem you hoped I might help you with. Surely I ought to be doing something about that? When will you give me a test so I can show what I've learned? At least help me see where I need improvement. There is a task I must accomplish by the end of this."

She hadn't forgotten her need to show Ray how much better than him she could be. She'd seen him in class today, smiling with Genna and Deshawna, planning out their next run on a new dungeon. At the time, Stelli hadn't felt much of anything, only the weight of her exhaustion dragging at her body. But now, breathing in the smoke of the fey fires and the bite of old blood on her armor, the rage stirred within her again. Her gloved fists creaked as they tightened around the reins, and her horse, a fey creature of much power itself, shied beneath her.

The ram-horned leader closed his eyes and drew air through his nostrils. "Ahh, the fires of mortality, they burn hard. It is something we fey lack, even those of us with the true magic."

"The true magic?"

The leader turned the full force of his gaze upon her and held it for a long moment. The sounds of the rest of the Midnight Huntsmen preparing for the second of the night's chases faded as though a veil had sprung up around Stelli and the Huntmaster.

"Don't tell me you hadn't come to understand yet, young huntress? What we truly are?"

Stelli looked at him. His red eyes glowed in the gathering haze of smoke and mist, and his dark visage was luminous as a moonbeam.

His aura pulsed around him, not so much a visible light as an agitation of the air around him. The pulse was rhythmic, and Stelli gasped to realize her heart beat in exact cadence with it.

She felt his presence through her entire being, through the essence that made her up. Somehow, her own energy had become tangled up with the drive of the huntsmen.

Suddenly, Stelli understood why her daytime sessions had become so numbing.

A wicked smile curved over the leader's face. "Yes, mortal. No bits of code or graphical trickery are we. When you ride with the Midnight Huntsmen, you ride with true fey."

True fey! She'd ridden by this creature's side for more nights than she could remember. How many nights? And if they were real, what about the rest of the things she'd thought were simple NPCs? How many living beings had she slaughtered under his watchful eye, how many "bits of code" that might have been just as alive as herself?

The stench rising from her armor clogged her throat.

The Huntmaster's grin shifted into a sneer. "Why do you recoil so? I thought you wanted to be strong, to be a huntress. Is my true nature enough to send you scurrying away so easily? But come, I am not so monstrous as you think. You find me in weakened state, to speak true. Myself, and all who ride with me through this false mirror of the Realm, we are all unjustly diminished. We are shades of our former glorious selves, unable to muster the power to escape this undeserved prison, let alone cause any real harm to the mortals who sport here."

Stelli held herself rigid atop her horse—her true fey horse, thrumming with *real magic*—as she wrestled with this glut of information. She didn't need to question the Huntmaster's words; the pulse throbbing through her entire being more than confirmed them. But could she handle the idea that faeries were real, and what's more, that she had been riding alongside them night after night, learning their bloodthirsty ways with the intent of using those skills against her friends?

It was too much, too *real*. How could she have let things go so far?

When had Feyland stopped being a game? She realized now that her friends had never stopped having fun, even if they did seek greater challenges. Their laughter and smiles at lunch proved that.

Stelli was the one who had changed things. Shame bloomed in her heart and spread through her body like a bruise.

At least she could take comfort in the fact that she had never found this quest fun in any way. It was all work for her, an unforgiving grind to get good, with no room for frivolous enjoyment. She'd taken no delight in any of her kills, and she had never resorted to making sport of any creature's death the way the other Midnight Huntsmen did.

She could stop herself before any more damage was done.

With a trembling hand, she gestured to open her in-game menu. All of a sudden, her lack of sleep was catching up with her. She'd log out, have a half night of rest tonight, and never play after hours again.

"And so you choose to run and hide. I'd not thought you so rabbit-hearted, mortal, nor so rabbit-stupid. You cannot escape from us. The Midnight Huntsmen have you in their sights now."

Stelli let her hand hover over the logout option. "You don't scare me. You said yourself you haven't got the power to cause any harm to mortals. I've neglected my friends for too long. It's time I treated Feyland like a game again. I thank you for your lessons, but now that I understand them better, I fear they are not for me. Good evening."

The Huntmaster's red eyes became slits, and suddenly his face was close to hers, impossibly close for two on horseback. He bore down on her mind with his will, crushing her until she slumped forward in her saddle with a whimper of pain. Her head felt full of stars, sparking and burning against the inside of her skull, and her body grew weak, so weak.

Without her permission, her hand moved away from the menu, away from the logout option, until it dangled useless and tame against her horse's flank.

Above her still, the Huntmaster bared his teeth. Their sharp points glinted in the light of myriad fey torches, and Stelli realized that the rest of the Midnight Huntsmen had closed in around them.

"No *thanks* are necessary, mortal, for I have *given* nothing. You bound yourself to the Huntsmen. You became one with Midnight. You gave yourself to me seeking power, and aye, you have found it. But that power belongs to the Midnight Huntsmen, and with the Midnight Huntsmen it shall stay."

The circle of lights closed in, and the pain in Stelli's head flared. Faces of the various huntsmen leered at her, faces she had come to know and respect as mentors over her nights with them. They terrified her now, their digital masks torn away to reveal the horrors beneath.

"No," she cried, but it came out as nothing more than a whisper. "Please..."

"Hear how she cries out," one huntsman jeered. "Hear how she squeals like a frightened piglet!"

"She will make good sport this night."

"Let us drink of her, Huntmaster."

"Let us grow strong off her power, Huntmaster."

Stelli shuddered, slumped numb against her horse's neck. Terror burned in her, but she could do nothing to fend off her oncoming comrades. Her lungs ached with the need to breathe, though she could not. They touched her with claws she'd seen rend the flesh from the bones of their quarry night after night.

"No," said the Huntmaster, and the word rang with power. The gathered huntsmen receded but a half pace, but it was enough to loosen the constricting hands around Stelli's lungs.

"No, we will not squander what we have to slake our thirst for a single night. The mortal needs her strength for herself, and you know it. Or are you all become dumb simulacra already?"

The huntsmen blinked and licked their lips, their eyes darting hungrily between Stelli and the leader.

A flicker of frustration crossed the leader's face, and he turned back to Stelli. "You see what I must contend with. My people grow stupid like prey, and they will soon succumb to the whims of the code ether that surrounds us in this place. Long have I fought against this spreading scourge, ever since one of our own trapped us here, but to little avail. But now, with you, with the fires of a mortal's determination, my people stand a chance. You would seek your strength with the Midnight Huntsmen? Then you will gain it only by strengthening the whole of the clan. Find the one who stole the greater part of our fey essence and open our way back into the Realm, and you will have the power you yearn for."

Air flowed rough through Stelli's throat, and her voice sounded like sandpaper, but the shackles of the Huntmaster's power still clutched at her limbs. "And will I be free then, if I do this thing for you?"

If she found some way to open a path into a mystical, dangerous realm of faeries and magic, would she be allowed to return to her mundane sim game and the fun she used to have playing the beginner "baby" levels?

Something in the way the Huntmaster's keening laugh echoed in the night told her that her chances were slim.

S telli fell back into her body with such force that she gasped. She felt as though she'd been thrust against the plasleather sim chair, and she might as well have been. The Huntmaster had forced her out of the game after his horrific revelation, as a show of his command over her. Even now, as she sat panting so her breath fogged the inside screen of her sim helmet, she still felt the strings of his power curling around her. He could compel her to return to the game anytime, she knew.

Her eyes burned. Her muscles ached as through she'd just run the mile in gym class. She couldn't seem to catch her breath no matter how long she lay there gasping like a fish.

Faeries. Real faeries. It shouldn't be possible. Real faeries! The dangerous kind. In a video game, of all places. In a place that was supposed to be fun.

And she'd gotten herself tangled up with them the moment she'd stopped allowing herself to have that fun. She'd run straight to them and begged them to teach her their ways, to give her some of their strength. Stupid! It didn't matter that she hadn't known, because now that she *did* know, it felt like she'd *always* known, somehow.

And now she was compelled to...what? To find some way into the Realm of Faerie? To track down a rogue faerie—probably a dangerous one, if he used to ride with the Midnight Huntsmen—and take the fey power he'd made off with back by force?

She hardly knew where to begin. She would have started laughing if she'd had the breath for it. Her eyes burned intensely.

A hand touched her knee.

Stelli yelped and jerked in the FullD chair. Had the Huntsmen followed her out of the game, somehow?

"Stelli! It's Grandma. Take that helmet off, dear."

Her heart in her mouth, Stelli struggled to pull the helmet from her head. She sat blinking, letting her eyes adjust to the darkness of the entertainment room around her. It was the dead of night, sometime after one in the morning, and the only sounds were the gentle hum of electronics and the air conditioning, as well as the rasp of her own frightened breath.

Grandma Marylan sat perched on the end of the second FullD chair, leaning forward, her hand still outstretched to touch Stelli's knee. Even in the shadows, the lines of worry stood stark on her face.

"Oh, Grandma," Stelli croaked. And then she couldn't stop the tears.

She let the helmet fall to the floor with a hollow thump and flung herself into her grandmother's lap. As if she were under a spell, Stelli heard herself telling everything that had happened, from her friends cutting her out to the terrible predicament she found herself in now. All the while, her grandmother smoothed a hand over her hair and down her back.

The strings of power that tethered her to the Huntmaster threaded through Grandma Marylan's fingers as she did. Stelli felt the tug and snag of them.

Sniffing, Stelli tilted her head up to stare into her grandmother's eyes. "What am I going to do? How can I possibly open a way into the Realm of Faerie?"

Grandma Marylan held her gaze for a long, silent moment, and Stelli was suddenly afraid that her grandmother was going to say she was imagining it all, that she just needed to sleep. Then Grandma Marylan cupped Stelli's face in both hands and smiled.

"'Mortal effort shall open the door.' It's what all these young faerie types seem to think. I can bet you these huntsmen of yours will find their ideas of the situation aren't quite on the mark, but they'll bluster and blow nonstop until we try it their way. So, we might as well get it over with. Then we can move on that much quicker to solving the real problem."

"Wh-what's the real problem?" Stelli asked.

"The problem is that you aren't having a lick of fun! Stelli, you haven't been yourself for weeks now. You've been like a shadow, like there are whole pieces of you that have been sucked away. It's a game, honey. Even a professional player knows to keep the fun in the fore-front. If you put too much of yourself in it, why, then it becomes like a *job*. And I can tell just by looking that you've got too much of yourself tied up in these huntsmen and 'getting good' at Feyland."

"But now I have to be serious, don't I? There's real faeries involved. They've got me in their grasp. They want me to *go to* the Realm!"

"Yes, you'll have to extricate yourself from this little mess," said Grandma Marylan, still smiling, "but it's still just a game. Not the Realm, of course. But Feyland is a game."

Stelli swallowed. She still felt shaky, like she might just fall apart if she leaned too far one way. "You really believe me? That there's real faeries and the Realm and everything?"

A faraway look shimmered in Grandma Marylan's eyes. "I do. I've seen a glimpse..."

She shook herself, motioned for Stelli to stand, then heaved herself up to her feet as well.

"Put that helmet of yours back on, honey. Let's sim a little together."

Stelli gaped. "What, now? I mean...are you...are you coming with me?"

Marylan busied about getting her own simming gear on, wriggling her hands into the gloves, plucking her helmet from where it rested on the chair. "Only partway. It's your quest to fulfill, so you'll have to be the one to do the work. But I have something that might help you a bit."

Grandma Marylan jammed the helmet over her gray hair and sat gingerly in the seat. By the time Stelli picked up her fallen helmet and raised it over her head, Grandma Marylan had flexed her fingers to open Feyland.

"Play your Spellcaster, dear. Come meet me in town."

A wave of relief washed over Stelli at the suggestion. She didn't want to touch her blood-soaked Mercenary character again if she could help it. But would she be able to accomplish anything as her Spellcaster? Her daytime sessions had grown steadily worse over the weeks, until she felt like she was always at level one.

Stifling her doubts, Stelli crushed the helmet onto her head and flopped back into the sim chair.

It's just a game, she told herself as the golden *F* logo danced before her.

But the strings of power pulling taut around her wouldn't let her believe it.

S he met her grandmother in a tavern in the first area town. The place was as stereotypical a fantasy tavern as you could hope for, with ale and music and a loud clientele ready to grant a quest or pick a fight, whatever the player chose. At this late hour, there were few actual players logged in, so despite the fact that Stelli had to weave through the packed house to reach the table her grandmother had picked, they were actually quite alone.

Unless some of these NPCs were *real faeries*.

But Stelli didn't get the same feel from them as she did from the

Midnight Huntsmen, so she tried to put the possibility out of her mind as she sat down across from her grandmother.

Grandma Marylan looked supremely over-leveled sitting there as her Kitsune character, bristling with knives, a pair of bows and a quiver full of yellow-fletched arrows slung over her back, her leather armor clearly broken in and fully functional. Even the way she held herself broadcast the fact that she could take out every NPC in this tavern in a few effortless moments if she wanted.

Stelli felt like a twig beside her.

Grandma Marylan nodded to her as she sat, and opened her inventory menu. "We won't waste time. The sooner you get this done with, the happier you'll be. Just give me a moment to un-equip..."

There was a click, and then a flare of light on the table. The light receded to reveal an ornate hunting knife, its hilt and blade both etched with mystical runes and flowing script. Grandma Marylan smiled and pushed the knife toward Stelli.

Stelli shook her head. "Your famous knife? I can't take that—it's, like, your signature weapon! Everyone will know I didn't earn it."

Grandma Marylan had won the recognizable blade as a drop from some tough boss fight early on in their time simming together. Stelli didn't remember much about it because, she recalled with shame now, she'd been KO'd pretty much right off the bat in that fight. But her grandma had used the knife almost exclusively ever since. The image of Kitsune Marylan wielding her iconic knife had become rather famous in the servers they tended to play in.

"Nonsense," Grandma Marylan said. "You have need of it. If you can't find a way to get into the Realm with that knife, I'll eat my bow. Plus, once you get there, having this will surely make things easier for you. Take it!"

Grandma Marylan pushed the knife closer, and Stelli took it. The moment her hand closed on the hilt, a warm feeling suffused her.

Magic.

It was like the feeling of the strings that even now bound her to the Huntmaster, so very like it, but *stronger.*

"That knife belongs to a faerie huntsman named Sealgaire,"

Grandma Marylan said. "He gave it to me after I helped him find his way home."

"Is he...is he the one who stole the Midnight Huntsmen's power?" Could Stelli use the knife to track him down?

Grandma Marylan chuckled. "Oh, he's the one you're looking for, I'm sure of it. You just talk to him and tell him to set his mess right."

Stelli put the knife away in her inventory, wary of the way its warmth still radiated over her.

Grandma Marylan pushed her stool away from the table and rose with a grunt. "Well, I'm too old to be prancing about in the sim world at this hour. I've got to get to sleep. You wrap this business up and get to bed yourself, honey. And do me a favor? When you see him, tell him I said hi, and I've not forgotten his promise. Okay? And have *fun*."

Stelli nodded, too nervous to form words. She thought her stomach might turn itself inside out if she opened her mouth.

"Good night, then." Grandma Marylan kissed her forehead and logged out.

Just like that, Stelli was alone in the crowded tavern. Alone with the unnerving magic of the knife her grandmother had been using for ages.

Alone with her task.

Should she log out and log back in as her Mercenary character? But no, her Merc wouldn't have the knife. And how was she supposed to use the knife to get to the Realm, anyway?

Well, how did one get anywhere in Feyland? The rings of faerie mushrooms were the usual way between levels. If anyplace in this digital world would allow her to cross over, it would be them. She hoped.

She left the tavern and walked out into the night, along the path that would lead her to the very first faerie ring in the game. The one in the forest just outside the town walls was closer, but the Midnight Huntsmen made the darkness beneath those trees their primary hunting grounds. The longer she could go without seeing them, the better.

Her white Spellcaster robes were coated in dirt by the time she reached the mushrooms. Pale moonlight drenched the grass and the ribbon of the road she'd walked, giving the clearing an ethereal glow designed to take a new player's breath away, while still beckoning them onward into their faerie-land adventures.

Stelli brought the knife out of her inventory, hesitated a moment, then swiped the blade in the air above the circle of mushrooms.

Nothing happened.

Except, before she had time to feel silly or frustrated or relieved, a whispery voice echoed from behind her, as if carried on the breeze from very far away.

"Mortal effort shall open the door."

Stelli gripped the knife tighter. Her grandma had said those words; something about the faeries always thinking that was the way.

A sudden thought came to Stelli, and with a quick motion, she drew the blade of the faerie knife across her left palm.

Her HP bar shrank a little, and, though the graphical design of Feyland didn't include blood for player character wounds, a line of red blossomed along with the pain.

She held her hand over the mushroom ring and let the blood drip onto the dirt.

The breeze from behind her grew into a gust and then a gale, and Stelli stumbled forward to stand in the center of the circle.

Her view darkened as it did every time she traveled between levels, but this time, the blackness carried a tinge of malice, and she felt as though somewhere above her—she didn't dare look up!—a pair of eyes looked down on her.

When the blackness drained away, she found herself standing on the bank of a slow-moving river that sparkled with the orange-gold glow of twilight. Her knees buckled under her, and she collapsed into the growth of high grass and mud beneath her feet. Her cut palm stung at the touch of the grit. She hissed and winced, but did not cry out.

The riverbank crawled with fey folk. Some were tall and beautiful, dark or fair of complexion and graceful as dancers; others were ugly in their naturalness, seemingly made of stone or bark or fungal growth. But all were terrible to behold, and their power was tangible even from a distance.

They, like the knife, felt *like* the Midnight Huntsmen back in the game world of Feyland, but so, so much more.

"Ssssweet thing, sweet mortal," hissed something behind her.

Stelli whipped her head around to see a water hag pulling herself from the edge of the water, dripping with brown weeds and stinking of the silty river bottom. Her beady eyes rippled like deep pools.

Stelli recoiled as best she could, and her cut hand plopped into the water.

The hag came up. "Oh, but you're just a morsel. Who has been feeding on you so, to reduce you to such a tiny sip? Oh, have they left nothing for poor Hagitha? Poor, poor Hagitha."

Her heart thumping, Stelli brought the faerie knife up. The edge gleamed in the twilight as if it had been gilded.

The hag lurched backward with a screech. "To the hunt she belongs! Oh, forgive poor Hagitha, she did not know, she didn't!"

"Shh," Stelli said, but it was too late. The hag's cries had pulled the attention of the other gathered fey folk to them. Their presences loomed closer, dark and foul, until it was all Stelli could do to draw breath.

Oh, man, she had to do something now. Something. Anything.

It's just a game, came her grandmother's voice from her memory. *Oh, and have* fun.

Finding a hidden well of strength, Stelli threw herself to her feet and whirled about, holding the faerie knife before her.

"I come seeking the faerie called Sealgaire," she shouted. She got all the words out, though her voice broke. "I come to implore him to put right what he has wrought in the, uh...in the Realm of Feyland."

Role playing had always been her strength. She might not be the best in a fight, but even her friends had often admitted that she shone when she talked with the NPCs.

From the fearsome bunch of fey folk leering at her, one stepped forward. His clothing and armor marked him as a huntsman, though his aura was not as strong as the other fey folk around him. He struck her as being somehow diminished, not at his peak strength. Like so many people had been saying about herself, she realized.

"I am the one you seek," he said. "You gave slow chase getting here, young mortal, especially for one who thought to ride with the hunt. With a grandmother like yours, I expected something more of you."

Stelli scowled and thrust the knife point toward him. "My grandmother said to tell you hi, and that she remembers the promise you made her."

The huntsman—Sealgaire, she supposed—flinched, and the others around them laughed. The sound crawled up Stelli's spine like spiders, but she made herself hold her posture.

"Yes, I've not forgotten it, either. It is why I called you here."

Stelli lowered her arm a bit. "Wait, what? You called me here? The Midnight Huntsmen *made* me come here."

"And I called you to join the Midnight Huntsmen. I tried to keep my promise by my own power, but I soon found I could not do so without calling on your aid, much as it galls me to pull on mortal effort once more."

"You sent me that quest?"

Sealgaire nodded.

"Why?" Stelli jabbed with the knife again. "So you could steal the last shreds of their power?"

"So you and I could both regain our true strength. They've been feeding on the both of us ever since I worked such sloppy magic in my desperation to escape. What power they have was never theirs to begin with."

Stelli huffed and adjusted her grip on the knife. Her cut palm ached. She wanted so badly to go to sleep.

"I don't understand," she said.

"Your grandmother helped me escape that false Realm after I found myself trapped there," Sealgaire said, wearing the same faraway look Grandma Marylan had when she'd said she'd believed Stelli's story. "She did this because I coerced her into assisting me by holding your mortal essence hostage. But I was not careful when I pulled your essence from you, and some of it leaked out of my hold, along with a measure of my own fey power. The residue of that combination had an effect on those bits of code I'd been riding hunt with. It wasn't long after my return here that I realized the effect, that the fake fey I'd left behind had soaked up that stray power and mortal essence and come to believe that they were true fey. Once they learned to catch hold of those frayed threads of magic, they naturally tugged to unravel the rest of the weave. It has been a struggle for me to hold on to what reserves of magic I still retain, as I know it has been for you and your own strength."

Stelli gaped as he spoke, her horror growing with every word said in such a matter-of-fact tone. This person, this creature, had *ripped out her soul?* And he'd just let some of it splash on the ground—oh, whoops, there goes a little piece of what makes you you. No big deal.

No freaking *wonder* she didn't remember the boss fight where her grandmother had won this knife.

And no wonder she'd been feeling so much like rubber anytime she played away from the Midnight Huntsmen. If Sealgaire's story was true, they'd been siphoning off even more of her mortal essence with every hunt she rode with them.

Stelli squinted. Did this make it Sealgaire's fault that her friends had cut her out? Had he made that happen? And if he had, had it been on purpose, or simply another sloppy, unintended consequence?

Sealgaire closed his eyes and breathed in through his nose, and Stelli was reminded of her first interaction with the Huntmaster back in Feyland.

"Yes, I feel your anger. It's as strong as your hold on that knife. Help me set this aright, mortal, and you shall have your opportunity at vengeance. This I swear."

The riverbank around them grew silent, as if the tension of the gathered fey folk as they awaited her decision had smothered even the constant babble of the water.

What a threat this situation must be to them, Stelli realized. If digital copies of faeries could grow strong enough to send an invader to the Realm of Faerie, what more could they achieve if left unchecked?

Finally, Stelli let her knife arm rest at her side. "I'll help you, Sealgaire. But, you ought to know, I'm not much good in a fight. I get KO'd a lot."

Sealgaire smiled, showing all of his teeth. "Then, mortal, which part of the hunt do *you* find the most fun?"

S telli bore two bloody slashes on her left palm when she logged back in to her Mercenary character. She came directly from the Realm of Faerie, with Sealgaire in tow and bound, the point of the knife held under his chin. She'd been afraid she'd lose it in the transition between characters, but Sealgaire had laughed at her fear.

They emerged into the game world precisely where the Huntmaster had placed his hold over her. The Midnight Huntsman were gathered in the clearing, their horses stamping, their fires blazing. They had just run a hunt, and were cleaning their kills.

All activity stopped the moment Stelli and her "prisoner" appeared.

"I return, Huntmaster," she called. She kept her voice strong but demure, as if she had accepted her subservient place and confidently completed her master's bidding. "I bring with me the thief."

She pushed Sealgaire forward until he fell to his knees before the ram-horned leader of the false huntsmen.

The Huntmaster rose from where he sat on a cushion of pelts amid the fallen leaves. His hand trembled as he reached toward Sealgaire.

"Yes," he said. "This power...long have I... Yes. You have done well for us, mortal."

"I have done better," Stelli said. She let a hint of surety bleed into her expression, hoping to lend her performance an edge. "I got him to tell me how he achieved his crime, and from that, how to put it aright. We have only to bring him to the source of our strength. We can tap into what remains to us in order to force him to relinquish his."

The Huntmaster narrowed his eyes. "Are you certain? You know we do not suffer outsiders to look upon the source of our power."

"But, sir," she said, really leaning into her role now, "this one, like myself, once pledged himself to be one with Midnight, did he not? So let him be one with Midnight."

All around her, the Midnight Huntsmen started whooping and crying in excitement. The sound echoed in the trees, and what carrion birds had perched above to await their chance at the scraps of the hunt took flight.

It took the Huntmaster many tries to get them to calm down enough to proclaim they would make for the stone of power, and once he said so, the clamor started up again. The whole clan tromped through the forest, shouting and carousing. Stelli worked to keep from being trampled at the front of the column.

Though she was leading Sealgaire as her false prisoner, he lent her his support where he could. Together, the two conspirators arrived at the site of the glowing boulder, the one Stelli had seen on her first night with the Midnight Huntsmen.

The glow had grown since she'd seen it last. The pulse of power from it was apparent, and in its strength, she felt the signatures of... herself. Herself and something more, something fey, like the feel of the air in that other place, in the Realm of Faerie.

With this proof of the truth in Sealgaire's claim—her own strength pulsing out of that rock and into the gathered replicas of fey hunters—Stelli let her anger build again.

Turning the faerie knife in her right hand, she pulled off a deft slash to the cords that bound Sealgaire. The ropes fell to the ground with a dull thump.

"Now, Sealgaire!"

But she didn't need to call out. The moment he had the use of his hands, Sealgaire turned them both toward the glowing boulder. A breathless moment stretched into forever as fey magic coalesced between his outstretched hands and the boulder.

A squeak of protest came from someone right behind Stelli. She thought it was the Huntmaster.

Then the boulder exploded.

Bits of rock flew everywhere, slicing trees and leaves and huntsmen in their wake. Some of the huntsmen took so many stones that they faded into the smoke of defeat, their screams drifting away on the wind. Stelli took a bunch of shrapnel, too, but the pain was the dull kind felt during normal play of Feyland.

She gritted her teeth and drew her sword.

The space where the boulder once sat glowed the same orange-gold of twilight she'd seen in the Realm of Faerie. It was her power and his, hovering there, waiting for someone to pick it up. The light flickered over the faces of those huntsmen that hadn't expired, including the Huntmaster. His fury rolled through the clearing in palpable waves.

"Stelli, the knife!"

Hoping she wouldn't hurt herself or her ally, Stelli threw the knife toward Sealgaire. He caught it, flipped it to catch the silver light of the moon, then showed his teeth again.

"Now we come to the part *I* find most fun."

The fight began. Stelli found herself first tangling blades with the Huntmaster himself, as he had been directly behind her. But he soon broke away from her, and before she could give chase, three false huntsmen swarmed up to get their blows in.

She was forced to parry, dodge, strike, almost faster than she could think. Every lesson she'd learned in her rides with the Midnight Huntsmen, every move she'd trained herself to use, she pulled out now in the fight for her own strength.

It was hard work.

It wasn't fun.

Many times, so many, she nearly fell, nearly left Sealgaire to pull both their weights in the fight.

Somehow, she kept on. She beat back a blade, then took the

opportunity to finish off an enemy. While the smoke of his defeat blew in her face, she whirled to slice an arrow right before it could strike her.

Other arrows hit their mark. She was looking rather like a porcupine, she thought. A really, really tired porcupine.

There were just so many of them.

Until, finally, Sealgaire finished one false hunter, and all that remained was the Huntmaster, fighting with Stelli clear on the other side of the meadow.

The glowing power hung before Sealgaire, and none stood between him and it. The light cast deep shadows over his fey visage.

If he took that clump of power now, his and hers all mixed up, with his own knife back in his hands, would that leave Stelli at his mercy?

Would he leave her to dwindle away in the game of Feyland?

The whoosh of the Huntmaster's blade grew loud in her ears, and she realized her adversary had caught her off guard. This was it. Her HP was low enough that if she took this hit, she'd be logged out. She'd leave the game without a good portion of her soul.

She closed her eyes and relied on her reflexes to bring her sword up to block.

A warbling ping of blades clashing nearly deafened her. When she opened her eyes, she found the Huntmaster staggering away, clutching his bleeding hand. His sword lay on the ground at Stelli's feet.

Sealgaire's faerie knife vibrated where it had embedded itself in a nearby tree.

Sealgaire approached, one hand still held out from his throw, a ball of light growing around it. Just the orange light, none of the gold.

Her light.

"I promised your grandmother that if she helped me, your essence would be returned to you in full. I keep my promises."

Then Sealgaire touched her forehead with his glowing hand, and warmth of a different kind than she'd felt from the knife washed over her. It filled her up, slowly at first, then sort of all at once. All her cracks, all the places she hadn't realized felt so empty all this time—the warmth filled them all in.

Beside her, the Huntmaster's eyes turned flat, dull. Still red, still full of threat and the desire for the hunt, but merely...designed that way. Nothing but pixels and some behavioral codes.

Seeing his men defeated, his own health at low, he spouted a scripted line, then turned tail and ran into the dark of the forest.

Stelli watched him go with a strange sense of melancholy. She had, in a twisted, unnatural kind of way, enjoyed her time riding with the Midnight Huntsmen.

Sealgaire flexed his fingers, then pulled his knife from the tree. He looked the blade over with an appraising eye.

"And so I am whole again. As are you, young mortal. Would you take the opportunity at vengeance I swore to you?"

Stelli looked him up and down, read the stance of a true fey hunter, saw the way the thrill of the hunt burned at full strength inside him.

She shook her head. "No way, man. That's not my idea of a good time. I'll just, uh, get you back home. I'm sure you're not too interested in spending more time here than you have to."

"Indeed."

He handed the knife to her handle first, and she took it with a sigh. Now that all the fighting was over, her left palm ached again.

But she sucked it up and made a third line with a quick motion. Wincing, she held her hand out and let the fresh blood drip.

"Here," she said, nudging the knife toward her unlikely partner. "It's yours, isn't it? You said it still holds some of your power."

Sealgaire eyed the knife, swallowed, but finally shook his head. "It was a gift. Offer it back to your grandmother, but if she'd rather you had the use of it, I have no issue with such an arrangement. Who knows—with the way things are stirring in the Realm these days, you may have need of its power for yourself."

With that enigmatic comment, he took her bleeding hand, pressed it with his own, and was gone.

The vacuum of his leaving was enough to make her stumble. Alone now in the clearing, Stelli took stock of herself.

She was whole, yes. She felt good, yes. She'd even, up until the fight got really hard there at the end, had a little fun tonight.

How long had it been since she'd had any fun in this place?

Stifling a yawn, she lifted her uninjured hand, put the knife back in her inventory, and swiped to bring up her in-game menu. She'd give the knife back to Grandma Marylan tomorrow, when they simmed together after school. Maybe she'd see if her friends wanted to play, too, but if they were too caught up in their big fights, that was okay. There were some role-play-focused groups she could join that tended to hang around the lower levels. They might be fun to mess around with for a while.

She was strong enough now to choose her own fun.

But first, she thought as the golden light of the logout screen engulfed her, she'd get some freaking sleep.

ABOUT THE AUTHOR

Brigid Collins is a fantasy and science fiction writer living in Michigan. Her short stories have appeared in Fiction River, The Uncollected Anthology Volume 13: *Mystical Melodies*, and the *Chronicle Worlds: Feyland* anthology. Books 1 through 3 of her fantasy series, Songbird River Chronicles, are available in print and electronic versions on Amazon.

Find out more about Brigid at:
backwrites.wordpress.com

twitter.com/purellian
bookbub.com/authors/brigid-collins

THE CALL OF THE HUNTRESS

JAMIE FERGUSON

S alome was her father's daughter.

I knew that long before she was born, from the way she kicked and tossed herself around in my belly.

Unlike my moody, tempestuous child, I was calm. Thoughtful. I liked to take my time, to analyze...to be careful. I'd learned caution as a child, watching the intrigue in the court of my parents, the prince and princess of Judea, and the machinations of my family to gain and hold on to power by influencing the imperial family of Rome. Then, later, I had to pretend to love and care for my grandfather, who ordered my father strangled to death, and then forced me to marry my half-uncle when I was thirteen.

I hated Salome's father, the vile, corpulent beast I had to act like I was pleased to marry. And I hated the child he planted inside of me.

Herod II, who we all called Phillip—there were so many Herods that it was, secretly of course, a joke, as was my own name, Herodias —was an evil, despicable man.

Oh, he was nice to the soldiers, the money makers, basically everyone male. But he was not nice to women, or slaves, or the poor or unfortunate. I once watched him poison three men in one evening, in front of me and two dinner guests who drank wine and made jokes during the event. My husband laughed as the men died, and made one of our slaves, a learned man from Greece who'd been captured in one of the many military skirmishes, take notes about the horror and misery the dying men went through on a piece of parchment.

I did not laugh, I did not joke. And I did not drink my wine.

No man, no matter how rich, or powerful, or noble of lineage he is, has the right to be so foul, so cruel, to another.

Those men, each forced to drink a different variant of poison, should not have died.

If Phillip had drunk poison and died, I would not have cried.

But—later, always later, because I knew to never allow him to see how I really felt lest I, even with my royal blood, be punished—I cried for those poor, innocent men, whose names I did not know.

Perhaps they'd had wives, and children, back in their homelands, who would never know what had happened to them.

But I did.

Over the years, I dreamed of escape from the hateful man I'd been married to—and from the child who I did my best to love, but who returned my affection by disobeying me and getting her father to void my rules, my expectations, my punishments. Salome would whisper jokes about me to Phillip in my very presence, and the two of them would laugh at my expense.

Thankfully, she was my only child.

And then I realized there was a way out. It was a word I hadn't known when I was first married, but once I learned of it, I latched on to it with all my might: Divorce. All I had to do was find a new husband so that I could justify leaving Phillip and ensure he wouldn't force me to return—or worse, have me killed in punishment.

I didn't realize that I would be trading one prison for another.

I rested a hand on the railing that bordered the wide stone patio and watched the winding train of people and donkeys climb up the hill to the palace. The setting sun warmed the side of my face, the light midsummer breeze rustled my hair, and the leather straps on my new sandals had been tied too tightly and were digging into my skin. Antipas, my second husband and the tetrarch of both Galilee and Perea, stood nearby, joking with some of the men and women who'd joined us to celebrate Salome's arrival. I tried to ignore the way his eyes kept wandering down Tamara's body. She was the wife of one of the local noblemen and, unbeknownst to her husband, had become Antipas' latest conquest.

I'd thought Antipas would rescue me from the cruelty I'd endured from his half-brother, Phillip. And he had. For the first few months I'd convinced myself I was in love with Antipas. I'd believed the lies he told me, and thought myself safe and fortunate. But then I learned that other forms of cruelty, while less visible and less brutal, can cause just as much pain.

Tamara walked over to stand next to me, her long, linen skirts rustling, the outlines of her large breasts clearly visible through the light fabric of her tunic. My back stiffened, and I kept my gaze fixed on one of the donkeys in the front of Salome's retinue.

"You must be so excited! How many years has it been since you saw your daughter?" Tamara asked in her nasal, high-pitched voice. Her rose perfume tickled my nose, and I stifled a sneeze.

"Excited" wasn't the right word. Nervous, perhaps. Apprehensive. Uneasy.

"Over six years," I said. With the strength of years of practice at pretense, I met the other woman's eyes and gave her a small, polite smile. I fingered the small, silver disc that hung from one of my bracelets, the round shape so simple and non-descript that none here in the land of Galilee would realize it represented the moon—and therefore the goddess of the moon, the hunt, and protector of women: Diana.

I'd spent part of my childhood in Rome, sent there by my mother after my father's death so she could play her games of politics and intrigue without the burden of dealing with her youngest child. I visited Diana's temple for the first time when I was nine, and a sense of calm and peace I'd never felt before came over me as soon as I passed through the marble columns and stood inside the main chamber. It was as if I'd met my first true friend, someone I could tell my secrets to, and share my fears and burdens with. I took advantage of every opportunity possible to return to the temple, and learned ways to keep something representing Diana close to me at all times, while hiding my belief in the goddess lest that complicate my future. Many in Galilee despised the gods of Rome I'd grown up believing in, and I did not want to give the people reason to dislike me even more than they already did.

"It must have been so hard to leave your child," Tamara said. "Salome was just a little girl at the time."

"She had just turned twelve when I left." I raised one eyebrow. "I was but a year older when I married her father."

"Yes, but to have her mother leave and marry... Why, I suppose Antipas is Salome's half-uncle, isn't he?" She raised a hand to her mouth, her eyes wide, as if she'd only just realized this fact even though I'd overheard her telling someone about it a few days earlier.

"He is," I said, amused by her attempt to act surprised. I'd long since ceased being annoyed when people brought up the facts of my divorce. If they really wanted to complain about intermarriage, they could look at the rest of my family tree—and, often, at their own. The only questionable thing I'd done was remarry while Phillip still lived. No one seemed concerned that *he* had gotten remarried. But, then, I was a woman.

"I have heard that man, what is his name? The hairy one who wears animal skins, and hangs out by the river. He says divorce is wrong, that what you did was wrong."

The woman was sleeping with my husband, behind the back of her own, and yet felt she had the temerity to imply wrongdoing on *my* part?

"His name is John," I said. I gave her a sideways glance, my features calm and regal. "And that is not what I have heard he says."

I had disguised myself and gone down to the river several times to hear the man speak for myself—with an escort, of course, as there was no way I could sneak out of the palace on my own. Antipas, just like Phillip before him, had guards at the gates. It would be impossible for me to leave lest I learned to walk on air.

And so, standing near the river disguised in worn robes made of rough linen, under the watchful eyes of five of Antipas' similarly camouflaged men, I listened to the young preacher speak to the crowd. John spoke out against my husband's choice to marry me, yes, but for a reason even I couldn't contest. For years Antipas had had disputes with the king of Nabatea, the father of Antipas' first wife. The king grew even more angry when Antipas threw the king's daughter aside for me, and the former peace between our lands became the strained and fragile thing it was today.

I had not known my plan to seek a new husband would have had such consequences. At the time all I could think of was that Antipas was a way out. I had been so miserable, every one of my days spent trying to avoid Phillip, or to please him, or both—while trying to manage my impudent and unruly daughter, a task even the gods would have struggled with. But the slight improvement in my own life wasn't worth the risk my actions had created for the people who lived in the contested territories.

I squeezed the silver disc that hung from my bracelet, and kept my eyes locked on Tamara's until she blinked and looked away.

"Oh. Well. Perhaps I misunderstood his words. I mean, um, it must have been so hard to leave your daughter," she said, the words spilling out in nervous rush. She pressed her lips together, ran a hand through her hair, then let out a high-pitched giggle. "Oh, the things we do for the men we love!"

"Indeed," I said, then turned my gaze to the north, so if she continued the conversation she'd be speaking to my right shoulder. The woman might be sharing my husband's bed, but I was still the wife of the tetrarch. At least I would be as long as I pretended not to notice his many, many dalliances. And as long as I kept my looks, and behaved properly, as a woman of my stature and pedigree should. I had just turned thirty-four and couldn't pull this off forever—but my husband was over two decades older than I, and eventually would become uninterested in replacing me, and more in ignoring me and focusing on his many gluttonous habits.

Or at least I hoped he would.

Salome's carriage had almost reached the palace gates. I smiled at Tamara, the trained warmth in my expression a contrast to the iciness I felt on the inside. "Let's prepare to greet my daughter."

The preparations had already been made, of course, so I slipped off to my quarters, made sure my hair was unmussed, and then rejoined my husband and the others on the patio. I stood next to my husband, held my breath, and watched my daughter make her entrance.

Trumpets blared in welcome as Salome stepped out onto the wide stone patio. The pretty twelve-year-old girl I remembered, with her pouting mouth and tousled hair, had become a striking woman of eighteen. Her dark curls hung loose, her lips were red and full, and long eyelashes framed eyes the color of the first shoots of grass in springtime. She'd gotten the eyes—and her height, for she was clearly several inches taller than me now—from her father, but the rest marked her as my daughter. She scanned the crowd—for we had become a crowd, as it seemed almost every person of any note had managed to find their way here tonight—and I realized she was looking for me.

Remembering my role I stepped forward, my arms held out to greet my daughter. Her eyes brightened as they met mine. Yes, Salome had been a horrible child to raise, lying, playing games, and forever pitting me against her father. But she was *my daughter*. I should never have left her in Rome. I should have brought her with me when I married Antipas. I swallowed past a lump in my throat and opened my mouth to greet her.

"Salome, my daughter! Welcome!" I hurried forward, the tightness across the tops of my feet reminding me I'd forgotten to retie my sandals when I'd gone to my quarters.

"Mother!" she cried.

We embraced, and I blinked back tears. Salome was here! My daughter, the baby I'd held in my arms, sung to sleep—the child who I'd abandoned in my own quest to have a better life—she was here!

I took a step back and looked up at my daughter, this child-turned-woman who looked so like me except for her light green eyes. My hands clasped hers, and I had a real smile on my face for the first time in I didn't know how many years. My baby, my little girl, was here at last!

"It's so wonderful to see you, my daughter," I said. I shook my head. "It has been far, far too long."

"Welcome," Antipas said, as he walked up to stand next to me. He bowed to her, then made a flourish with his right hand. "I am Antipas, tetrarch. My home is your home. Come, Salome. I will introduce you to everyone."

He held out his arm. Salome withdrew her hands from mine, blinked, and then took Antipas' arm. She tilted her head up to him and smiled, her expression charming, beautiful, and not at all that of a child.

I knew that smile. That was the smile I'd used to convince Antipas to bed me, and then to wed me. I kept the pleasant look on my face, but my insides felt as if they'd been turned to ice.

Members of my family plotted against each other on a regular basis; every few years someone was poisoned, or mysteriously fell from a window, or the like. My own mother had been accused of complicity in my father's death and, since as a young girl I'd over-heard some of the conversations between her and several of her co-conspirators, I knew the accusations were true.

I learned very early that I had two choices: embrace the intrigue and use others for my personal gain—at least until I was murdered, framed, banished, or executed; or do my best to be honorable in spite of my family and station. My actions to woo Antipas had been borne out of desperation—not to gain power or control, but instead they'd been an attempt to escape the constant misery of my first marriage.

The goddess Diana, who I loved and thought of as a friend and confidant, even though I would of course never meet her—Diana would choose the honorable path. And so that's the path I'd chosen.

As Salome walked away, on the arm of my husband, I realized my daughter had made a different choice.

My life, which had been mostly tolerable as long as I ignored Antipas' philandering, changed after Salome's arrival.

On the surface, she was the perfect daughter. She stayed close by me, fetching me water or wine. She rubbed my shoulders, or my neck. She insisted on going through my wardrobe and helping me plan what to wear.

I was perfectly capable of selecting my own clothing. My neck felt fine. My shoulders were sore, but only because I kept tensing them whenever my daughter was around.

And every night, Salome dined with me and Antipas, and whoever he deemed worthy enough to join us—really, to join *him*. As his wife, I was just there for decoration, like a potted orchid. Salome was a charming dinner companion, her hair perfectly coiffed, her gowns proper and respectable while revealing hints of what lay underneath, her expression demure, her comments perfectly timed, and her jokes filled with just the right combination of humor and mockery. She was respectful to me, said and did the right things, the things a daughter should do.

But I remembered the script well, and I knew exactly what she was doing.

I just didn't know what to do about it.

One evening, after Salome had been at the palace for almost a month, I asked her when she planned to go back to her father's house in Rome. It was Antipas' birthday, and guests were streaming in to attend the long and elaborate celebration. Salome and I sat in a small room near the dining hall, waiting until most of the guests had arrived so that we'd have a large audience to watch our entrance.

"I'll go back someday," she said, waving a hand in the air. Several tiny wisps of hair hung around her face as if they'd escaped the pins that held the rest of her dark curls on top of her head, but we'd had our hair done together, and I knew the entire look had been carefully constructed. "I've been enjoying meeting the people of Galilee—and, of course, spending time with you and Antipas."

Lately she'd been spending less and less time with me, and more with the other noblewomen—and, I suspected, with some of the noblemen as well. I doubted she was sleeping with any of them—not that I knew that for sure, of course, but she was far too sharp to risk being caught dallying with anyone.

"Perhaps you should travel more, then," I said, doing my best to sound nonchalant. "You could visit your uncle Agrippa, or perhaps your cousin Berenice."

Salome rolled her eyes. "Agrippa is an overgrown child, always wanting to play children's games instead of discuss adult topics, and

Berenice is one of the most boring people I've ever met. I'm having fun here. The people in Galilee are so different, and so interesting. Speaking of the people, what do you think about John, the preacher who speaks out about you marrying Antipas?"

Her light green eyes locked on mine, a smile playing on her rosy lips. Something about her expression unnerved me, although nothing she'd said seemed out of the ordinary.

"He's not talking about me," I said. "Not really. He believes that my marriage to Antipas increased the risk of war with Nabatea, because Antipas' first wife is the daughter of their king. That's all."

"And did it increase the chances of war?" my daughter asked. She adjusted her shawl, and raised her eyebrows.

Salome wasn't stupid. She knew relations with Nabatea had been deteriorating since Antipas threw his first wife aside for me six years earlier. So...why was she asking about this?

"It did," I said. I held her gaze. "And you know it did. Why are you asking me?"

"If it were me, I would have had the preacher killed years ago," she said, her voice so cold and firm chills ran down my spine. Then she tossed her head, stood up, and laughed, the light, happy sound jarring. "Tonight's festivities promise to be quite entertaining. Come, Mother, let's go greet our guests."

The festivities were indeed entertaining. There were dancers, singers, jugglers, and even a man who swallowed fire. There were so many courses of food that I lost track—roast pheasant and pomegranate seeds, dates stuffed with almonds, curried eggplant, plates of bread fresh from the oven, goat cheese, and of course plenty of wine. It all smelled wonderful, but my stomach felt as though it had been twisted into a knot, and I had to force myself to take a few bites here and there so as to not draw attention to myself.

My daughter, on the other hand, had no qualms about being the center of attention. She flitted about the room as if it were her birthday, not the tetrarch's. Antipas' eyes followed her as she moved around the room, and instead of being annoyed, he smiled as he watched her.

The night grew late, the wine continued to flow, and the revelers became more and more raucous. I sat next to my husband, who had ignored me most of the evening, and rubbed the silver disc on my bracelet, wishing the goddess Diana could help me. I wanted to retire to the serenity of my chambers, go out on my balcony, and look up at the moon...but what I *really* wanted was to leave this place entirely, to be free of my husband, my daughter, this entire life. I pretended to take a sip of wine, and was about to stand up when a gong rang out. The hall grew quiet, and then my daughter stepped out into the center of the room.

"Antipas, I have three birthday gifts for you. The first one is a dance," she said. She smiled at the gasps and cheers of the guests, bowed to my husband, and gestured to the musicians to begin to play. And then my daughter began to dance.

Salome moved her body as if she were one with the music. She threw her head back, her hips swinging from side to side, her arms high in the air, then curving in sinuous motions in time to the beat as she pulled her scarf off her shoulders. I pulled my eyes away from her and looked at my husband. His eyes were fixed on my daughter, his jaw hanging open, an expression of primal lust on his face. I turned away from him in disgust, and even though I wanted to leave, I couldn't help but watch Salome dance. She laughed, the sound throaty and sensual, and then pulled her long curls free from their confinement, tossing her head in the air. Finally, she stopped right in front of Antipas, just as the song ended. The room was silent. Her skin was coated with a faint sheen of sweat, and the round shapes of her breasts moved slightly as she caught her breath.

The hall erupted in cheers, the loudest of which came from my husband.

Salome smiled, and waited until the din subsided.

"That was your first birthday gift," she said. Her pink tongue flicked across her lips, like that of a snake. She glanced at me, her eyes full of mockery and mirth, then she looked away as if dismissing me. "Your second gift is the gift of action and power, the kind of gift a strong woman gives to a strong man."

Salome gestured to someone at the end of the hall. Three of Antipas' soldiers walked into the center of the room, two of them holding a man dressed in animal skin. His arms were bound behind his back, and a cloth had been tied around his mouth to keep him from speaking. It was John, the man who preached peace to people down by the river. The man who said Antipas' marriage to me had increased the risk of war.

"If it were me, I would have had the preacher killed years ago."

My daughter's words from earlier in the evening echoed in my head.

"No," I whispered. I stood up. "Salome, no!"

Antipas shoved me backward with one arm, his eyes not leaving Salome's face. I stumbled and tripped over my chair, falling to the ground, and then I heard my daughter speak.

"My second gift to you is this man, and the power his death will bring you. By your leave, Antipas?"

Antipas grinned and nodded.

"No!" I yelled. I pulled myself to my feet. "He's done nothing wrong!"

I took a step toward them just as the two soldiers pushed John forward. The third soldier raised his sword high in the air, and then...

...John's head fell to the floor.

The hall was quiet.

I pressed my hands to my mouth, my eyes wide, the only sound I could hear that of my blood rushing in my ears.

My daughter smiled at Antipas, picked up a golden platter, and placed the head of the preacher on it.

My husband smiled back and stood up.

"Thank you for these gifts," he said. The guests began to clap and cheer. Antipas waved to the musicians. They started to play again, and the guests began to talk, and some to dance, and many to drink.

Salome set the platter with the head on it on one of the tables, next to a plate of half-eaten leg of lamb, then walked over to my husband. He took her arm, and they walked out of the hall without even a glance in my direction.

My entire body felt numb as I watched them go.

I, and everyone else in the room, knew what the third gift was.

I went back to my chambers, put on my nightdress, and laid down on my bed. My daughter had just stolen my husband. Yes, I had lured Antipas away from his first wife, but that wasn't nearly the same. And that poor, poor preacher. I'd heard John speak by the river, and his words had been about kindness and hope. Yes, he'd spoken out against Antipas...but what John had said had been true. Antipas had divorced his first wife without thinking through the political ramifications—or perhaps he had known them all along. Either way, what had happened was my fault. If I hadn't stolen Antipas from his first wife, there would still be peace in Galilee, and the preacher would still be alive. I hadn't done anything nearly as brazen and horrible as what my daughter had done, but John's death was on my shoulders.

And in the morning, I would have to face my husband and his soon-to-be new wife: my daughter.

Finally, I threw off the bedcovers and crossed the marble floor to the door that opened on to my little balcony, the stone cool under my bare feet. I pushed aside the long, heavy curtains that kept the wind and rain out of my room, walked over to the railing, and looked out at the night. The garden below—*my* garden, the one thing in my life that truly gave me joy—was dark, the night air filled with the scents of lavender, rosemary, and jasmine. I'd filled the little plot with flowers, bushes, and herbs I tended to myself, with assistance from the palace gardener when I needed extra help, or when my husband showed up and I had to pretend I wasn't digging in the dirt myself like a commoner.

I stared up at the sky, at the stars, the moon, and the tiny strips of clouds shot through with moonlight. From where I stood, the town in the valley below the palace, and the nearby villages scattered about the hills, were all hidden, although the sky was so bright that I could make out the dark shapes of the buildings just past the town. Off in the distance were tiny dots of light from fires burning where the preacher John spoke to his followers every night until they ran out of energy and fell asleep.

John would never speak by the river again.

I took a deep breath of the air, focusing on the smell of lavender, willing it to calm me like it had years ago when I'd been married off to my first husband at the age of thirteen. After seeing me rise exhausted morning after morning, one of my maids put together sacks of lavender seeds, tucked them in a chest in my dressing room, and told me to place them by my pillows to help me sleep. I didn't tell her that I hadn't been able to sleep because each night, after my husband had visited my chambers, I cried and shook for hours, alone in my rooms...but I saw the way she looked at me, and I knew she knew.

I learned quickly, and within weeks I'd figured out what to expect from my husband, what he wanted—and what he didn't want—me to do. I learned how to laugh at just the right time, when to act innocent and naïve—or worldly and provocative, when to pour him another glass of wine, and when to slide my dress off and stand naked before him.

He rarely stayed in my chambers for long after he got what he'd come there for.

And after he left, I would go to my dressing room, bury my face in the lavender-stuffed pillows, and cry myself to sleep.

Tonight, the scent wasn't as calming as it normally was. It could have been that the scent of jasmine was too strong, or maybe the lemon tree was mingling with that of the lavender.

Or perhaps it was that I knew my daughter was sleeping with my husband right now.

My daughter, who had just orchestrated the death of a man. And for what? Power? Control?

After year and years of acting the way I was "supposed" to, following my own mother's example and using people in order to gain power, or leverage, so that I could keep myself safe, years of watching others be mistreated and die, of pretending to be someone I didn't want to be... I was tired.

I looked up at the moon, rubbed the silver disc on my bracelet, and remembered the first day I'd stepped into the temple of Diana in Rome. How peaceful I'd felt, how safe. How for the first time I'd felt like *me*. I'd felt that way every other time I'd gone to her temple, as if I'd stepped into a sanctuary where I could drop the artifice, the pretense, and just be myself. I'd never had a real friend—I'd learned early that no one was truly trustworthy. But I thought of Diana as if she were my friend.

The last time I'd been to her temple by myself had been almost twenty years ago, before my marriage to Phillip, and before my world had changed to one of even greater wealth and privilege than I'd grown up with—and with those changes came the addition of many, many rules. I could no longer go to a temple on my own. The one time I'd tried, I'd ended up going with an entourage, as befitted the wife of a nobleman. I did not try again. And now I lived in Galilee, where the people didn't worship Diana. They had their own gods; some similar, some different, and some new, like the one that man John down by the river was always talking about. But the goddess Diana was not one of them.

I leaned against the stone wall of the palace, and closed my eyes. If only I lived in a different world entirely. One where there was no need for subterfuge, politics, and deadly games. One where there were no poor people, nor wealthy, just people working together. I took a deep breath, and focused on the scent of lavender, willing myself to be calm, and not think about having to face my husband and daughter in the morning.

After a few minutes I gave up. I opened my eyes, then my breath caught as I saw a woman sitting on the corner of the stone railing of my balcony.

Who was she, and where had she come from? The only avenues to my balcony were through my bedroom, and the door in the tall stone wall that bordered my garden. But the door bolted from the garden side, so no one could enter without my knowledge. She must have broken through the gate, or someone else must have let her into my chambers earlier in the day. But...I had looked out into the garden before retiring for the night, and I would have seen anyone there. I was sure of it.

And yet, I felt unafraid.

"I hope I didn't alarm you, Herodias," she said. She smiled at me, her face brightening as if she was genuinely happy to see me. It made me feel warm inside.

"Only momentarily," I said, and smiled back. The woman looked familiar, although I couldn't remember ever seeing her before. Her black hair had been pulled back in long braids. She wore a short-sleeved tunic made of light-colored fabric that looked almost silver in the moonlight and, oddly, dark trousers, like a man would wear. Her arms were muscled, and she held a small, silver horn in one hand.

"I am sorry I haven't been able to visit you before," she said. She slid off the railing on to the balcony, and waved her free hand at the sky. "Tomorrow is Midsummer, when the gates between worlds and planes are open for but a moment. Even now they wear thin, so when I heard you calling me, I was able to cross over to your side. I am so glad to finally see you in person!"

I blinked. What she'd said didn't make any sense—other than that tomorrow would be Midsummer, which was indeed true. But what did she mean by gates between worlds? And planes? What was a plane?

I realized I should be more curious about who the woman was than about the words she'd used, but somehow that seemed less important. I felt as comfortable with her as if we were old friends who were catching up after years apart.

"Would you care to sit?" I asked, gesturing to the chairs and table that sat at one end of the balcony. I took a few steps toward them. "I can call for wine and food, if you'd like."

"I cannot stay long," she said. "Tonight is the full moon, and I must lead the Wild Hunt."

I stopped in mid-step, and would have lost my balance if I hadn't spent years focusing on keeping every movement of mine as graceful as a cat. I now knew who she must be, but…it wasn't possible.

"Diana?" I whispered, and turned, my eyes meeting hers.

"Oh, I—I am so sorry," she said. She laughed, the sound so warm and inviting that, even as confused and awestruck as I felt, I joined in. "I was so very happy to see you that…I forgot you wouldn't… Yes, I am Diana."

"You…" I bit my lip. "You're a *goddess*. Why are you here talking with me?"

"But I *have* spoken with you before, Herodias," she said, her voice soft and low. "You walked into my temple in Rome years ago, a young girl, and you caught my attention. I do not know why, but you stood out, like a candle glowing in the darkest night. Several times since then we have spoken in dreams that you do not remember, because in those dreams you asked me to make sure you forgot lest you be even more unhappy with your life when you woke up. But this is not a dream. This is real."

She took a step toward me and placed her free hand on my left forearm. I jumped—it felt as if I'd been struck by lightning. It took me a moment to realize Diana had jumped as well. Her eyes were wide. Her touch on her skin was now warm and pleasant, the odd electric sensation gone.

"Can…can you give me back those memories?" I asked. Could she really be Diana, the goddess I'd prayed to since I was a child?

She wrinkled her nose, the expression sweet and charming—words I wouldn't have expected to use for a goddess, but which fit perfectly.

"It was only a few times. Five, I think. Maybe six. I can help give part of them back to you," she said. "But for you, they were dreams, not reality, so I can only unlock the remnants that are left in your mind. Here."

She removed her hand from my forearm. My skin tingled where she'd touched it. She took a deep breath and touched the tips of her fingers to my forehead. I closed my eyes, and then…

…I walked with Diana along a beach, looking up at her—for I was but a young girl at the time, and shorter than she. We both giggled as a wave came in and immersed us in ankle-deep water, then receded, leaving white foam that tickled my skin...

...the two of us sat outside of her temple in Rome, except it wasn't the real Rome, because it was the middle of the day and no one else was there, plus there were palm trees planted near her temple instead of the tall pines I knew were there in the real world...

...we flew through the air, like birds, yet we had no wings, and I laughed and laughed at the freedom I felt—not because I flew, as fun as that was, but because the ability to fly meant I was able to make choices, decisions of my own...

...we sat next to a circle of gray stones pointing to the sky, each of them taller than the tallest man I'd ever seen, and Diana was telling me how a thousand years before the people of that land had danced inside the circle at midsummer and midwinter, and that drums inside the circle sounded louder than outside of it, and that the stones themselves had woken up a little at the solstices...

...I stood on a pinnacle of rock on a high, high mountain, looking down at the layer of clouds below, but I wasn't afraid of falling because Diana was there holding my hand, and I knew I was safe...

...and then I opened my eyes, and the face of Diana, my friend, who I had spoken to in my dreams—for now I remembered them, and knew them to be true—looked back at me.

Diana couldn't be my *friend*. She was a goddess!

"It's different, somehow, seeing you in real life, instead of in another plane," she said, her voice low.

She tugged on the end of one of her braids. I remembered her doing the same thing when we'd walked around the circle of rocks in my dream. Or had it been a dream, if I'd been the only one dreaming? I didn't remember much of what we'd talked about, but I did remember the happy, comfortable, *right* feeling that had been through the handful of dreams we'd met in.

But this wasn't a dream where I walked along a beach with a goddess, imagining we were friends. This was reality.

And in reality, the goddess I'd sent my pleas, my confessions, my emotions to for over two decades stood on the balcony of the palace where I was the wife of the tetrarch.

I took a few steps backward, straightened my shoulders, and put on my regal face, pushing the inner me down, down, like I did every single day. I dampened the joy and happiness I'd briefly allowed myself to feel. I stared at her, my face composed and calm, while my mind raced. I had to be dreaming. Or...perhaps I'd been drugged, and the "memories" were hallucinations. Neither choice seemed to fit— but they both seemed infinitely more plausible than the appearance of a goddess on my balcony.

"I am dreaming," I said, my voice as firm as if I were instructing an errant maid. "I'm going back to bed."

I began to turn back toward the doorway to my chambers, then froze as she reached out and laid a hand on the side of my arm.

"Please, don't," she said. "I realize this must sound crazy, but it's true."

I could feel the warmth of her hand on my skin through the light fabric of my nightdress.

Maybe this wasn't a dream after all.

I turned back toward her, and took a deep breath.

"I don't understand," I said.

"I wish...oh, life is what it is." She clasped her hands together. "I know you think of me as a goddess, but I am not. I mean, I am—in a sense, compared to what you are familiar with. But I am really just a person, like you are. From your perspective, it appears that I have power. But I don't—or at least, I don't have the power you, or the people who worship me, think I do. I live in a different plane. Sometimes I hear the people who speak to me, like when I first heard you, back when you were a young girl and entered the temple they built to honor me in Rome. But I cannot see the people I hear. I cannot address their concerns. If they are in peril, I cannot help them. I am bound by the rules of the worlds, and may only intervene in the land of dreams."

"Am I dreaming?" I asked.

She shook her head. "Not this time. This time I am here for real.

I...wanted to meet you in person. We have been friends in your dreams for years, and for the first time I was able to time passing through the walls between worlds to see you. I can still visit you in your dreams, but now you will remember them. I know this sounds strange. But it is the truth."

I bit my lip. I now had the memories of the conversations I'd had with Diana over the years in my dreams, and in them she had always been like me—not like the goddess I knew her to be.

Finally, I nodded.

"I believe you," I said. "And...I would very much like to see you again. I am glad you're my friend."

Not only was she my friend, she was the only friend I'd ever had.

She glanced up at the moon, then looked back at me.

"I must go," she said, her voice somber. "Tonight I ride in the Wild Hunt, and will lead the host as we chase through the minds and dreams of those who have done wrong to others."

I blinked. "How do you know who to hunt? And do you...kill them?"

She shook her head. "No, although there have been many times when I've wished we could. We hunt them in their dreams, chasing their spirits through the otherworld, inflicting the pain and fear and anguish on them that they've caused to others. Sometimes a person we hunt at night will realize the error of their ways and change. Not always, of course...but that is the hope."

Could my daughter change? My husband? If they did, that wouldn't bring John back to life. But maybe they would learn, and treat people better in the future.

"I know this must be confusing, but..." She took a deep breath. "Come with me, Herodias. I know you're unhappy. You have been unhappy the entire time I've known you. We've spoken of it in your dreams. I can't fix your life, but if you would like, you could come with me on the Wild Hunt—and then to the plane where I live. There you would be happy. You could be yourself—you wouldn't have to worry about rank, or power, or any of the things you've told me about over the years."

"I couldn't leave..." I said, my voice trailing off.

Or could I? What was keeping me here? Now that Salome had taken my husband, I'd have to leave the palace and go stay with one of my relatives in another land until...what? Until I found yet another husband, and sat over yet another court, with simpering people who pretended to be noble but would applaud the murder of an innocent man while they cheered and drink wine?

Unlike my daughter, and my own mother, I'd never wanted power. I'd used my wiles to lure Antipas away from his first wife, but only because I'd believed that to be the only way to escape the horrible marriage I'd been forced into when I was only thirteen.

But...where exactly did Diana live? And I'd have to go with her on the hunt, chasing people through their dreams? I'd seen people die, but I'd never been on a hunt—much less a *dream* hunt. I ran a hand through my hair.

"I promise you will be happy," Diana said, her voice soft. She glanced up at the moon. "But I must go, now. Please, come with me. I won't be able to come back to your world for many years, until the planes and worlds align once again. Come with me on the hunt, and then to the land I live in."

To leave my lecherous, cruel husband, and my conniving, murderous daughter...

I took a deep breath and smiled at my friend. "I would love to go with you," I said.

"Oh, I'm so glad!" she said. She faced the moon, held the small silver horn up to her lips, and blew. It sounded like the pealing of bells, but bells richer, warmer, and fuller sounding than anything I'd ever heard of. I felt an almost overpowering urge to run toward the sound, to join in the hunt—for in the sound of the bells it was clear what kind of call it was.

"Diana?" I asked.

She turned toward me and met my eyes, her own filled with worry.

"You may change your mind," she said. She pressed her lips

together. "Once we leave, there is no way to turn back. But...as much as I would love to have you go with me, my friend, it is your choice."

I shook my head. "I'm not changing my mind. Do not worry. But... may I suggest some people to hunt tonight?"

Behind her a darkness had formed in the cloudless sky, a writhing, winding shape in the night, growing larger as it moved closer and closer to us. I could make out the shapes of horses, people astride them, large, baying dogs, and other creatures I did not recognize and could not name. It was a fierce, frightful sight, but I was unafraid. Diana, the goddess, and my friend, would be by my side.

"You certainly may," Diana said, and grinned.

The wild host grew even closer, then stilled as they hung in the air over my garden, the garden I would never see again.

I grinned back. I couldn't undo John's murder, but I could make sure Salome and Antipas paid for it—if only in their dreams.

My friend stepped off the balcony on to the back of a beautiful black mare, the horse's coat dappled with moonlight. Diana held out her hand to me.

I swallowed, and then hitched up the skirts of my nightdress and mounted the horse behind her.

I took a deep breath, soaking in the energy of the night, of the hunt, and felt the rightness of what we were about to do. "Let the hunt begin!"

ABOUT THE AUTHOR

Jamie focuses on getting into the minds and hearts of her characters, whether she's writing about a saloon girl in the American West, a man who discovers the barista he's in love with is a naiad, or a ghost who haunts the house she was killed in—even though that house no longer exists. Jamie lives in Colorado, and spends her free time in a futile quest to wear out her two border collies since she hasn't given in and gotten them their own herd of sheep.

Find out more about Jamie at:
jamieferguson.com

facebook.com/jamie.ferguson.author

twitter.com/jamie_ferguson

instagram.com/jamie.ferguson.author

goodreads.com/jamieferguson

pinterest.com/jamieauthor

bookbub.com/authors/jamie-ferguson

MURDER'S REVENGE

ANNIE REED

B artending at a strip club in a dodgy dockside neighborhood in Moretown Bay wasn't how an elf with royal blood in her veins was supposed to spend her nights.

Running for her life from the Wild Hunt wasn't how said elf was supposed to spend the night either. But then again, Twig had never been a normal elf.

"Hang out in the woods, gaze at the trees," Twig muttered to herself as she gunned her motorcycle down a garbage-strewn alley, the Wild Hunt hot on her heels. "What would have been so bad about that?"

Pretty much everything, which was why she'd left her family behind more than a decade ago. Let them live on their pine-studded island out in the middle of the bay contemplating their navels. She'd wanted adventure. She'd wanted friends who weren't snooty old elves mired in tradition. She'd wanted her life to mean something.Well, she'd gotten all that, and look where she'd ended up. Leading the Wild Hunt on a not-so-merry chase around the backstreets and alley-ways of a Pacific Northwest city, hoping she could stay alive long enough to see the sunrise and the end of this murderous night.

So far she hadn't managed to get more than a half block ahead of the hunt, and she was damn good on a motorcycle.

She should have expected that. Murder was leading the hunt, and he knew her. Knew her tricks (or at least most of them) thanks to the years she'd spent riding with his "club."

Club. Ha! Murder's pack of hardcore bikers was little more than a gang of motorcycle-riding thugs and criminals.

That was bad enough, but tonight that gang had been trans-formed by the magic of the Wild Hunt into a pack of super-charged, nearly unbeatable creatures of legend.

And she'd managed to piss off all of them.

~

The night had started off like any other normal night at Snow's Palace, the strip club her friend Jocko the dwarf owned. Changeling dancers worked the poles behind the bar where Twig served watered-down drinks to the club's patrons. Surfer music, the only type of music Jocko allowed in his club, blared from the sound system. The air was thick with the smell of cigarettes and alcohol, sweat and repressed sex.

Twig liked the club. It had been her home on and off ever since she'd left the stodgy elves of Marlette Island behind. Jocko and the changeling dancers and all the other women Jocko "rescued" from the streets had become her family. The dwarf had a heart nearly as big as he was, and at six feet plus, that made his heart a damn big one. He towered over her and always would, thanks to her elven heritage which would perpetually make her look like a human teenager who'd just begun to hit her growth spurt, only with ears that had very, very long, delicate points.

Ears that could hear magic.

The everyday magic in the world. The magic of a cast spell or glamour or veil.

And most especially the untamed magic of the Wild Hunt.

The very first hint she caught of the hunt's magic had sent a shiver down Twig's spine and raised the hair on the back of her neck.

And on the heels of that first hint of the hunt's magic came the unmistakable sound of the huntsman's horn, deep and resonate and mournful. The sound vibrated inside Twig's chest and spread out through her body in the way she imagined humans might feel severe cold.

The hunt was coming to Moretown Bay.

No one else in the club reacted to the horn. The changelings kept dancing, the customers kept stuffing dollar bills in the dancers' G-strings, and the endless surfer music kept right on assaulting every-one's hearing.

Twig had a very bad feeling about this.

And not only because she seemed to be the only one who could hear the horn.

What was the saying? Ride, hide, or die? The hunt chased down the unwary in its path and offered them a choice: join the hunt or die, and the hunt wasn't overly particular about who it conscripted into its ranks. It would streak through the countryside, the hunt master— the most powerful fae lord in the land, or so said the legends handed down by her kin—dictating the course, and woe be to those unlucky enough to cross its path.

Twig had discovered in the years since she'd left her kin behind that the real world operated quite differently.

The Wild Hunt wasn't just one hunt, not anymore. Like everything else in the mortal world, the hunt had adapted to a more modern way of thinking.

The Wild Hunt had gone franchise.

In today's world money had almost become a minor deity in its own right. The fae who controlled the Wild Hunt had adapted to this new measure of power. On this one night of the year when the Wild Hunt was allowed to intersect with the mortal world, multiple hunts crisscrossed the globe. Anyone with enough money to buy a spot in one of the hunts could become hunt master and take on the mantle of power that came with the title.

But there was another level to the hunt, and that level couldn't be purchased with mere money.

If the master of a particular hunt was a truly greedy and malevolent creature with a score to settle, the hunt and all those who rode with it could be directed to exact the hunt master's revenge.

All it cost was a piece of the hunt master's soul.

The huntsman's horn blared louder into the night. This time the sound drowned out the music and the half-shouted conversations going on around her. Again, Twig was the only person who seemed to hear the horn.

She was afraid to ask Jocko what that meant. Her ears were good, but they weren't that good.

But in the next instant she realized she didn't need to ask Jocko. She didn't need to ask anyone.

A mark had appeared on the back of her hand.

A tattoo of a stylized skeleton that hadn't been there before.

Her mouth went dry. She recognized that skeleton. She'd hoped never to see it again.

She held out her hand in front of her, staring at it like it belonged to some stranger. Her heart pounded as the sound the hunt grew ever closer, and an undeniable urge to flee got stronger and stronger.

Words suddenly appeared on the back of her hand, dark and heavy beneath the mark of the skeleton. The whole thing looked now like a tattoo she'd had her whole life, only Twig didn't have any tattoos.

Just two words: *Death Reaper.*

They were enough to deliver a message that Twig understood all too well.

She fought against the nausea that threatened to buckle her knees and bring up her dinner in a sick rush.

She knew now why no one else in Snow's had heard the huntsman's horn. She also knew why this particular Wild Hunt had come to Moretown Bay. She even knew who'd paid a king's ransom and given up a piece of his soul to lead this particular hunt.

Murder.

He'd brought the hunt to her city

And tonight, Twig was the hunt's prey.

The damp cold of late October stiffened Twig's leathers. Misted the faceplate on her helmet. Slicked up the pavement beneath her motorcycle's tires so much that she almost lost control of her bike as she slid into a quick turn at the end of an alley behind an abandoned warehouse.

Her heart pounded hard as she fought to keep her bike upright.

She couldn't afford to go down. The hunt would be on her in an instant, and Murder would tear her limb from limb.

He'd save her ears for last.

Twig's ears had been her ticket into Murder's gang—what megalomaniac wouldn't want to have an elf around who could hear someone using magic to plot against you?—but she'd never truly been one of them. The only reason she joined the gang in the first place was to rescue their captive, a gentle water spirit enslaved by Murder and forced to do his bidding.

She'd been intent on betraying Murder and his gang from the beginning, but it had taken years for her to earn the water spirit's trust. The spirit had been badly abused by Murder and his buddies and didn't trust any corporeal being. The spirit's magic had given the club—and Murder in particular—the kind of power mere mortals could never hope to attain, and Murder had wielded that power like a malevolent demigod. His gang became as wealthy as corporate raiders and as feared as the fae kings of old, thanks to the water spirit's magic which Murder twisted to his own dark purposes.

And Twig had taken all that power away when she finally freed the water spirit from its prison.

The gang hated her, Murder most of all. They'd tried to take her out once before by using another spirit being, this one a dark and angry creature, but that attempt had failed. She'd thought that had been the end of it, but it looked like Murder had found another way —a *legal* way—to kill her.

Because in this world where mortals and magic folk lived side by side, the law forbade anyone from using magic to intentionally harm one another—except on the night of the Wild Hunt.

On that one night of the year, all rules were off for those who rode with the hunt. And for all those who opposed the hunt as well.

But only the most foolhardy or the most powerful had any chance of opposing the hunt and defeating it.

Twig wasn't powerful. Foolhardy? Maybe. She wouldn't have an answer to that question until the sun came up.

If she was still alive by then.

She righted her motorcycle at the end of the alley at the last possible second. The tires caught and held as she made the turn and gunned down a side street. Another alley opened up on her left and she shot across traffic, barely missing a speeding taxi that blared its horn at her as she raced down this new alley.

Murder and his minions didn't have to worry about slick pavement or colliding with traffic. The magic of the hunt kept their motorcycles a good five feet off the ground even as it cloaked them with the images of beasts from the Wild Hunt legends of old.

Hell hounds with fire-red eyes and lolling tongues that dripped flame that sizzled and smoked when it hit the wet pavement. Massive horses with flowing manes and tails made of hissing snakes whose hooves struck sparks when they hit the non-existent ground. Demons rode on the back of the horses, nightmare creatures with flayed skin and forked tongues hanging from open mouths filled with razor-sharp teeth.

But worst of all was the dragon that brought up the rear of the hunt. Its three heads spat fire at her as its leathery wings beat the night air, and the stench of it overpowered the wet city smell of diesel exhaust and moldy garbage and the ever-present musty, fishy odor of the bay.

Murder sat astride the back of the dragon. He hadn't bothered to take on the form of a demon like the other members of the gang, or even cloak himself with the visage of a demigod, which was his right as the hunt master.

Of course not. Murder thought of himself as a demigod in his own right. Let mere mortals wear the veil of the hunt if they didn't think their human forms sufficiently worthy. Murder knew his own form was the ultimate shape he could wear to strike fear into the hearts of his enemies.

He could have used the magic of the hunt to kill her at a distance. It would have been easy. Let the dragon's fire burn her alive, or let one of the demons bite her head off with its sharp teeth.

But Murder liked to kill up close and personal. He always had, and he'd always gotten away with it. He'd want to savor her death.

Watch the life leave her eyes and know he'd finally gotten the better of this little elf who thought she'd beaten the powerful Murder.

It didn't matter how big the hunt was that was chasing her. How many buddies he'd brought along with him, or how many innocents he'd conscripted to ride with him tonight. She didn't have to worry about them. Murder wouldn't let anyone else try to kill her. He'd reserve that pleasure for himself.

And that, Twig hoped, was her one key to surviving this night—Murder's need to face her down on his own and make her death last.

～

Trouble had been Twig's introduction to Murder's gang.

Trouble wasn't the woman's real name, of course, just like Murder had a real name he'd long since abandoned. Trouble had been known as Leslie Claire, and she had a sweetly round face, an infectious grin, and a friendly nature. Basically the last person you'd ever expect to find riding with a motorcycle gang like Murder's.

The gang had come to Moretown Bay one summer night over a decade ago on their way back to their home turf a few hundred miles to the south. They'd stopped at Snow's Palace, the strip club where Twig worked on and off as a bartender. Twig hadn't been living in the city long at that point—still "fresh off the island" as the club's owner, Jocko, liked to say. She hadn't made many friends outside of Jocko, and she'd initially only made friends with him to piss off her family.

Jocko was a dwarf of extremely impressive stature. That alone would have been enough to shock the stodgy royals in her bloodline, but Jocko was also a former vice cop. He had a soft spot for women in trouble, and the kind of women he rescued from life on the street weren't exactly the upper crust of Moretown Bay. Twig was pretty sure word that she was consorting with a most unsuitable dwarf had made it back to her family, and that gave her rebellious heart a definite happy.

Or at least it had at the time. Her family had since disowned her, a wound that still stung her heart when she least expected it.

Twig's diminutive size and elven features made her look like a perpetual human teenager, and she was pretty sure that was why Jocko had hired her. She hadn't exactly been a woman in trouble like a lot of the dancers and other women he employed, but she hadn't been worldly wise either, thanks to the reclusive nature of her kin.

Jocko had introduced her to a woman who'd taught Twig how to use her natural elven abilities to protect herself from people who would try to take advantage of her small size and young-looking face. By the time Murder's gang had stopped in for drinks and a few private dances at Snow's, Twig could more than take care of herself.

Maybe that's why she'd felt a kinship of sorts with Trouble. Two women—one elf, one human—who didn't look like they belonged in the world they found themselves in. Especially since Trouble couldn't have been much older than Twig looked.

Over the watered-down drinks that Twig served up to Trouble, she learned that the woman had never intended to join a motorcycle gang.

"Jessie—he's my guy," Trouble said. "That's him over there."

She pointed to a man in his late twenties with a shock of nearly white blond hair and a full beard to match. He sat at a corner table with two older men. All three of them wore black leathers emblazoned with a stylized skeleton on the back of the jackets along with the name of the club: Death Reaper. Trouble wore a similar black jacket. All three men were staring at the dancers working the poles on the stage behind the bar, Jessie and one of the other men with wide grins on their faces. Occasionally Trouble's guy made some remark to the older man who wasn't smiling, but even with her sensitive hearing, Twig couldn't tell what they were saying over the pounding music and other half-shouted conversations going on in the packed club.

She had no difficultly hearing Trouble, though.

"His dad—the guy he's talking to—he's the head of our chapter." Trouble took a sip of her drink and grimaced. "Hate the kind of drinks we get in strip clubs." She shot a quick glance at Twig. "No offense intended, but you can hardly taste the booze in these things."

"Drinks aren't exactly the reason people come here," Twig said.

"No shit," Trouble said with a grin. "Me, I'd rather just buy a bottle or two and drink down by the waterfront, you know? But I go where Jessie goes."

"You like the life?" Twig asked, just to make conversation. "Traveling. Riding bikes." She gestured with her head toward the table where Jessie sat. "Putting up with all the macho bullshit."

Trouble nearly spit out her drink around a sudden laugh. "Yeah, it's a bit much, right? But these guys. If you're in their good graces, they'd die for you. And fuck up anybody who disrespects you. That's important, you know?"

From the look on Trouble's face, Twig guessed that no one in Trouble's past had respected her as a person. Twig could commiserate. In her family, only her grandmother had listened to Twig and treated her like the individual she was. As far as Twig's parents were concerned, she was just another elf with royal blood in her veins, and she was to comport herself as such.

Not that she had to worry about those things anymore.

"They're my family," Trouble was saying. "We take care of each other."

Just like Jocko and the dancers and Twig took care of each other.

By the time Twig's break came around, Trouble was insisting that Twig go outside with her to see Jessie's bike. Before extending the invitation, she'd gone over to the table where Jessie sat to ask permission, or so she'd told Twig.

One of the older men, the one who never smiled, had taken a good long look at Twig. She could practically feel his dark eyes sizing her up. He'd said something to the man sitting next to him, and that man had nodded, a gesture so subtle Twig might not have caught it if she hadn't been looking.

He was powerful, that second man. He had the sound of magic around him. Twig heard it, but just barely. He wasn't using any, not now, but woe be to anyone who crossed him. Twig had apparently met with his approval, though.

She didn't know it at the time, but Trouble had been recruiting her. The man with the magic was the gang's enforcer, and thanks to her ears, he'd pegged her as someone who might be useful to the gang—if she joined voluntarily. So Jessie had sent Trouble to talk to her, to "feel her out" and see where the conversation went. Trouble went back to report to Jessie and his dad, and they'd liked what they heard.

So Trouble took Twig out to see Jessie's motorcycle. "It's way more comfortable than it looks," she said, "at least the part where I sit. I don't get the high handlebars, but I don't do the driving."

Jessie's bike was a huge Harley, tricked out like crazy, and yes, with extremely high handlebars. But it wasn't Jessie's bike that drew her attention.

A smaller bike sat two over from Jessie's. Not a Harley, but Twig didn't know enough about motorcycles to guess the brand. Not that the motorcycle itself was all that important.

It was what the motorcycle held trapped inside the chrome: a magical spirit that was quietly weeping for its lost home.

A water spirit the gang was punishing for some infraction by bringing it close to the bay that had been its home, while keeping it imprisoned in hard, unforgiving metal.

Twig's heart broke at the mournful sound of it.

She tried to communicate with it, but the spirit shied away from her. It was too broken to trust her, but she couldn't just leave it to its fate. The spirit was sentient and beautiful and belonged in the water, just like the spirits she and her grandmother had heard sing from the depths of the bay when she'd been a child. She just couldn't do anything about it right now. She had no clue what kind of magic she'd need to set it free. She'd need a wizard for that, maybe someone Jocko would know. And she'd need the spirit's cooperation.

That would take time.

"We're heading out later tonight," Trouble said, then she sighed and lifted her eyebrows in invitation. "I could use some company besides the guys, you know? There are a few other old ladies back home, but they're *old,* you know? They don't really get me. I think we could be good friends. Jessie said it was okay to ask you, so do you want to come along? It'd be fun to have you around."

Twig liked her life at the club, her life with Jocko and the dancers, but she couldn't leave the water spirit like this. The only reason to trap a magical entity was to use its magic, and eventually the spirit would become so disheartened it would die. It sounded like it was already well on its way, and she just couldn't leave the spirit like that. It belonged in the water where it could live out the rest of its naturally long, long life. But it had been so damaged already, she'd need time to become its friend. To earn its trust.

"It would be an adventure," Twig said, stalling.

"If you're worried about the guys," Trouble said, "I'll protect you."

The thought was so ludicrous, Twig couldn't help it. She laughed out loud. "You?" Trouble didn't look like she could protect herself, much less anyone else.

"Yeah." Trouble didn't look offended. She just walked around to the front of Jessie's bike, got a good grip on the frame, and lifted the front part of the bike off the ground like it was no heavier than a sack of flour. "Me," she said with a grin.

Damn. She hadn't even used a spell. Twig would have heard if she had.

Twig could have done the same thing. Elves were strong and quick on their feet, but for a mere mortal to do something like that? Trouble had a serious amount of muscle hiding beneath her leathers.

When the gang left the strip club that night, Twig rode behind one of the other members, a short guy in his thirties with tribal tattoos curling around one side of his neck. The guy said his name was Marco and told her up front that his old lady was waiting for him back home and she'd bust his chops if she thought he'd tried anything funny with Twig. Twig told him she'd be sure to behave herself.

She didn't say goodbye to Jocko. She couldn't afford to have him ask her why she was leaving and have anyone from the gang hear her. She didn't even let herself think about the reason. She didn't know if the magic she'd heard swirling around the gang's enforcer would let him read her thoughts. Only time and experience would give her a clue just how far his magic went.

She could also admit to herself that she was more than a little afraid of Jessie's father. She could take care of herself—she'd been taking care of herself ever since she'd left her family behind—but Murder scared her. No one gave themselves a nickname like that without earning it.

But Trouble was Jessie's old lady, and Jessie was Murder's son. Trouble had vowed to protect Twig, and Trouble said that meant Jessie would protect her too. At least until Twig got a man of her own within the club, and then he'd look out for her.

So Twig had simply left Jocko a note and rode off into the night with the gang that would become her family for the next ten years. It took her that long to make friends with the water spirit and to hide the fact that was her real purpose with the gang. She never did become anyone's "old lady," but earned her keep on her own by using her ears to listen for magic that anyone planned to use against the gang.

But eventually things had gone wrong. The enforcer began to suspect her true purpose. By the time she fled the gang, racing back to Moretown Bay on the motorcycle that housed the water spirit, Trouble had died in childbirth along with her baby, and Jessie had killed himself in his grief. Murder had quietly been going insane with his own grief and his unquenchable rage at his inability to save his son and grandson. His inattention to the gang had been the only way Twig had been able to sneak away with the water spirit.

The enforcer, though... He figured out what Twig had done. He'd followed them back to Moretown Bay, intent on killing Twig and reclaiming the water spirit's prison before Twig could release it. Instead, Twig had killed the enforcer with Jocko's help, released the water spirit, and been welcomed back into the dwarf's extended family.

She thought she'd been safe.

She'd been wrong.

And now she was fleeing for her life.

~

This time around, she couldn't call on Jocko for help. She didn't want him to fall victim to the Wild Hunt. To be conscripted into its ranks and forced to hunt her down.

That would break the oversized dwarf and his huge, compassionate heart.

She couldn't go to her family for help, either. The magic and might of the elves who were her kin might be able to fight off the magic of the hunt—Twig's father had far more magic in the tips of his fingers than Twig had in the points of her ears—but her family had made it clear that they no longer considered Twig family. She wouldn't be welcome, and they wouldn't do anything to help her.

No, she was on her own. Even Trouble and Jessie, who'd vowed to keep her safe until she became someone's old lady, couldn't help her now.

She'd led the hunt on a frenzied chase through the neighborhoods near the docks, down streets lined with boarded-up warehouses and empty storefronts. She'd kept to the working-class areas, avoiding the tourist section where people might still be out dancing and clubbing until dawn. The hunt had come for her. She didn't want anyone else to die at the hunt's hands this night.

She made two quick turns after she barreled out of the end of this particular alley. The streetlights in this section of town weren't working, either shot out by gunfire or sparked out by magic. Elves had good eyesight, but even she couldn't see everything in the dark. The headlight on her bike helped, but she was going too fast to read street signs. The ones that hadn't been torn off their posts, anyway.

Snow's Palace was in a dodgy part of the city, but there were worse areas. Places where goblin gangs sold drugs on street corners, and warlocks sold far worse things from back alleys. Even the cops that dealt with magical crime didn't patrol those sections of the city.

The magic of the hunt had been overpowering Twig's sensitive ears since the moment the chase began, so she supposed she could be forgiven for not hearing the surge of sound and magic coming at her in a wave until she made a quick right turn at the next corner without stopping.

A huge bonfire filled the street in front of her from sidewalk to sidewalk, lighting up the night with dancing shadows. Goblins capered in the firelight, hooting and screeching as they circled the bonfire.

Twig couldn't get around the bonfire, not on the street, and goblins filled the sidewalks on both sides. They were high, she could tell that much. These weren't drug dealers. They were customers, and the drug had driven them out of their little goblin minds.

She had no weapon with her except for an iron knife tucked into a special pocket in her boots. She hadn't taken the knife out—it wouldn't work against the riders in the hunt. Beneath their enchanted appearances, they were merely human. The slice of an iron knife wouldn't affect them any more than the slice of a kitchen knife.

Iron would kill goblins, but there were too many of them. If she slowed down to stab enough of them to get them out of her way—not to kill, just to incapacitate—the hunt would catch up to her. She couldn't try to go around the goblins either. In their drugged state, they wouldn't give her the wide berth that most goblins gave elves.

Not that they'd know she was an elf until they caught her and ripped off her helmet. All of her elven assets were hidden beneath the helmet and her leathers.

Her only choice, and an insane one at that, was to turn her bike around and try to go *under* the hunt. She was small enough. Even on a motorcycle, she might be able to use that five-foot space between the hunt and the street to her advantage.

Murder wouldn't expect it. He'd seen her race around corners and down alleys and cut across speeding cars. He'd seen her handle a bike like it was part of her body, using it in a way no one else in his club ever had. But he'd never seen her turn around and play chicken with an enemy.

All this went through Twig's mind in an instant.

She had no other choice. Dawn was still at least an hour away.

The Wild Hunt would be done at the rising of the sun, whether or not the hunt caught their prey.

She couldn't let them catch her yet.

And she had no other damn choice.

She worked the throttle and the brake in a combination that kicked the motorcycle into a stand on the front wheel, the back of the bike rising up beneath her. Then she twisted her body and the bike in tandem, turning the bike nearly one-hundred eighty degrees, until she was almost at a dead stop facing the leading edge of the Wild Hunt.

The devil dogs went crazy with blood lust. They howled and snarled, flames dripping from their mouths at their desire to rip her to shreds now that she was almost within their reach.

Not that Murder would let them, which no doubt made their hunger all that much worse.

Twig gunned the engine and her bike shot forward. She leaned low over the body of the bike as she sped beneath the devil dogs, and raced beneath the sparking hooves of the horses with their demon riders.

She heard Murder shout to the lead hunters to turn around, turn around, but the hunt wasn't as nimble as Twig and her bike.

In the end she nearly made it, but the hunt's turn around the bonfire did her in.

When the lead rider in the hunt dipped low to slow his speed enough to circle around the bonfire, the rest of the hunt followed.

The Wild Hunt rode through the night like a giant whip, one rider after the other connected by magic, like the harness of a huge wagon train from the old west connected the carriage to the horses that pulled it. When the lead rider dropped closer to the ground, the rest of the hunt followed suit.

The last horse in line before Murder and his three-headed dragon dropped low enough to clip the handlebars on Twig's bike with one hoof.

The front wheel of the bike wobbled, and Twig lost control. The tire skidded on the wet pavement. This time Twig couldn't bring it back straight, and she felt the bike starting to go into a slide.

She prepared herself to leap from the bike, hoping that her elven reflexes would let her duck into a roll and then regain her feet running. She wouldn't be able to outrun the hunt, but maybe she could find somewhere to hide. She only needed an hour to beat the hunt. Then she'd have another whole year to learn how to prevent Murder (and what was left of his soul) from ever using the Wild Hunt to try to kill her again.

That's when Murder passed overhead, and she felt the teeth of one of the dragon heads latch onto her leathers.

As her bike slid away on its side trailing sparks even on the wet pavement, Murder's dragon lifted her into the air. The bonfire singed the bottom of her boots as the hunt finished its circle around the drugged-out goblins. The leathery wings of the dragons beat against the night air as another one of the dragon's heads got a better grip on Twig's body, and she winced against the pain.

The Wild Hunt erupted in triumphant cheers as they sped off down a darkened street and out of the city proper. Night air rushed against Twig's helmet, assaulting her with the stench of rusted metal and fetid water and motor oil.

She knew where the hunt was taking her. The shipyards to the south of the city. Manufacturing had slowed to a crawl, and most of the shipyards were abandoned. The ones that were left wouldn't care what Murder and the hunt did with his prey. After all, killing her this night was legal.

Twig sent a silent goodbye to Jocko and her friends and the gentle water spirit she'd released into the bay. She even said a silent goodbye to her kin, though they had disowned her. She'd lived far longer than her appearance indicated, and it had been a good life. Trouble and Jessie hadn't been able to protect her after all, but that was all right. She'd tell them that when she saw them again, which would be soon now.

Dawn was less than an hour away, but she wouldn't see it. Murder would make sure she was dead by then.

The hunt set Twig down in what had been the parking lot for a busy manufacturing center, before most of the manufacturing centers on the south side of the bay went out of business or simply closed up shop to move overseas. The oil-stained concrete was cracked and broken, with only a few stunted weeds poking up through the cracks and what was left of the faded white lines that had delineated parking spaces.

The building to the south of the parking lot was dark and deserted. Broken windows stared at the parking lot like the rheumy eyes of an arthritic mortal contemplating the ruin of his life. A few empty hulks of abandoned cargo ships littered the bay itself, and the water at this end of the bay was foul with spilled oil and half-dead reeds and garbage.

Murder and the rest of the riders had shed the trappings of the hunt. Now they were just a group of men and motorcycles armed with the only weapons they needed to end Twig's life.

Not knives or guns, but chains. Heavy iron chains and sturdy locks.

Twig knew these men, but not the way they looked now. Marco, the man she'd ridden behind when she'd left Moretown Bay all those years ago, was a haggard forty-something. He had new scars on his face and new tattoos on his neck, and he looked at her like she was a disgusting bug in his dinner.

The way the other men looked at her was even worse.

They wrapped the chains around her wrists and her ankles, locking each in place.

Then they locked the other ends of the chains to the back of their bikes.

She'd been right. Murder was going to have her torn limb from limb, and she couldn't do anything about it. Marco knew about her knife. He'd taken it away from her and thrown it away into the night. She didn't have any spells that she could cast, and even if she did, those spells wouldn't be effective against the thick iron of her chains.

She hadn't been strong enough to fight against the three-headed dragon that had held her in its clutches. Before the dragon let her go, Murder had fastened the first of the chains on her.

The iron chain locked in place around her neck.

Only after the lock had snapped in place did the dragon fade from existence. It had done its job, after all. Murder no longer needed to maintain the illusion that his motorcycle was a deadly beast that could snap her spine merely by clenching its jaws.

Twig's elven strength and speed were useless now. The iron chains that held her were as effective as the bars of a cage.

Murder held the other end of the chain around her neck. He stood in front of her, a good foot taller than she was, and bounced his end of the chain against the palm of one hand.

"This isn't going to be pretty, elf," he said.

She didn't give him an answer.

"What's going to pull off first?" he said. "A leg? Maybe one of your hands?"

He reached down and ran a fingertip around the tip of one ear. His skin was rough against hers, and she shook her head, glaring at him.

He snorted out a laugh. "Too bad I can't wrap a chain around your ears. I'd like to pull those things off your head, but I guess pulling your head off your body will have to do."

"Jessie wouldn't want this," Twig said.

The last of his laugh cut off abruptly, and he yanked on the chain. The thick links dug into the back of Twig's neck.

Murder glared at her. "Well, Jessie's not here, is he?"

"He did that to get away from you," Twig said.

He yanked on her chain again, this time jerking her chin up so that she was nearly nose-to-nose with him as he bent down over her.

"He did that because he was a pussy," Murder said, his words hissing out between clenched teeth. "He let his old lady get in his head. Made that broad his whole life."

"He couldn't stand the thought of life with only you in it," Twig said. "Trouble and his baby were the only things he loved. Or didn't you realize that?" She smiled, even though it was the last thing she felt like doing. "I'll be seeing them soon. I'll be sure to tell them what you did to me. How you ended my life. Think he'll be proud of his old man?"

She was goading him deliberately. If he got mad enough, maybe he'd snap her neck. That would be a better death, a quicker and less painful death, than being torn limb from limb and bleeding out on this soiled and broken concrete.

She wasn't sure if she was telling him the truth about Jessie. She'd grown close enough to Trouble over the years to know that Trouble had grown disillusioned with life in Murder's gang. She was too decent, too good of a person to let her love for Jessie blind her to the evil things that Murder did, and the things that Murder convinced Jessie to do. Trouble didn't want her baby growing up in that culture. She didn't want her baby to be influenced by his grandfather. Twig was pretty sure Trouble had almost talked Jessie into leaving after the baby was born.

Only they never got the chance.

Twig kept her gaze locked with Murder's. She was getting to him. His eyes had narrowed, and his face had gone ruddy with the extent of his rage.

"Did you know that they promised to protect me?" She let her smile grow larger even as her blood grew colder. She was committing suicide here, just like Jessie had, but she couldn't think of another way to beat him. To steal from him the kind of death he'd planned for her. "Bet Jessie never promised to protect you. He didn't—"

"Shut up!"

Spittle flew from his lips as Murder shouted at her. He yanked her off her feet with the chain around her neck, the muscles in his arms bulging even as the bones and ligaments in Twig's neck crunched again the hard iron links of the chain.

If the chain had formed a noose around her neck instead of being locked in place, she would be choking and unable to breathe. Instead all of her weight rested on the delicate bones of her neck, and she swore she could feel them giving way.

She wondered if she struggled hard enough, would she be able to wrench her neck and break it herself?

Murder was yelling at her, incoherent in his rage. Shaking her, but not hard enough to snap her neck. She flexed her legs, dragging the chains wrapped around her ankles, getting ready to kick Murder in the gut as a way to swing her body like a pendulum so she could finish the job he'd started, when her ears picked up a sudden rush of magic.

Familiar magic.

The sound of magic she'd first heard trapped inside a motorcycle as a mournful water spirit wept for its lost home.

The water spirit had heard her mental goodbye. It had left its home in the depths of the bay and brought its magic in an attempt to rescue its friend the same way Twig had saved it from captivity.

And the spirit hadn't come alone.

Light brighter than the sun spilled across the concrete. Golden light so bright it was nearly white.

Golden light the same color as Jessie's hair.

Murder hadn't felt the water spirit's presence. He had no magic of his own. His power over magic had died when Twig had killed his enforcer. But he didn't need magic to see the ghost of his son.

Murder let go of the chain holding Twig aloft so suddenly that she had no chance to stop her fall. She landed in an awkward bundle on the concrete. Her left arm collided with a thick loop of chain, and she felt the bones in her forearm break.

The pain was enormous, and for a moment Twig had to fight against the dark fog that threatened to envelop her mind.

Twig had heard the sad, faded magic of ghosts before. She sensed them in the same way she sensed the water spirit and other non-corporeal beings.

But she had never *seen* a ghost before. Not like this.

Jessie stood in front of his father nearly as present in flesh and bone as he had been on the day of his death. Trouble stood next to him, a baby cradled in her arms. Her friendly, open face wasn't nearly as *there* as Jessie's form, but she still nodded in Twig's direction and gave her a smile.

Told you we'd protect you, girlfriend, Twig heard in her head as clearly as if Trouble had spoken out loud. *Just needed a little help, you know? Or we'd have been here sooner.*

The water spirit. It had shared its magic with Jessie and, to a lesser extent, with Trouble.

Her friends had come to rescue her.

But what could their magic do against iron chains?

Enough, as it turned out.

None of Murder's buddies had any magic. Marco was a thief, a wiz with lockpicks and combination locks. Other members of the gang had similar talents, including a crazy old guy who could make explosives out of common kitchen ingredients, and another guy who could scale walls nearly as well as an elf. What made them into a badass gang was the force of Murder's willingness to do anything and everything necessary to make other people afraid of him. They'd grown used to relying on Murder's strength of will and his reputation. When that deserted them, and without the added strength the Wild Hunt had given them, they didn't know what to do.

Jessie's sudden appearance had unmanned Murder.

He cried and shrank back from the vision of his dead son.

"No," he said, his voice now that of an old man's. "You can't be here. You can't be real."

Jessie gave his father a sad, rueful smile. "It's time to own up to what you did," he said.

His voice had a wispy feel to it. Gooseflesh crept up on Twig's unbroken arm as she forced herself into a sitting position, biting back a cry of her own as the bones in her broken arm shifted.

"No!" Murder's face had turned pale in the predawn light.

Jessie turned to look at Twig. "You don't know what really happened. You think you do." He turned his gaze on all the men his father rode with, looking at each in turn until they all backed away. "You all think you know what happened, but you don't." He turned back to his father. "Do you want to tell them—or should I?"

The water spirit's magic took on the sad tones of an elegy, and Twig had a bad feeling she knew what was coming.

"You killed your own son," she whispered.

Murder had been the one who'd told them he'd found Jessie's body. That Jessie had taken his own life. Everyone in the gang had assumed Jessie had been despondent about Trouble and the baby, and they never questioned what Murder had told them. Murder himself had been nearly out of his mind with grief.

But he'd lied. Twig knew it from the look on his face as much as from the magic surrounding Jessie and his family.

It hadn't been grief that had driven him mad. It had been guilt.

"You killed him," one of the gang members said. Twig thought it might have been Marco, but she wasn't sure. "That's fucked up, man."

One by one, the gang stepped away from Murder and the ghost of his son. They unlocked the chains that held Twig to their motorcycles, and unwrapped the chains from around her wrists and ankles, taking as much care with her broken arm as they would with their own, and then they drove away.

Throughout it all, Jessie stood and looked at his father as Murder simply stood there, head hung low, and gazed at the length of chain he still held in his hand.

The chain that was still locked around Twig's neck.

His power was gone now, and everyone knew it. He could still kill Twig, but it would be a hollow death. He'd gain nothing by it, not even revenge, and he knew it.

"Enough," Jessie said. "You've lost a piece of your soul this night. Don't do this. Don't lose the rest."

He took a ghostly step toward his father and laid a noncorporeal hand on his shoulder. Murder flinched as if the touch had burned him.

"Give me the key," Jessie said softly.

He held out his hand, waiting.

It took a few moments, but Murder eventually dropped the key into Jessie's hand. It fell through the ghost's fingers and landed practically in Twig's lap. She didn't have to be told what to do with it. She unlocked the chain from around her neck and scrambled to her feet.

Trouble floated across the concrete to stand next to Twig. *Baby's a cutie, don't you think?*

Twig couldn't turn her head to look at the baby—her neck was too sore—so she shifted her body to see a baby who'd never drawn a breath in the real world. He had Trouble's round face and his father's golden white hair, and yes, he was a cutie.

"You okay?" Twig asked, looking at the ghost of her friend. The sky in the east was getting lighter, and Trouble seemed to be fading the closer it got to sunrise.

Trouble shrugged. *It's different here, but it's all good.* She glanced over at Jessie, who also seemed to be fading with the light. *Still have my guy, you know? Love's all that matters, really. Way better than hate. Remember that, okay?*

Twig wasn't a hugger, but she wished she could hug Trouble. And the water spirit who'd made all this possible.

Jessie looked over at Twig, smiled at his family, then turned back one last time to look at his father.

"I forgive you," Jessie said.

He words echoed in the nearly empty parking lot long after he and his family had faded away.

Murder had fallen to his knees next to his motorcycle. He had his hands over his face and he was weeping.

He still held his end of the chain that had been wrapped around Twig's neck.

She could have taken his motorcycle and she doubted he would even notice, but she wanted nothing more to do with him. He was broken. His friends had deserted him. He'd never be a threat to her again.

Her neck still hurt and her arm throbbed, but the pain was lessening. Elves healed quickly in comparison to mortals. It would take her a couple of days, but she'd be back to normal in no time. In the meantime, she could walk her own self back to where she'd wrecked her bike and see if the goblins had left anything worth salvaging.

She'd survived the Wild Hunt. Yes, she'd had help from her friends—magical and ghostly friends—but she'd still survived. And she hadn't put Jocko or the women at the club in danger in order to do it.

Maybe there was a lesson in that. Even a solitary, rebellious elf who'd been disowned by her kin needed family and friends in order to survive. She'd have to learn to ask for help even if she thought she didn't need it. That might be the hardest lesson to put into practice, but maybe she'd start by asking Jocko to help her with her bike.

And if that went well, who knew? She might even give the big guy a hug.

One step at a time.

All it took was one step at a time.

ABOUT THE AUTHOR

A frequent contributor to the *Fiction River* anthologies and *Pulphouse Fiction Magazine*, Annie Reed's recent work includes the urban fantasy mystery novels *Unbroken Familiar* and *Iris & Ivy*, and the near-future science fiction short novel *In Dreams*. Annie's also one of the founding members of the innovative Uncollected Anthology, a series of themed urban fantasy stories published three times a year written by some of the best writers working today.

Annie's full-length novels include the Abby Maxon private investigator novels *Pretty Little Horses* and *Paper Bullets*, the Jill Jordan mystery *A Death in Cumberland*, and the suspense novel *Shadow Life*, written under the name Kris Sparks, as well as numerous other projects she can't wait to get to.

Find out more about Annie at:
annie-reed.com

BB bookbub.com/authors/annie-reed

ABOUT A PROCESSION OF FAERIES

The *Wild Hunt* is the fifth volume in the anthology series *A Procession of Faeries*. If you enjoyed this collection, check out the others—and follow the series on Facebook!

www.ingramcontent.com/pod-product-compliance
Lightning Source LLC
Chambersburg PA
CBHW070307280626
47159CB00017B/563